Panda
Ray

ALSO BY MICHAEL KANDEL

as author
STRANGE INVASION (1989)
IN BETWEEN DRAGONS (1990)
CAPTAIN JACK ZODIAC (1992)

as translator of Stanislaw Lem
THE FUTUROLOGICAL CONGRESS (1974)
THE CYBERIAD (1974)
THE STAR DIARIES (1976)
A PERFECT VACUUM (1978)
HIS MASTER'S VOICE (1983)
FIASCO (1986)
HIGHCASTLE (1995)

Panda
Ray

a Novel by

Michael Kandel

St. Martin's Press ☒ New York

Design by Songhee Kim

Edited by Gordon Van Gelder

Library of Congress Cataloging-in-Publication Data

Kandel, Michael.
    Panda Ray / by Michael Kandel. —1st ed.
      p.   cm.
    ISBN 0–312–14387–7
    I. Title.
    PS3561.A462P36   1996
    813'.54—dc20   ,   96–3484

First edition: July 1996

10 9 8 7 6 5 4 3 2 1

Part One

One of the great achievements of Greek mathematics is the construction of the regular pentagon.

—L. FEJES TÓTH

Too Much Science Fiction?

A hallway, long walls of shiny tiles. They are a pastel terra-cota color. In the air, the smell of chalk. Mingled with the sharp chalk smell are the smells of white paste, apples, beaverboard, poster paint, and disinfectant.

We are in the west wing. After we turn a corner, our finger running along the slippery cold tile, we come to room 16, where a few people stand waiting. They are polite but impatient, one man impatient to the point of muttering. In room 16, on the other side of the beige door with the little square window at head height—and note the chicken wire in the glass, an array of symmetrical hexagons filling a square—Mrs. Palmer looks up again at the wall clock. She sighs. It is a sigh from the depths yet contained carefully in her throat and kept inaudible—for the reason that she is a teacher, and teachers must smile at the world through thick and thin. Smiling is in their job description.

Mrs. Palmer—first name Jane—had been up at five this morning. She hadn't slept at all well, worrying about her errant Roger. Her teenage son, her cross and curse. Now in Mexico. He went off a week ago with that irresponsible Coyle kid, despite her long talk with him, despite her desperate threats. The Coyle kid drank and probably took drugs and for sure drove without a seat belt. The Coyle kid's car: not inspected, souped up illegally, falling apart. God, who looks after drunks and fools, preserve my son please on the highway. She could throttle him, her only child, her impossible Roger, throttle him blue and keep throttling.

Mrs. Palmer had been up at five this morning. It was now four in the afternoon and there was still an hour to go, four parents to go, and she had not only a headache but one of her dreaded full-ax headaches: the whole blade of the ax embedded in your skull, at the top, longitudinally, working the split methodically—twisting a little to the left, twisting a little to the right—to pry the bone apart and slip deeper into pounding brain. They were running late—but didn't they always run late?—and the parents would feel shortchanged even if she gave them half an hour each instead of their fifteen minutes. What, only fifteen minutes to discuss our lovable Johnny, our gifted and talented Brenda, our troubled Keith? Stuttering Belle, slow David? What was wrong with this school? Why couldn't Lincoln schedule parent-teacher conferences more conveniently and more often? Why did they always run late? Why, why? Therefore Mrs. Palmer had not an hour to go but more like an hour and a half, maybe even two hours. She looked at the clock and told herself that the delicate word choices and wide smiling might have to continue until 6 P.M. Her smile, her teacher's badge and shield, displayed bright teeth and hid fatigue. But fatigue, like sour breath or a greasy face, only became more difficult to hide as the sun sank in the sky outside and the shadows lengthened.

When Mr. and Mrs. Dean left, full of pride in their unremarkable Angela—the child's success was due solely to the simple but effective trick of following directions—Mrs. Palmer straightened her back, girded her loins, and put the next folder in front of her. She centered it on the desk, aligning its edges with the edges of the desk: a rectangle within a rectangle, all the sides equidistant and parallel. Adults liked to see order in a fifth-grade classroom. It reassured them that the evil of the modern world had not made its way yet into this sacrosanct storybook oasis.

A knock at the door—a polite, dry knuckle on hollow steel—and Mrs. Zimmerman entered. They knew each other. Brian Zimmerman had been in Mrs. Palmer's class—what, five years ago? More than five. The father was not in attendance, but as Mrs. Palmer remembered now, he rarely showed himself. A sales manager. He had a thin mustache, a fussy, twitchy mouth, and he dyed his hair a ridiculous boot-polish black. Mr. Zimmerman was the kind of mouse-man who let his wife do the talking.

Mrs. Zimmerman, when Brian was in Mrs. Palmer's class, had helped out some—not a lot, but some—on field trips, bake sales, fund-raisers. Therefore a valuable parent: Be particularly careful not to antagonize this one. She was also the aunt of another child here, Cathy Carmichael. Mrs. Zimmerman showed up at PTA meetings every other month. When she stood and spoke, which was rare, she spoke slowly and deliberately, in a way that made everyone, even Mr. Sykes, wait in silence for her to finish.

Fifteen minutes for Christopher, Mrs. Palmer thought hopefully. But then the folder before her reminded her of Christopher's problem, his peculiar problem. So she revised the fifteen minutes to twenty, thirty. She took a breath and got to work: Shake hands, do have a seat, then the standard few pleasantries back and forth, cordial and impersonal. And now, clearing her throat, opening the folder, your son.

Christopher Zimmerman. Ten years old. Straw hair and freckles.

"Christopher," Mrs. Palmer began, "possesses quite an imagination."

Mrs. Zimmerman's face expressed nothing. The lines on her broad forehead were all straight, horizontal, parallel, a musical staff without notes. She blinked slowly, as if to say: Go on, I am all attention. The clock on the wall, a plain factory-style clock, made a slight whirring noise, but its hands did not move. It, too, was waiting blankly.

Mrs. Palmer went on. "I don't wish to alarm you."

Mrs. Zimmerman was not alarmed. She was not a woman who got alarmed; Mrs. Palmer remembered that now. No flicker of distress—or flicker of pleasure, either—at the fact that her son was imaginative to such a degree that the teacher felt obliged to bring it up first thing at a parent-teacher conference.

"An imagination is a wonderful thing," Mrs. Palmer intoned, because much-used phrases are difficult not to intone; they all but intone themselves. "Many children here, if I may be frank, would do well to have more of it. Oh yes. We nurture it, we encourage it, we bend over backward not to stifle it, but there you are."

Mrs. Zimmerman wasn't helping. She blinked again: the blink of a cat on a summer porch.

"But, of course, to excess . . . Well, nothing is ever good to excess, is it?"

Mrs. Zimmerman nodded her agreement: Nothing was ever good to excess. One nod. If you told her the world was coming to an end, she would look around, verify that it was indeed coming to an end in assorted flames, screams, and tumultuous rumbling, and turn back to you and say: Yes, what is your point?

"I would suggest," said Mrs. Palmer, feeling more and more stupid, but it had to be said, "that you might want to set up an evaluation for Christopher with Mr. DiVincenzo. He is our school psychologist."

"Christopher's imagination," said Mrs. Zimmerman slowly, very slowly, "is so excessive, you are telling me, that he needs to see a psychologist?"

A pause for Mrs. Palmer to take a breath before she continued uphill against a steepening grade.

"Well, Mrs. Zimmerman, let me give you a few examples of what I mean. And you can judge for yourself."

A nod. One nod.

"We were discussing Shakespeare in class. The Globe Theatre. What the theater was like back then, you know. How women weren't allowed to appear on the stage, and men—boys—played their roles?"

"Yes."

"And Christopher said. And he said it quite earnestly, Mrs. Zimmerman, as if he had been there, a fly on the wall, though of course it was all a joke. He said that Shakespeare wore a dress, always wore a dress, when he wrote his plays. That he wrote them in a little paneled room on the second floor, third door to the right, and for *Macbeth* he chose a white dress with green embroidery and a green plush sash. The Bard of Avon, Christopher told us, also had a blond wig with lots of ringlets which he used to cover his bald spot. Also, there were long earrings in his ears, and they jiggled as his quill pen scratched across the page. Christopher went on like this, Mrs. Zimmerman, until the class was in stitches."

"My child appears to be a comedian."

"Another time, when we were talking about the dinosaurs becoming extinct because a large meteor hit the Yucatán Peninsula, he raised his hand and said it wasn't a meteor at all. He said that the dinosaurs had wiped themselves out by ESP."

"ESP?" Mrs. Zimmerman now leaned forward a little and gave Mrs. Palmer a quizzical look, as if maybe Mrs. Palmer and not her son was the one who needed to be evaluated by Mr. DiVincenzo.

"You know—parapsychology, mind waves." Mrs. Palmer was always uncomfortable using long words with parents. Long words tended to make them defensive or sardonic. She shouldn't have said *parapsychology.* "Christopher told us the dinosaurs developed these powers because they had been around for so long as a species. He said that whenever a species survived more than five million years, it developed extrasensory powers because of the genes on the seventh chromosome from the left evolving." She winced. She shouldn't have used *extrasensory,* either, or *chromosome.* Though little Christopher had used those words. "He said that the exact same thing happened with the trilobites."

"Trilobites?"

"They're animals, something like horseshoe crabs, who lived in the sea in the early—"

"I know what trilobites are, Mrs. Palmer."

"Oh, I'm sorry, I'm sure you do. But you see, Christopher rattled on and on about it, the war of the dinosaurs, the war of the trilobites, how in each case after five million years they killed each other off inside of two months with blasts of mental energy—"

"And the class was in stitches."

"Well, I think some of the children were actually beginning to believe it. Your son was so serious and full of all these details. The way he described and explained . . . I've never seen anything like it—well, only once before—in all my years of teaching. So I think, Mrs. Zimmerman, that Christopher is maybe, I mean, at that age. Does he spend a lot of time reading comic books or too much science fiction?"

"No, he does not. We have rules in our house."

"Is he quiet at home, does he keep to himself? Because a child can retreat into a dreamworld, you know, become introverted in response to social pressures or maybe a personal problem. And that can be so unhealthy. When we were doing math—this was only last week—I introduced infinity, showed the children the sign for infinity, but then Christopher started talking about scarlet people on another planet who look like moths on top and plumber's helpers on the bottom—that's what he said—and they do their mathematics all backward. They start with infinity and work their way in from both directions. He wanted to go to the blackboard and show us, but I said no, enough was enough."

Mrs. Zimmerman closed her eyes and pursed her lips. Not the

slightest cloud on her lined brow. "Perhaps you are making too much of this," she said.

Mrs. Palmer's head pulsed with the embedded ax, which was deeper now, going deeper, but she kept her smile intact. "Mrs. Zimmerman, I am only thinking of the child's welfare. If he has a problem . . ."

"Brian, you may recall, had a problem."

Brian?

Oh yes, Brian. True. He had been loud, disrespectful, sometimes disruptive. Wouldn't do his homework. Refused on principle, as if the assignment was beneath his dignity. Not that that was so unusual. Early onset of teenage hormones and arrogance. Look at her own son gone to Mexico despite her threats.

Mrs. Palmer remembered how a month ago she got so provoked, she smacked Roger in the mouth as hard as she could and wanted to shake him if not choke the very life out of him with her bare hands, because of what he dared say, the ungrateful puppy, about his departed father. But the boy was too big, bigger than she, with his stupid weight-lifting arms, back, and shoulders. When she slapped him, all he did was laugh. Her only son, her cross and curse, laughing at her.

"What grade is Brian in now?" inquired Mrs. Palmer.

"Twelfth," said Mrs. Zimmerman. "And he's settled down completely."

"Well, that's wonderful."

"Yes. He's begun looking at colleges. His grades couldn't be better. He's in the honor society. He plays intramural soccer. He does volunteer work at the nursing home. He's thinking of going into patent law."

"You must be very proud."

A memory came, vivid, though it was more than five years ago. Once, after class, Brian said something strange to her. With an angry face, a red and twisted face. He said he didn't have to do what other children did because he was different, not only different but "really, really different," more than anybody knew. Then he lowered his eyes and bit his lip, as if he had blurted a government secret and this might cost him his freedom if not his life.

Was such a thing work for Mr. DiVincenzo, or was it just another stage, where typically a child's comic-book fantasy became a little too real, spilling into life and mixing with fact, competing with fact? Mrs. Palmer had let it pass—and evidently she was right to have let it pass, because behold Brian now, going into patent law.

Most children straightened out when they got older.

Though you never knew for sure. It was so hard to tell from a face, from a pair of eyes. The eyes were certainly no window to the soul; they were a wall that perplexed, deceived, and mocked. When would her Roger straighten out? He was nearly twenty, his birthday in November. A few young people never straightened out, growing more disturbed and antisocial with time. They sank. Jack Bethany, for one example. Jack was in juvenile court and most likely on his way to the penitentiary. And yet in the fifth grade he hadn't been that bad. Just boys-will-be-boys bad. Plenty of mischievous, mean-streak boys, after all, grew up to become bankers instead of bank robbers.

After they hot-wired cars and stole hubcaps, they pumped gas. Life took the trouble out of them.

Brian Zimmerman had turned out just fine. Christopher would turn out just fine, too, like his older brother, and not end up in a padded cell on some funny farm, forgotten by humanity, remembered only by his fifth-grade teacher.

"I really don't think we have to worry about Christopher," concluded Mrs. Zimmerman.

Mrs. Palmer practically blushed. She was growing old-maidish, afraid of too many things. A child's overactive imagination didn't mean, for heaven's sake, schizophrenia.

Except . . . except that Christopher had gone into such detail. Unusual detail, inexhaustible detail. And his eyes, as he spoke, had shone. But they had shone not with the light of humor or with the impudent wit of a class comedian . . .

Those gray-blue eyes had shone with the pleasure of disobedience.

But how exactly, with these stories, these elaborate jokes, was he being disobedient? And disobedient to whom? It made no sense. A mystery.

"Still, I will have a little talk with him," said his mother, rising.

"He gets along perfectly with his classmates," said Mrs. Palmer, rising with her. "He seems self-confident, too, even though he's small, the smallest in his class. And never any problem learning. He's a good child, Mrs. Zimmerman. I was just concerned, you know . . ."

9

"Yes, I understand, thank you."

A handshake, a smile and nod on either side, and another parent out the door.

Next were Mr. and Mrs. Boileau, deeply concerned about Karen's poor showing in the science fair. This was the first time her project—food color and watercress—didn't place, didn't even get a lousy honorable mention.

"Karen is destroyed," began Karen's mother, a woman with so much mascara, she looked like a circus clown playing a woman.

Mrs. Palmer gestured for them to be seated, showed all her white teeth in a smile that despite herself was becoming, with each passing minute, less a smile and more a skeleton's fixed grimace at Halloween. She took another glance at the clock above her—the plain face, the thin black hands pointing down, an angle of maybe sixty degrees between them—and felt unutterably tired.

The Rules of the House

2

Gray clapboard. Peeling paint.
The house at 54 Wilson is three stories and more than a hundred
years old. It has a rusted rooster weather vane, also a big microwave
antenna dish angled on a steep, scallop-shingled roof. There is a
high hedge all around. Plenty of shade, here and the entire length
of the block, from all the old maples and oaks. The narrow street
is like a tunnel: thick trunks on either side and an arched ceiling
of boughs. The sidewalk is broken everywhere by gnarled roots, so
we have to watch our step. Impossible to skate or even bike on such
a sidewalk. Moss. Ants. Layered leaf stains. Acorns crunching underfoot.

Kaelin was at the kitchen window, watching, chewing her lip.
She had a way of twisting her fingers, too, when she was nervous—
her right hand twisting a left fingertip as if it were a knob, her left
hand twisting a right fingertip as if it were a knob. But Kaelin was
nervous all the time, even in her sleep. Anyone would have been,
growing up in that family.

She blew out a breath when she saw Christopher—but didn't
blow too loud—she never did anything too loud. When she cried,
for example, her head would be deep under her pillow, letting escape only the tiniest bleats of sorrow, all but inaudible. Else Mother
would ask questions.

Kaelin gestured as he came around the walk to the back, gestured through the window, a raised, timidly crooking index finger
that whispered: Mayday, Mayday, red alert.

Christopher pretended he hadn't noticed his sister at the kitchen window. He pretended so well, you would have thought—if you didn't know him and his sister better—that he really hadn't noticed her. Entering, he took the pebbles for the pebble puzzle out of his jacket pocket. From a half-cupped hand he dropped them into the shoe box under the sink, adding to the fifty-some already collected. Then he poured himself a glass of milk from the refrigerator. He drank, his Adam's apple moving. He wiped his mouth, washed the glass and put it carefully in the drainer, and went into the hall. Not hurrying, unconcerned—as if going to his room, which was up on the third floor, as high as you could get in this house, his little room adjacent to the attic. Except that in the hall he turned unexpectedly and went quickly down the steps to the basement, where Kaelin was waiting.

"Have you done anything wrong?" she asked in a low voice, by the washing machine, ostensibly busy sorting light and dark clothes from a laundry basket.

He fiddled with the brace and bit lying on the workbench, a couple of screws, a carriage bolt. He wandered over closer to his sister.

"Mother wants to see you," she whispered. "She said I was to tell you as soon as you got home. Did you do anything, Chris?"

Christopher mumbled, but it wasn't words. He walked past his sister and looked at the boiler. Had he done something he shouldn't? Of course he had—children were always doing something they shouldn't, otherwise they wouldn't be children, would they? His pebbles . . . but they were not a thing anyone would notice. They looked like ordinary pebbles. Only if you happened to try to put them together—but why would anyone do that?—and discovered that they fit exactly, like jigsaw pieces, fit much better than any jigsaw pieces. But Christopher had no intention of ever putting them together; he would let them lie inconspicuously mixed in the box under the sink and in the flowerpot under the back steps. There were also a few in a row on his bookshelf upstairs. The pebble puzzle remained his secret that way. A kid had to exercise his upsilon a little, didn't he? What was the harm in a little upsilon exercise, if no one saw and no one knew?

"You did something, didn't you?" Kaelin said.

"Maybe," whispered Christopher. It could have been a hundred things. Dogs barked. Cats meowed. Children misbehaved.

"Chris. You're in trouble again. When her face gets like that . . .

You better be careful. Please, Chris. I don't want—to lose another brother."

"What?"

"Nothing."

"What?"

"Nothing."

"You never lost a brother."

"Hush."

"You're telling me there was a brother before Brian? I don't believe it."

Mouthed more than whispered: "Later, maybe, I'll tell you. Not now." They were good at lipreading, brother and sister, and good at secrets. From long practice.

But time was up: Mother knew that Christopher was home, and she was expecting him, and if you kept her waiting, you would have to explain. Christopher, what were you doing all that time in the kitchen? Were you talking to Kaelin? What were you talking about?

Christopher climbed the basement steps, and—a small, quiet, nondescript child—he seemed to grow even smaller and quieter and more nondescript as he climbed. He assumed the drab innocence of a stationery watermark. But a mother's eyes can see through such protective coloration, and Debra Zimmerman's vision was twice as acute as any mother's.

She smiled when her son appeared before her. But the smile was only one-cornered: a bad sign. This was more serious, he realized, than his using a little upsilon to change pebbles. This was much more serious. On the screened-in front porch she rocked slowly in the white swing seat, a crossword book in her lap. You could hear the trees rustling overhead like surf.

"You've been traveling, haven't you?" she said.

He said nothing. Maybe turned a shade paler.

She looked down at her crossword puzzle, thought a moment, filled in a word. Letter by letter, vertical. Clicked the ballpoint.

"I can't imagine how, at your age," she said to the puzzle book. "Unless it's Gramps. It must be Gramps."

Christopher started to deny it but stopped himself in time, choking back the denial. You didn't lie to Mother; she was death on lies. She always knew. Silence was safer, meek silence, an abject head and limp, nerveless hands.

"Poor Gramps grows foolish," she said with a dry tsk. "I think it is time for him to go to that place, that life-care facility, the community in Florida."

Christopher knew that his grandfather hated the idea like poison centipedes. Literature for the facility lay on the coffee table in Gramps's house on Walnut Street. You couldn't help seeing it as you went in and as you left. Gramps wasn't allowed to throw it out or even cover it with a magazine. It was there as a warning, a reminder that the old codger better behave. The brochure had glossy pictures of palm trees and, in the foreground, happy, lean people with white hair who were playing golf or tennis. It was a fate worse than death. It was a living death.

Gramps would say, "Just throw me to the alligators. That would be more merciful, more honest, and more ecological." Because Golden Years—the facility community—was right next door to the Everglades.

The Everglades reminded Christopher of the Permian period: heavy air, insects humming, an occasional lazy slap in warm brown water, and the trees like mournful, molting posts.

"Traveling," said Mother, "is bad enough. But, Christopher, talking about it?" She looked at him.

He was fingering a scab on his knuckle and thinking of Gramps banished to a swamp. A fly, furious but helpless, buzzing in an upside-down glass. How long before the fly ran out of oxygen?

Christopher felt ill.

"You know, dear, that you are not supposed to talk." Mother spoke very, very softly now. "None of us may talk—about we all know what—on the outside. That is one of the rules of the house."

Tears welled in his eyes. Tears for Gramps—and for himself, too. His punishment would be crushing and crippling. It would be a permanent crippling, because he had broken a rule of the house and been caught.

"I'm sorry," he said, his words strangled. "It was only a joke. They didn't believe me." People were stupid. They would never believe him, not in a million years. Neither the children nor the adults. He had just done it to amuse himself a little. What was the harm? Why turn this into a federal case?

"You are not sorry, Christopher, you are defiant. You knew you were doing wrong. That was the whole fun of it, wasn't it?"

"They didn't believe me, really," he croaked.

"You're supposed to blend in, you know that. Telling them about William Shakespeare's private life isn't blending in, is it, dear? Or about the dinosaurs psi-suiciding. You were showing off, Christopher, that's what you were doing. Showing off and defying your mother."

She regarded him awhile, then resumed her puzzle, filling in a word. Horizontal.

He kept his pulse steady, which was like juggling without moving your arms. Lub dub, lub dub.

"Defying your mother is natural, I suppose," she continued as she filled in letter by letter. "Boys growing up, growing rebellious. It's natural. But you see, dear, we Zimmermans cannot afford to be natural. Alas. We are not natural to begin with, now are we? But you know all this, you know all this. Please don't play stupid. You are an intelligent boy. All my children are intelligent. Don't pretend you don't understand why we must keep our lips buttoned about ourselves, completely buttoned, no exceptions ever. Puberty no excuse, senility no excuse. We are not in a position, our family is not in a position, to be human. That's it in a very plain nutshell. And you know this, Christopher dear."

Yes, he knew it. And his punishment would be excruciating and unspeakable. It struck ice into him. For he would not be judged as a tiny child with freckles. Ah no.

"A full confession," Mother said after a pause, filling in another word, vertical, this a long vertical, "might mitigate your situation some. Demonstrating to us that you are not set in your defiance, that there is perhaps hope for you, although frankly it doesn't look like it."

A lighter sentence, in other words, in exchange for snitching on Gramps. But Gramps hadn't done anything wrong. Gramps was Gramps. If Christopher had only kept his mouth shut at school, Mother would never have found out about the trips.

"Gramps didn't do anything wrong," he mumbled, hanging his head, thinking of the poor fly trapped under a glass in the Everglades and slowly suffocating.

Mrs. Zimmerman considered her small, pale son, her youngest. Her eyes narrowed. "Young man," she said at last, with all the warmth and compassion of a slab of granite, "go to your room. No dinner tonight for you, and no television."

He knew. This evening, while he was under house arrest in his room, his fate would be sealed by family council. But sealed or not, come what may, he couldn't, no, he couldn't snitch on his grandfather. Gramps was defenseless. The poor old man hadn't been right in the head since the death of Emily, his lifelong wife. Emily passed away a few years before Christopher was born, but Christopher had seen a picture of her. Faded, watery eyes, an angular jaw, a sweet but savvy smile.

Christopher was the only protector of his grandfather, the only companion of his grandfather, the only friend, aside from Panda Ray maybe, of his grandfather.

He went to his room, up three flights of stairs, thirty-six steps in all, and shut the door behind him. Patted Buzz, his trusty robot dog, in the closet, as he always did. Sat on his bed and sighed, a sigh from the depths. So young, so unformed, with hundreds of thousands of millions of billions of things yet to do and taste and know and become, and to have to face a firing squad in the morning. Or worse.

He put his head on his pillow, groaned, and the lights, as if taking pity on him, dimmed and went out by themselves.

3

A steady ticking in the dining room, from the antique captain's clock atop the sideboard. The clock: dark wood, scrollwork, a cosine hump between sphinxlike shoulders, and the hours in serifed Roman numerals, dull gold. With a little brass-cased hole centered under the face, for the windup key. The hands are raised, with maybe thirty degrees between them: it is less than five minutes to 10 P.M. Dinner is long over, but the whole Zimmerman family, minus Christopher of course, has assembled around the table.

Debra Zimmerman sits at the head; her husband, Monty, sits at the foot. Her son Brian is to her right, her daughter Kaelin is to her left. Kaelin stares at the antique clock, which ticks steadily.

"I call this family council to order," Debra Zimmerman began. "The subject is Christopher."

No one said anything, so she went on:

"The problem is his rebellion. Now in the fifth grade, he has traveled with Gramps and spoken of it at school."

No one said anything, so she went on:

"An open-and-shut case, I would think, particularly since the boy refuses to snitch on his grandfather. But before we reach our decision and take action, every member of the family must be heard and polled. We observe due process. This is the United States of America. Monty?"

Mr. Zimmerman winced, squinted, touched his mustache. "Well, dear, as you say, an open-and-shut case."

"So what do we do?"

Mr. Zimmerman shrugged uncomfortably and seemed to have difficulty finding a place to rest his eyes. "Well, I suppose we have no choice," he murmured. "We do what we must do."

She nodded not once but twice, slowly.

"What we . . . have done before," he added, looking at the ceiling, "in similar . . . in similar . . ." Trailing off and not resuming.

"Brian?" Debra Zimmerman said, turning to her son.

Brian was tall, clean-cut, well groomed, collegiately sweatered. A pleasant smile and a popular vagueness around the eyes and mouth. He was the student-government type. The face—nothing distinctive about it, a generic face. Brian said: "I agree with Dad, of course. We have no choice, do we? The family comes first, it always comes first. It has to, right?"

"So what do we do?"

"We do what we did the last time, what else?" answered Brian smoothly. "Same situation, really, except that Christopher is in the fifth grade and I was in the seventh. We neutralize him."

Debra Zimmerman nodded, again twice, and turned to her daughter. Directed upon her daughter two eyes of ice.

"Kaelin?"

Kaelin knew that Mother was scrutinizing her, searching her. That Mother suspected. She had to be extremely careful. She must not let her feelings show.

She tried to smile, but it was impossible; the smile spasmed in an ugly way. Take a deep breath, girl, she told herself. Control, control, or the dragon will eat you, too. But she couldn't take a deep breath, not for the life of her. She said in a voice much too thin and high:

"He is responsible. He must accept responsibility."

Mother nodded.

"His age is no excuse," Kaelin said, and the words were so painful, like walking on broken glass with bare feet, that they made her whimper inside. Please, God, she prayed, don't let my eyes fill with tears. Keep them dry, dry. Else the dragon would open its huge jaws, and the rest would be, as Shakespeare the transvestite put it so dramatically in *Hamlet,* silence.

She made herself think of Harve. Tan, beautiful Harve in jeans. Focus on Harve, girl. She had to save herself for Harve.

"So what do we do?" asked the monster that was also her mother, in a soft, dragon purr.

What Kaelin wanted to say more than anything in the world was something in this vein: Oh please let's give Christopher another chance. One more chance, please. He's so young, so small, with his freckles and pebble collection and the hair that falls over his eyes. He'll behave. I'm sure he'll behave. I promise, I swear to you on my honor, that he'll behave!

What she said instead, somehow without collapsing, was: "We neutralize him."

Mother nodded twice.

But let us not blame Kaelin. She had no choice.

She remembered the first time she took her little brother to the dime store in Wenderoth. The store was closed now, unable to compete with the new mall in Quail Ridge. That was five years ago, five and a half, right after Brian was neutralized. Chris wore shorts, pale blue shorts, and a blue-and-white striped shirt, and he clung to her hand. She took him up and down the aisles, all around the store, showing him what was there. Pinwheels, beach slippers, whistles, bottles of cleaning fluid, lampshades. And after she bought whatever it was she bought, maybe a thimble and a spool of thread, and they went outside into the sun, she saw that both his pockets bulged, that he had shoplifted. Breathless, she pulled him into an alley and behind some garbage cans and there emptied his pockets—toy soldiers—and smacked his little face. He howled, struggled, kicked, but she held him close and hissed into his ear, as if to brand him with her words, "If you're going to steal, Chris—for God's sake, steal with your hands, not with your head. Never, never with your head, or Mother will take it right off. Do you hear me? Do you understand?"

Why were boys so much trouble? Trouble-loving from the cradle? Why were they so stubbornly, irresistibly drawn to danger? To electrical sockets, to high places on furniture and in trees, to unfamiliar, growling animals at the zoo? To dares and double dares? Drawn to testing, mocking, tricking, facing the adults in power.

She would never forget Brian's face, red and twisted, when he screamed at his mother that last night.

The clock in the dining room ticked.

"Then it is settled," said Debra Zimmerman, tapping the table with a finger, tapping once, twice, as if it were not a finger but a gavel. "We scoop the child out."

The Flashlight Test

Moonlight. Midnight. Rustling trees. A cricket chorus. High on the roof, the bdellium dish hums subliminally, because Mother is at the transmitter talking again to Mrs. Fxn, about things arcane, obscure, and far beyond the scope of this or any other book.

The door creaks open in Christopher's room, and a shadow slinks in. It takes a long time closing the door after it so the latch won't click. The shadow holds its breath. Twists its fingers fretfully, its left fingers, its right fingers. It is Kaelin. More frightened now than she's been in her life, because this is disobedience no matter how you cut it. Coming here, she places her head in the noose, in the lion's mouth. If she is caught . . .

She reached out across the moonlight and put a hand on his arm.

His eyes opened.

"Chris," she said. His name was lost in the dark rustling outside the window, but he caught it even so, and understood—all Mother's children were intelligent—that what happened next, whatever it was, would change his life.

"Are you awake? Chris?"

He moved his arm a little.

"Chris. They're going to scoop you out."

He heard his sister, heard the terror in her voice, but wasn't sure what scooping out meant. It sounded surgical. How did you scoop out a person? A person was not a pumpkin on a Halloween doorstep.

"Like they did to Brian," she whispered.

"What are you talking about, Kaelin?" he whispered. "Brian's not scooped out."

"He is. He is."

"How can he talk if he doesn't have lungs? How can he eat if he doesn't have a stomach?"

"Chris, don't be dopey. It's not your body, it's not your organs, it's your upsilon and omicron they take away."

Silence.

"I don't believe you," said Christopher finally. "Mother wouldn't do that." Dismemberment he could imagine, bamboo slivers shoved under fingernails, boiling nitric acid thrown in the eyes and face, two hundred volts applied through sharp-toothed clamp electrodes to toes, nipples, and genitals. Burial alive in an African anthill, smeared with molasses, he could imagine.

But your upsilon and omicron, that was your very soul. To touch that was unthinkable. Mother wouldn't do that.

Not even Mother.

"Brian's not scooped out," he said. His sister sometimes got a little crazy from all her fear.

"All right, I'll prove it to you."

"How are you going to prove it to me?"

"The flashlight test."

Even though he was doomed at dawn, Christopher Zimmerman pricked up his ears. His big sister knew lots of things he didn't, but usually she kept them to herself. Whenever she let something out, it was always something great. Like the time she taught him how to see fish under the ice of the pond behind the shopping center on Bailey's Path, or see the marbles making their inexorable way through Stupid Loomis's intestines in the cafeteria at lunch. And you saw the fish and the marbles not in X-ray black-and-white but living color.

He sat up in bed. "The flashlight test?" he breathed, all attention.

Kaelin showed him. You took an ordinary flashlight, removed the batteries, removed the little bulb, then you whistled down the tube, a low moany whistle full of air, like this, until the sound got that funny swell in it. You quickly screwed the case back together—like catching a fly in a jar—but the batteries and bulb stayed out. Then you simply turned the flashlight on.

At the push of her thumb, light poured from Christopher's old dented metal Eveready. It was a sad orange light, a sunset kind of light, but perfectly strong and even, not a ripple or kink in it, as if it had come flowing out of an overturned can of paint.

"Now watch," said Kaelin. She put her hand over the glass and blocked the light. Only a thread of orange glowed in a crack between two fingers.

"So?" Christopher didn't see what was special about that.

She went over to the window, crouching. He followed.

"We need an animal," she said.

"Call a bat."

"No. Mother might hear."

"What time is it?"

"Twelve-fourteen." Kaelin always knew what time it was.

"She won't hear," said Christopher. "This is Tuesday. She's talking to Mrs. Fxn."

"We can't take the chance. Sometimes the reception is bad."

Christopher elbowed his sister aside, put his chin on the sill, and called into the night, called a bat as softly as he could. There was no answer. They probably couldn't hear him over the wind in the trees, even with their keen ultrasonic ears. He was about to call louder when suddenly there was a flutter and flap in the dark, and a bat came up through the air in the jumpy-jerky way of bats.

Kaelin took it, held it still, and turned the flashlight on it so the beam was aimed at the wall over Christopher's dresser.

"So?" he said.

"Look at the light."

He looked and saw only a circle of sad orange on the wallpaper, which had a green-and-purple fleur-de-lis pattern with vertical lines different distances apart. Not random distances, note, but arranged according to a proportion discovered by the ancient Greeks and given new life, in integers, by an Italian mathematician in the thirteenth century. And given newer life, in topology, as recently as twenty years ago, by a brilliant British physicist who loves to play games.

"So?" said Christopher.

Then he realized that the bat—patient, squirming only a little— was being held in front of the flashlight, blocking the light.

But apparently not blocking it at all. The orange light was going straight through it. Somehow. There was not the least blur or shadow or hint of a bat in the bright disk on the wallpaper.

As if the bat were not in Kaelin's hands. Except it was.

She released the animal. It opened its wings, made a few quick odd angles in the room, and flew out the window, to return to hunting bugs and communing with its dark furry family below the treetops and above the street.

"And here. Look."

Christopher came closer and saw that there was a spiderweb in the upper left corner of the window, milky in the moonlight. And in the center of the web, the spider that had built it was still working, adding finishing touches. It was a wolf spider, fast, with a big body and hairy, predatory legs.

Carefully, so she wouldn't disturb the web, Kaelin got up on the sill with her knees and put her hand slowly out, until it was on the other side of the spider. She turned on the flashlight.

"See?"

Her outstretched hand, fingers closed, was bright orange in the light—and did not contain the shadow of the spider so busy between flashlight and hand.

"It goes through animals," said Christopher.

"Because they have no upsilon, no omicron," she whispered. "Now come." She tiptoed to the door and crooked a finger for him to follow. They slunk out and slipped down the hall, brother and sister, and tiptoed down the stairs to Brian's room on the second floor, not daring to breathe and even slowing their heartbeats. Below them they could hear, with their far hearing, Mother talking.

No static tonight. The subether was clear. Which meant that they had roughly half an hour in which they wouldn't be noticed, unless they did something incredibly stupid like yelp from a stubbed toe or knock over a lamp.

Father was snoring. The snoring of a bear in its den, a peaceful and comforting sound. What a pity that Mother never slept.

Brian, too, was snoring when they crept up to his bed. He didn't wake as Kaelin gingerly took his hand from the blanket and placed it over the upturned flashlight. He only grunted, shifted, and made a few wet tasting noises before he continued with his snores, which were higher and more nasal than Father's and nowhere near as sonorous.

Christopher looked at the ceiling and saw a full moon of sad orange light.

Through Brian's hand.

Kaelin put her hand over the flashlight, and the light was blocked. Christopher put his hand over the flashlight, and the light was blocked. Their eyes met. Christopher looked with dawning horror at Brian, and understood now what Kaelin had meant when she said before, in the basement, that she had lost a brother.

Christopher had lost a brother, too.

Brian turned over, away from them, mumbling, sleeping, his retrieved hand shoved under the pillow. He was there in the flesh, yes, but only in the flesh. He would get up in the morning and go to school, but it would be only a body, Brian's body, getting up, having breakfast, taking his book bag, and walking to the bus stop. Brian's body, not Brian. Brian was gone.

Christopher could hardly believe it. His own family. He stared at his brother as one stares at one's first corpse. A real-life corpse, not in the movies or on television. An actual dead person.

Kaelin tapped him on the arm: time to go. They tiptoed back upstairs. Mother was still on the transmitter, but they could tell, from the intonation, that the chat was winding down. You couldn't just say over and out to Mrs. Fxn when you were done. There was a whole protocol of leave-taking on Mrs. Fxn's planet.

Back in Christopher's room, Kaelin said: "You better run."

He said: "Come with me."

A pause, a wrenched "I can't."

Christopher was so awfully young to run away by himself, and so small. But Kaelin couldn't go with him.

For one thing, they would probably be caught anyhow. Kaelin didn't think it was possible to escape from Mother, no matter what you did, no matter what hiding tricks you used. But even if it was possible, Kaelin didn't want to run. She wanted a normal life here in Wenderoth.

"I just got a boyfriend."

"Harve."

"Yes, Harve." Her eyes welled. "He's only human, he's not a genius, but he's cute and sweet. He likes me, he really does. He took me out for ice cream last week after school. He has a car."

She wiped at her tears. She wanted to be a normal girl that someone would someday take to the senior prom. She didn't want to be a freak.

A mutant.

An alien.

A monster.

"Harve's all right," said Christopher, annoyed by her tears.

Kaelin did something then which she rarely did, almost never did. She put out her arms and took her brother and hugged him tight. "I'll always love you," she said with a sob. "Oh Chris, please run. Don't let them scoop you out." She held him for a moment, then fled on tiptoe.

Alone, Christopher flicked his flashlight on and off a few times, then sighed, opened it, and replaced the batteries and bulb. He turned the flashlight on. It was regular again, getting dim the way all flashlights seemed to do the moment you bought them. He put it back on the shelf. He was extremely tired. A glance at the clock: no wonder, it was going on one.

And he had to pack.

He went to the closet and pulled out Buzz. Buzz was covered with dust and needed WD-40. When the poor thing wagged his tail, it squeaked like a windshield wiper. The squeak was a reproach from an old friend. Christopher had been too busy lately for the dog, caught up with—what? His pebble puzzle? Daydreaming?

He took a dirty undershirt off the floor and wiped away the cobwebs. He got out an old can of silicone spray—there wasn't much left in it, but there was enough—and loosened up Buzz's limbs. The dog crooned. The liquid-crystal eyes were dull but affectionate as always. Devoted as always. A hundred years might pass, but Buzz would be as true as the day he was assembled.

"Shh," said Christopher.

He ran a diagnostic, plugging the dog into the closet Atari, which was also covered with dust. He had a bad moment when the computer beeped okay. Did Mother hear that beep? He waited, praying that she hadn't.

If she had, his goose was cooked.

The clock ticked and the crickets outside sang, and Father snored, but there were no doors opened, no footfalls on the stairs below. He was safe.

Christopher put a toothbrush, comb, grammar book, and a few clothes into his knapsack. A penknife. Two Band-Aids. Only the necessities. He couldn't take all his treasures. When you were on the run, you needed to travel light.

He made a copy of himself, using a towel, a yellow plastic ruler, his collection of baseball cards, and some string. This was forbidden, but it didn't matter now, he was already a criminal. The copy would get up in the morning when the alarm went off, take a shower, and with any luck make it through breakfast and school before Mother caught on. Giving Christopher precious hours. Giving him and Gramps a head start.

He put the knapsack on his back, tightened the shoulder straps, turned off the lights, and said to Buzz, "Now we have to be very quiet. Understand?"

Buzz nodded.

Christopher got on the dog, clasped his hands around the dog's shaggy carpet neck, locked his ankles under the dog's galvanized belly. They rose and went out the window, they soared over the rustling trees, through the moonlit night, toward Walnut Street and Gramps's house.

Tongue lolling, Buzz panted, but the panting didn't make much noise. Mother didn't hear.

The stars twinkled. Christopher had never seen so many stars before. He had never been up so late before. He felt light-headed.

He held on.

5

Snoring. The wheezy, sniffling snores you would expect from a withered old man. On his pillow the hair is a dull dishrag gray. It is the hair of a derelict in an alley, not the hair of a sage in a temple. He has sunken cheeks, from extracted molars. He has a large wen on his forehead above the left eyebrow. No, this is not the kind of prettied-up senior citizen we see in *Modern Maturity* ads for mutual funds, trusses, or high-fiber cereal.

He smiles faintly. Why is he smiling? He is visiting with his Emily. Such visits are ordinarily not permitted, but an exception was made in his case. After all, he and Emily did spend fifty-five years together, quarreling seriously only twice in all that time.

A knock at the window, timid ten-year-old knuckles on double glass.

A more insistent knock.

Gramps woke and saw, in his window, the muzzle of Buzz, the pale face of Christopher.

"They scooped out Brian," Christopher said when his grandfather came, slippers flopping, and opened the window. "And I'm next."

Gramps opened the window more so they could come in. "Have to watch my back," he muttered as he lifted the sash. "Easy does it. No jerks. One fluid motion."

When boy and dog alighted in his bedroom, he closed the window.

"Fresh air," he said, hitching his pajamas. "Used to love it. Still do. But you think about drafts on muscles at my age."

"Gramps," said Christopher. "Mother will be after us. She knows."

The old man held up a hand, patted the air, as if to say: Now let's not get excited.

"They're going to scoop me out," said Christopher, "and send you to that Golden Years place in Florida."

Buzz wagged his tail happily. The dog had not been programmed to register human tragedy.

"We have to run!" Christopher exclaimed.

Gramps shook a finger. "Tomorrow, bright and early, after breakfast. Breakfast first. Bacon. Last chance to get some real saturated fat and no-nonsense cholesterol into the old bloodstream. Because it'll be nothing but cold, dry rations for weeks, my boy, maybe months. You'll be sick of it. No Big Macs where we're going, no Quarter Pounders. Just trail mix, peanut butter, and pitted prunes."

"Mother could be here any minute."

You never underestimated Mother.

Gramps touched his grandson on the forehead, brushed aside some straw hair. He saw puffy eyes. The kid was half asleep. "Go on, lie down," he said, gesturing at the bed. "I'll need a few hours anyhow to pack the bathroom for us."

Christopher yawned and climbed up on the bed without even removing his knapsack. He was asleep the moment his head sank into the pillow hollow, still warm, that Gramps's larger, gray head had left.

Buzz looked around for a closet, found one, and made himself comfortable, with a couple of low snuffles, among some shoes, boxed tax records, and a tripod that once belonged to a telescope.

"Poor kid," the old man muttered. "Debra's on the warpath again." He shook his head and turned on the lamp, adjusting the shade so the light wouldn't hit Christopher in the face.

The packing he had to do was really only last-minute things. Most of the supplies had been stocked in the bathroom for a couple of weeks now. Gramps had been around long enough to know which way the wind blew—and he wasn't about to be shipped off to any old-age facility-community near Naples, a spotless institution, a cluster of white buildings between a golf course and the Okaloacoochee Slough. No sir.

He had been planning this escape for almost a year. That was why he replaced the tiles. A lot of trouble, those tiles. The measuring, the cutting. Murder on the knees. And of course then it was so tempting to take the kid for a spin or two, to try the tiles out. He should have known better. He *did* know better, but hell, it had been so tempting. To show the kid what the Mayan temples were like before the white man came. How the mastodons ran in high grass. The big meteor rain, that glorious nonstop fireworks display before the air got thick, and the volcanoes growling and booming so much, it was like getting a full body massage though you stood miles away.

And the civilization on IV Gamma Seven Zee Prime of M928, their sidesplitting knitting contest every hundred years.

Now he'd have to take his grandson with him. That was not part of the plan. But what choice did he have? You couldn't reason with Debra. Even when she was a little girl, you couldn't reason with her. Little Miss Inflexible. Everything set in concrete, hewn in stone. He remembered the way she had to have her toast buttered in the morning. How she explained it to her parents slowly, patiently, as if they were mentally deficient.

He didn't understand this neutralizing business. Neutralizing children, for God's sake. What was the world coming to?

From the dresser he took underwear, socks, handkerchiefs. A bow tie, in case there was a social occasion. You never could tell. He was old and dried up, but not that old and dried up. The universe was a big place, and there were ladies out there on the Seven Seas who might take a shine to him and not mind a little partying, a little lighthearted seduction. Emily wouldn't object, bless her. She understood about loneliness and physical needs.

A small bottle of Old Spice, just in case. There was room for it.

He checked the vanity under the bathroom sink: Coleman stove, spare propane tank, snake-bite kit, water purification kit, flares, fishing gear, scouring pads. The tent, sleeping bags, and magnetometer were all neatly folded and fitted into the tub.

He checked the medicine cabinet and the food stored on shelves just under the ceiling.

Beef jerky.

Mercurochrome.

The Cutter's.

Swiss army knife.

Astrolabe.

He had bought so many bungee cords, the men were starting to make jokes at the hardware store.

No room for the dog, though. He hoped that wouldn't be a problem.

Christopher had been so thrilled, the first time. Full of questions. A lot of them good questions, too. Smart kid. He asked about the new tiles. "They make your eyes swim, Gramps," he said.

The whole idea. It had to be something that was repeating but not repeating. Not repeating but repeating. Until your mind hung between the two, undecided. It had to be a pattern symmetrical all kinds of ways—five, to be exact—yet making your eyes shift back and forth to follow this subpattern, then that subpattern, then another, until they went out of focus in the special way that enabled you, balanced, and with the proper positioning and timing, of course, to hook onto a cosmic string with your upsilon and omicron. Like thumbing a ride.

Gramps chuckled, thinking of Panda Ray enthusing about the great balance. He could picture that Dravidian head, round and black, bobbing as Panda Ray spoke in his choppy, bubbly, cheerful singsong.

"Bal-lance, bal-lance, yiss."

And then Christopher started asking about the traveling itself—where they went, how they went, in what sense they went—so Gramps sat the boy down and told him about the different modes.

Think of it as the Seven Seas, Christopher.

First there's the Sea of Is. That's the Sea we're in now, the Sea we're always in, just by living, breathing, being. We don't look on Is as a thing to travel through, because it's so much a part of the routine, so everyday and everywhere. Brushing your teeth, waxing the floor, putting a flea collar on the cat—what kind of journey is that? We take it for granted.

You don't need any special equipment or powers to navigate the Sea of Is.

In fact, you don't really have any say in the matter. There's only one way of getting *out* of the Sea of Is, and it usually hurts.

The next Sea—for that you do need equipment, something like these tiles, plus your upsilon and omicron. It's a complicated Sea and one of the harder ones to understand. The Sea of If. Some call it the Sea of If Then.

Let me try to explain it. Suppose you don't want to do your homework. It's adverbs.

"I hate adverbs," said Christopher.

Right. Me, too. You have all these adverbs to do, suppose, and you'd much rather watch television. Let's say there's a *Star Trek* festival on.

"I don't like *Star Trek*."

No? He doesn't like *Star Trek*. I thought everyone liked *Star Trek*. What do you like?

"Nova."

Okay, there's a *Nova* festival on, and you're stuck with pages and pages of words that end in *ly*.

"Not all adverbs end in *ly,* Gramps."

I know that. I'm not stupid. One foot in the grave, maybe, but not stupid. Go fast. Go slow. Be well. See?

"We have to do adverbial phrases."

Anyway, Christopher, let's say you'd love to watch television but you've been given this homework for tomorrow. However, if the teacher—

"Mr. Osborne."

If Mr. Osborne had been sick that day, if he had had to stay home with the flu, then he wouldn't have given you the homework assignment in the first place.

"If the teacher is sick, the substitute will give us the assignment."

But the substitute is sick, too. There's a lot of flu running around. A whole epidemic. Let's suppose they can't get a substitute for love or money, or if they do find someone, Mr. Osborne still has too much of a sore throat to give the assignment over the phone. He tries, but all that comes out is croaks. He gives up. He hangs up.

"All right."

Now, here you are at home with your adverb homework. And you want to watch the *Nova* festival more than anything. So what do you do? You travel the Sea of If.

"We don't have these kinds of funny tiles in our bathroom."

Pretend you're visiting with me. Come on, use your imagination. This is a thought experiment. Einstein did them. Your folks went to a World Expo in Nablus, and I have you for a whole week.

"All right."

So you travel the Sea of If. There you are now, on the Sea of If. And you come to the day—one of the days, one of the todays—where Mr. Osborne is home in bed with laryngitis.

"The flu."

The flu gave him laryngitis. And therefore he doesn't give *you* the adverb homework, neither in person nor through a substitute who somehow survived the epidemic.

"All right. Then what?"

You don't have any homework now. Hurrah. You can watch the *Nova* festival.

Christopher wrinkled his brow. "But . . . if I stay there, in that home, and watch television, then there won't be anybody in *my* home, the one here, and the homework won't get done, and I'll be in big trouble tomorrow."

True. Not to mention the problem, my boy, that there will already be a Christopher there, in that home, and that your folks in that home will not fail to notice that now there are two of you sitting in front of the television.

This is one of the reasons traveling the Sea of If is not recommended for tyros.

"What's a tyro? A kind of top?"

A tyro is a beginner, a greenhorn. As I said, the Sea of If is complicated, full of trouble, and can sometimes even be dangerous. I will not take you on it, so you don't have to worry about getting into awkward situations with other Christopher Zimmermans.

The next Sea is easy. You've already heard of it, though by a different name. The Sea of Was.

"The past."

Very good. The simple past. Time travel.

"But that's only half of time travel, Gramps. There's the future, too."

Okay. The future is another Sea. We haven't gotten to that one yet. The Sea of Will Be. They're two different modes, two different Seas, the Sea of Was and the Sea of Will Be. There's a good reason for this, but the reason is philosophical and I don't want to bore you.

"Will we visit the future, too, Gramps?"

If you behave. The future is not quite as simple as the past. But simple enough.

The next Sea, the fourth, is the Sea of Where, and in that one, like the Sea of Is, you don't even need a vehicle—unless you have to get someplace in a hurry. Your own two feet work just fine. This is traveling through space. Space travel. Though of course if you want to have a look at another galaxy, it's a hell of a lot more convenient to grab a cosmic string, bam, and you're there in a blink and a swallow. Unless there's a disturbance.

The Sea after that is the Sea of Will Be, which we've already covered.

The sixth Sea is the Sea of Isn't. This one we will *both* avoid. It's hard to return from. What is it? Well, perhaps the best way to explain it . . .

Let me see.

All right.

You know how you have psi, upsilon, and omicron? The Sea of Isn't is like pure omicron, if you can imagine pure omicron.

With psi, you toss a coin, a penny for example, and can tell whether it will be heads or tails before it falls. Or you can make it fall heads or tails.

With upsilon, you might make the penny square or octagonal, or maybe put a different president on it, Hayes instead of Lincoln, that kind of thing. Or change the color or size or metal or smell.

It's still a penny, though.

With omicron, say good-bye to the penny, because anything can become anything else, just about. You take the penny and turn it into a dime, a shilling—or an owl.

"Mother won't allow that."

I know she won't. Well, she's probably right, there. What would you want with a pocketful of owls?

In the Sea of Isn't, anything goes, nothing stays the same, and everything is in flux, changing, as if it's alive. . . . The Sea of Isn't, you might think of it as a dream place.

"That's six."

What?

"That's six Seas, Gramps. You said there were seven."

Right. The seventh and last Sea is the Sea of What.

"And what does that do?"

I have absolutely no idea. I've never been on it or near it. I was on the Sea of Isn't once, only once—an unnerving experience. I wouldn't have gotten out in one piece, I don't think, without old Panda Ray throwing me a rope. But the Sea of What—no, never been there. And I am not even sure I could get there if I wanted to. There's no entrance.

"Then how do you know about it?"

The grapevine, how else?

And Gramps stroked Christopher's head and wondered why it was that children, who knew so much less than grown-ups, always asked better questions.

Rose Tiles

It is dawn. We are in Gramps's bathroom. Everything is packed now. The bow tie and bottle of Old Spice, in the event that a little romance chances by, are included. From the kitchen wafts the smell of bacon. The bathroom itself smells of soap and mildew, with a touch maybe of the sewer, because with poor eyes, arthritis in fingers, and difficulty bending the back it is not easy to clean as thoroughly as one should, to get at all those hard-to-reach pockets and pools of effluvial bacteria. But let us not judge Gramps too harshly. He is not the man he used to be.

The tiles are shiny, being relatively new. They are rose-colored. No soap scum on them. No mold yet in the grout. They are rhombs and pentagons. Stars and suns. Asterisks, pentagrams, whirling wheels that are interrupted when your eye follows them in a spiral—interrupted by a different wheel, or a wedge, or a kind of wriggling zigzag ray outward. And each element—wedge, wheel, zigzag—is repeated in a pattern, a perfectly symmetrical pattern, until your eye again comes to an interruption and again you find yourself shifting to a different pattern and a different symmetry.

You notice now, looking closer, that all this variety, this pleasantly confusing order—or this pleasantly ordered confusion—is constructed of only two kinds of tile, and even those two kinds, you also notice, are similar: one becomes the other if you flip a corner in or flip a corner out. Flip it out, the tile is a kite; flip it in, the tile is a dart. Rose-colored darts and kites, fitted together to make rhombs and pentagons, stars and suns, fill the walls around the toilet, tub, towel rack, medicine cabinet, and vanity.

If you look more closely still, and have a protractor with you, you will discover that the dart-and-kite angles are 36 degrees here, 72 degrees there, 144 degrees here, 216 degrees there. These might not strike you offhand as interesting numbers, but being degrees, they are fifths and tenths of a circle. It might occur to you now that there is some connection between fifths and tenths of a circle and the pentagons and decagons we're seeing in such profusion in the patterns within patterns and in the patterns interrupting patterns in these new tiles on Gramps's bathroom walls.

There was once a secret society, set up by Plato himself, that considered the five-pointed star an occult figure. They believed that it had mystic power, that it partook of divinity. The reason: the pentagram's sides and intersecting diagonals are chock-full of golden sections. Everywhere you turn in a pentagram there are golden sections, side by side and within one another. The golden section, the divine proportion, is something extremely simple—as simple as adding a thing to itself. But that addition yields, in a few quite straightforward and innocuous steps—translate, transpose—an imponderable irrational, a number no calculator or computer can contain, and a number, *mirabile dictu,* that keeps cropping up in all sorts of common, natural places.

Pay attention now: there is nothing up my sleeve. Behold.

Add one to the golden number, and it is the same as squaring it.

Applause.

Take away one, and it is its inverse.

Applause.

What is the golden number? One and two—and presto chango, the square root of five.

One plus a one which is divided by a one plus a one which is in turn divided by a one plus a one also divided by a one plus a one likewise divided, and so on forever. And when forever arrives, they equal a combination of—yes—one, two, and voilà, the square root of five.

Applause.

An unknown squared, then subtracted by itself to equal zero. What could be simpler? One, two, and the square root of five all holding hands.

Applause.

The growth in the population of deathless rabbits, each rabbit pair begetting a new rabbit pair each month but only after their first month of life. One, two, and the square root of five solemnly posing for a family portrait.

Pythagoras. The perfect fifth. The fifth essence. Divide the number of darts by the number of kites. This is to this as that is to that. What could be simpler?

Powder on the floor to contain the demon summoned or to keep out Satan.

Five points, five sides, five angles.

Five fingers.

Five books.

Aliquot parts, everything fitting, mirroring itself, repeated and added to itself, recursive and wheeling constantly, now to the left, now to the right, radiating out as it wheels, rose-colored to the eye but also, though the eye cannot directly see it, full of ratios and full of gold.

The dawn, by coincidence, is also rose and gold. Its light filters through the small window above the tub.

Enter Gramps and Christopher, knapsack straps tightened and hickory-smoked bacon in their bellies. There is not much room for them in the bathroom, even though Gramps is rail thin and Christopher close to the low end of the spectrum of height for his age.

They shut the door. They lock the door.

Don't feel sorry for Buzz, who can't go along. He is perfectly happy in closets, perhaps because his fundamental optimism—he is only a machine—assures him that everything will turn out all right in the end and we will all be reunited. This is not actually the case, but what the dog doesn't know won't hurt him.

Gramps sat on the edge of the tub. Christopher sat on the john. Their knees touched.

They both stifled a yawn. It was early, and with the events of the last six hours neither had gotten a full night's sleep.

"And you brought your schoolbooks?"

Since Christopher would be out of school for an indefinite period of time, maybe as much as a month or two, Gramps's idea was to tutor him now and then as they traveled, whenever there wasn't much doing, so the boy wouldn't fall too far behind.

Which is why Christopher took his grammar book with him (if you noticed) when he left home: a little precognitive psi at work, nothing special.

"Just the grammar book," replied Christopher. "The other subjects I don't need to study."

"Hmm," said Gramps, screwing up his mouth and trying to look like a displeased teacher. It was a responsibility, being in charge of a child. "Bring a toothbrush?" he asked.

"Yes, sir," said Christopher.

The old man nodded with approval.

"So where are we going?" asked Christopher.

"The Sea of Was, for starters. We'll have to keep a low profile and we'll have to keep moving. They'll try to find us, you know. Your mother doesn't like to be crossed."

Curiously, it was on the very word *mother* that the doorbell sounded.

Gramps looked at Christopher. "You left a copy of yourself?"

"Yes," said Christopher.

"It must not have been a good one."

Christopher shrugged. Somehow, under his grandfather's wing, as it were, even with the dragon herself at the door, he wasn't afraid.

Gramps looked at his watch. "She didn't lose much time, did she. No, Christopher, your mother never did like to be crossed. We better hurry."

The doorbell sounded again, there was angry knocking, and then the front door flew open. Monty Zimmerman took three steps in, Debra behind him. They sniffed the trace of bacon, but the trace of bacon told them nothing. They looked around, and went quickly from room to room.

They found Buzz, who lifted his head. They moved on, leaving him. He lowered his head again.

Monty crouched in the hall, rattling a knob.

"What's that?" asked his wife.

"Bathroom door's locked," he said.

"Unlock it, then, you idiot," she said.

He did, the door opened, and they saw a normal bathroom. Nothing in the tub except for a ring of grime. No shelves near the ceiling. No unmanageable Gramps, no disobedient Christopher.

The tiles on the wall were not rose now but a robin's egg blue.

And they were square. A regular array of squares, squares repeating themselves up, down, left, and right, repeating themselves without mistake or variation, as it is with most bathroom tiles in most middle-class bathrooms. A fully periodic tiling, in other words—nothing the least bit aperiodic about it.

With square tiles, there were no surprises or perplexities, whichever way a looker looked.

The squares were like the squares that fill ordinary graph paper. Each blue tile was exactly like its neighbors, and all were oriented the same, all lined up vertically, horizontally, perpendicularly, the grout lines at 90 degrees and 180 degrees. The circle was divided by simple fourths, not by tricky fifths.

"They're traveling," said Debra Zimmerman, and there was black murder in her eyes.

Damage Control

The FBI agent who approached the main desk at Lincoln Elementary School asking to see the principal looked like a 1950s Clark Kent. He had thick dark Brylcreem hair and thick dark-rimmed glasses. He was tall, with broad shoulders and white teeth. His smile was constant and even, his skin pasty, maybe even clammy. He seemed uncomfortable in his well-tailored clothes. The name he gave the secretary, in a resonant voice, was Calvin Hornwood.

"You don't have an appointment," said the secretary, Betty. "Mr. Sykes has a lot of meetings." She used her twangy monotone, not wanting to show that she was impressed, quite impressed, with the FBI badge he flashed before her.

"It won't take long," said the agent. "Please see if you can fit me in."

"What is this in regard to, Mr.—?"

"Hornwood."

"Hardwood?"

"Hornwood."

"What is this in regard to, Mr. Hornwood?"

Betty's first thought was that one of the teachers was a drug dealer, child pornographer, or wanted in Tennessee for the execution-style slaying of a minister and his wife in their home on a shady street on a quiet Sunday afternoon. But which teacher could it be? That was the question. In her mind she started making a list.

The agent's smile widened, revealing more white. "We need some information, ma'am. It's important."

When Mr. Sykes heard that the FBI wanted to talk to him, he blinked, frowned, looked at his fingernails, which were manicured—Mr. Sykes went to a manicurist regularly, in East Carlyle—and said to Betty with a sigh: "Show the gentleman in."

The agent, shown in, presented—deferentially, apologetically— an ID that contained his picture.

"What can I do for you?" asked Mr. Sykes, who hadn't caught the man's name or really looked at the face on the ID. It was undoubtedly the FBI. The dark suit, the big shoulders, the careful politeness were dead giveaways.

Mr. Sykes turned to the secretary and told her she could leave. Betty left reluctantly, with sidelong glances. He got up, made sure the door was closed, made sure the intercom was off, resumed his seat, and folded his clean, pink hands on the desk before him.

"The FBI has been trying to track down a certain group of people," began the agent, "some of whom, we have reason to believe, are in central Pennsylvania."

They looked at each other.

"This group of people," said the principal of Lincoln Elementary, clearing his throat. "Some kind of religious cult?"

"No," said the agent.

"Terrorists?"

"No."

Another pause. They both smiled, Mr. Sykes smiling nervously, the agent smiling evenly. Mr. Sykes glanced at his watch and began fidgeting with his thumbs. He was almost twiddling.

"They are very secretive," said the agent. "But children, you know. You know how children are. Not always good at keeping a secret. At keeping the skeleton in the closet, the dirty laundry in the family. Children, bless them, are open, trusting, reckless, and forgetful. This is why we are going around to the schools."

"You think some of the children of these . . . people . . . are enrolled here, at Lincoln?" Mr. Sykes was having a problem with his throat. He couldn't seem to clear it. "Would you care for a cup of coffee?" he asked.

"No thanks."

Mr. Sykes flicked on the intercom and asked Betty for a cup of coffee. She brought it in almost instantly—steaming, black, in a plastic foam cup.

"No coffee for you?" Betty asked the FBI man.

"No thanks."

"Tea? We have tea."

"I'm fine, thank you."

They waited for her to leave. She left.

"What sort of secrets, generally, are these people secretive about?" asked Mr. Sykes, sipping slowly so he wouldn't burn himself. "I mean, to have some idea of what you're looking for."

The agent nodded. "Let's see what I can tell you. I can tell you that these people are very unusual. So unusual, that what a child of theirs might do or say of a revelatory nature—it would be strikingly different, the kind of thing everyone would remark and remember."

"Well, you know," said the principal, sipping, "all children are different. And many are remarkable, even in this sleepy community of ours. Many more than you might imagine. You would be surprised, Mr. . . . ."

"Hornwood."

"Yes. We have a child in the sixth grade who has appeared in a professional performance of the *Nutcracker.* It was televised. We have a child, he's in the junior high now, who's an inventor and already owns two patents. It's true his father helped him a little, but still. We have a spelling champ who last year, believe it or not, placed—"

"Mr. Sykes," said the agent, "we're not talking about gifted and talented. This is something that would be seen, rather, as abnormal."

The principal raised an eyebrow. "Abnormal. An imprecise and often judgmental word," he said. "We try to avoid it. Abnormal in what sense? These people, are you telling me that they are . . . pathological in some way? Dangerous?"

"They are abnormal in the extreme," said the agent. "But they hide it."

"They hide it. And you suggest—yes?—that a child, a child belonging to this group, may be indiscreet in school."

"That's right."

The principal fluttered a hand in the air. "What I'm getting at, Mr. . . . ."

"Hornwood."

"Mr. Hornwood. How would we know, how would we recognize, aside from the fact of its striking nature, as you put it, an instance of such indiscretion . . . on the part of this hypothetical, so-called abnormal child?" He was pleased with the sentence. Sometimes he came up with good sentences.

"You would know it," said the agent, losing his smile.

"I would know it." And the principal's squint held a glint of irony.

The FBI man thought, deliberated, and said: "I will tell you this, Mr. Sykes. But it's classified."

The principal nodded and leaned forward, gravely, as if he were a priest in a confessional.

"These people."

"Yes?"

"Are so different."

"Yes?"

"You might think of them as not quite human."

Mr. Sykes tried to digest that but had difficulty with it. He blinked and cleared his throat. He took a swallow of his coffee. "I'm not sure I understand you."

"You might think of them," said the agent in a lower voice, "as mutants."

"Mutants?"

"With powers."

"Mutants with powers . . . mutants with powers. Mr.—"

"Hornwood."

"Mr. Hornwood. I'm sorry."

"That's all right."

"But this does sound, you must admit, like something out of, I don't know, *Star Trek* or a comic book."

"They're not really mutants, of course," said the agent.

"They're not."

"No. I only said that to give you an idea of how different they are."

"You make them sound like something . . . supernatural. Or like, I don't know, monsters from Planet X." Mr. Sykes attempted a chuckle here, but it died when he saw the agent's face.

"Talk to your teachers. Individually, in private," said the agent, who was looking more and more like a 1950s Clark Kent. "See if they have anything to report, about any student. Anything that seems bizarre, unique, incredible." He reached over the desk to give the principal a card. "That's my number. You can call at any time, any day."

The principal pocketed the card, not looking at it.

The agent rose. "I can tell you this, Mr. Sykes. Not to alarm you, but you should know. We are concerned. These people—they may not be in your area, but if they are . . ."

"Yes?"

"In answer to your question before. Yes, it is possible that they are dangerous. They may be very dangerous."

The principal rose, blinking.

"But keep this under your hat."

"Certainly."

"We don't want hysteria."

"Of course not."

And on the dramatic note of hysteria the agent left—most likely to proceed to another school and talk to another principal, such as Josh Bentley over at Quail Ridge.

Betty stuck her head in—to learn, before anyone else, which teacher or teachers would be led away in shame and handcuffs. Mr. Sykes waved her out. She grimaced her exasperation and shut the door.

Mr. Sykes paced on his office carpet. He shook his head. He shook his head again. He sat at his desk and inspected his fingernails.

The phone rang. It was Betty reminding him that he had a meeting in five minutes at the district office with the assistant superintendent. Yet another meeting about revised estimates for next year's budget. Moving numbers around to conceal mismanagement or worse. He looked at his watch. He cursed under his breath. He called the assistant superintendent and left a message with the assistant superintendent's secretary: Something came up, Sal. Minor emergency. Can't make it. Sorry. Let's reschedule.

He told Betty to field all his calls. He pushed the forwarding button on the phone. He went and locked his door. Went and closed his blinds. Sat at his desk. Then he did something odd: he dropped his head and banged it on the desk and muttered, "Jesus, Jesus, Jesus." It was soft muttering but with great feeling.

He sighed. He wiped his face, using a cafeteria napkin. He finished his coffee. He opened the left desk drawer and took out a box, opened the box and took out a plastic toy, a green telephone. It had no cord or aerial, but it wasn't a toy; it worked.

He dialed with a sigh and a groan. This was not a call he wanted to make. He ever wanted to make. He had no choice, however, absolutely no choice.

"Hello?" he said into the plastic green receiver. "Debra? . . . Yes, it's me. . . . Yes . . . What you anticipated . . . I'm afraid so. I'm calling as you instructed me. . . . A man from the FBI . . . Yes . . . No . . . I didn't. Of course I didn't. . . . Yes . . . What? . . . Mrs. Palmer? . . . Christopher's class . . . Oh . . . You don't think that . . . Yes, Debra, I understand, but . . . Of course . . . We have to, yes . . . All right . . . I'll take care of it. . . . Whatever you say, Debra . . . Always . . . Don't worry, we'll take her out of the picture. Yes, silenced, she'll be silenced. . . . You're right, of course. . . . When? Well, tomorrow evening? There's a bake sale at the school. . . . George will handle it, he's reliable. . . . Yes, I will, Debra. . . . No, I won't. . . . All right . . . Yes, Debra . . . Good . . . Yes . . . Goodbye."

Mr. Sykes put away the toy telephone and banged his head on the desk again with a clenched-teeth "Jesus, Jesus, Jesus." One bang for each clenched-teeth Jesus. There was a growing red spot on his forehead. Jane Palmer had been with the school—what, twenty years? It wouldn't be the same place without her.

He got up, opened the blinds, unlocked the door, unforwarded his phone. He groaned. She had a son, too.

They always had family—a grieving spouse, and stunned, lost-looking children.

Mr. Sykes made a note to himself. He would have to say something at the funeral. Simple, to the point, official yet heartfelt.

After the second lunch period he went looking for George and found the custodian in the boiler room, a dim, humid area full of bandaged conduits, dented ducts, and strange echoes. On a workbench under a fluorescent lamp George was repairing something that looked like a television set or a VCR. Probably for himself. George had plenty of spare time.

The custodian's stomach was such a beer belly, his shirt was always coming out of his pants. He wore greasy suspenders. He had jowls, sad eyes: a classic bulldog face. He smelled of cigars, stale sweat, and hops. You could walk down an empty hall and know that George had been there.

"Bad news, George," said Mr. Sykes.

"I don't want to hear it," said George, looking up from the tangled guts of whatever kind of appliance it was he had opened. A vacuum cleaner, a typewriter, a microwave oven.

"I just spoke to Mrs. Zimmerman."

"Shit," said George.

"George, you know I don't like you using that kind of language on school grounds."

George made a disgusted face and spat.

"George, please don't spit on the floor. You know it's not sanitary. And it sets a bad example for the children." Not that children usually came to the boiler room.

The custodian had no more choice than did the principal. "What is it this time?" he growled. But meant: Who is it this time?

"Christopher's teacher. Mrs. Palmer."

George got up and wiped his hands on an old rag. They were calloused, tobacco-stained hands. Thick, misshapen paws more than hands. The nails horny and yellow, the fingers like short sausages. The top joint of one finger on his left hand was missing.

"Mrs. Palmer," he said. "Just about the best teacher we have."

"Yes."

"A good woman. Decent. Always cares about the kids. Does the fund-raisers. Stays late. One of the few who help clean up."

"Yes." The principal thought he might use some of that in the eulogy.

"Why?"

"The FBI came snooping around today. This morning. A Mr. Hardwood. Apparently Uncle Sam got wind of them somehow. And Christopher must have said something in class he shouldn't have."

"So what's the harm? For God's sake, who's going to believe a little kid with a tall tale?"

"Mrs. Zimmerman says that Mrs. Palmer is not a stupid woman and may put two and two together when government people come here and start asking questions."

"If you ask me, we should kill them." This in a throaty whisper.

"The government people?"

"No, *them.*"

"Don't be absurd. We can't. Don't even think like that, George. I didn't hear that. Remember Jim. Look what happened to Jim. Get a grip on yourself." Both whispering now. Two grown men whispering, heads close together, in the boiler room in the school basement.

Lest Mother hear.

"I don't know," mumbled George defiantly. "With a rifle, maybe. At a distance. From behind." But you could tell he didn't mean it. The way his eyes shifted.

Jim had tried a bomb, plastique.

For which he was tied into a pretzel. A screaming, pleading pretzel.

"Enough of that," said Mr. Sykes, smoothing down his hair and straightening his jacket, looking over his shoulder, looking around. The walls sometimes had ears. And you never knew when they did. He cleared his throat and said, louder: "So. There's a PTA bake sale tomorrow evening. At the talent show."

"I know that. It's on my calendar. I'll be working then. Dave is off."

"Mrs. Palmer will be there."

"You want me to do it at the bake sale?"

"Whatever accident you arrange," said Mr. Sykes, blinking, "I hope, George, you will do your very best to make it as painless for her as possible."

George wasn't prepossessing, wasn't a genius, but he had a heart and you could rely on him.

Mr. Sykes Says a Few Words

Where is Jane? Has anybody seen Jane?

Mrs. Bender, Mrs. Strapelli, and Mrs. Showalter are manning the table, but it is a big table—several tables put together, end to end—and when intermission comes, in five or ten minutes, the ladies will be swamped. All the brownies haven't been cut yet. The carrot cake hasn't been cut yet. Maybe more cups should be put out for the juice. And my God, where are the napkins? Did you bring the napkins?

Jane's chair is empty. She went to check something, get something—the milk for the coffee? yes—and she still isn't back.

The table is filled with goodies. Thirty parents (that's a lot) were generous this time. There are coffee rings glazed and with crumbs, peach pies made by good old Mrs. Wells, fruitcakes, brownies in ten varieties, fudge, plates of chocolate-chip cookies, pound cake, a pecan pie that looks bought, a lemon cake full of calories, a braided thing with dates and hazelnuts which is probably delicious, and blueberry and cranberry muffins.

Circles, squares, wedges all mixed. No pattern to it, no symmetry, and yet it looks as if it has all been carefully arranged for a magazine camera. Geometry doesn't apply to everything. It doesn't apply to dessert. We find ourselves salivating.

The PTA should clear a few hundred dollars on this bake sale, easy.

You can hear muffled singing through the doors to the auditorium. Other than that, the hall is still. Only George mopping at the other end. And the big percolator in the corner makes an occasional, sleepy, aquarium gurgle.

Mrs. Strapelli wonders if she'll have the chance, in all the activity tonight, to talk to Caroline or Dot or Denise, to pull them aside and ask a few quick questions. Probably not. She heard about it only yesterday. But she can't do anything now, with Mrs. Bender sitting right next to her.

Mrs. Bender looks perfectly normal, perfectly calm and proper. Not one bit like an adulteress, fallen woman, strumpet, harlot, slut. Mrs. Strapelli tries to imagine her in bed with football coach Steve Wanamaker, doing it—panting, moaning, climaxing—but can't. She can't even imagine Mrs. Bender in suggestive underwear or dabbing a little Indiscretion behind her ears. Mrs. Bender is a mainstay of the Presbyterian Church of Wenderoth. Who would ever have thought?

Mrs. Strapelli is salivating, but not because of the fudge or fruitcake. This is the juiciest thing that's happened in ten years. No, in twenty years. It is almost too good to be true. It is perfect.

The band is doing a march now. You can tell it's a march from the beat. There's not much in the way of melody to pick out and recognize. There never is. Mr. Moskowitz, always patient and mild, does his best with the children and the old battered horns. The clarinets that squeak, the saxophones that squawk. A glance at the program: intermission is next. Where is Jane? Where's the milk for the coffee? Could someone go look?

Intermission—

The auditorium doors part, and for the next fifteen minutes we have a roar of voices, bodies jostling, pocketbooks and wallets opening. Only one person minds terribly that there's only nondairy creamer for the coffee. People are watching their fat and cholesterol these days. Smoking less, too. Everybody is health-conscious.

Mrs. Wells's peach pies go first, predictably. Actually, Mrs. Showalter bought two and put them aside—for herself and her sister—almost the minute they were delivered, so there were only three on the table for the sale.

Mrs. Strapelli thinks this is another example of me-firstism.

The peaches come out of Mrs. Wells's own backyard and have a wonderful fragrance. The crust, flaky and light, is divine.

Mrs. Showalter, Mrs. Strapelli thinks, would go on a diet if she knew what was good for her. She looks stuffed into that dress. But her husband doesn't seem to care. They are low-class people, the kind who break wind in public and then pretend nothing happened.

Children run and shout in the hall. Mrs. Davis says they mustn't run because the floor is wet, just mopped. Parents look at children's paintings on the wall as if they were at a museum. Gaudy, smeared two-dimensional houses are mounted on the slick tile with little torn rectangles of masking tape along the edges. Lisa, age six. Mark, age seven. A cluster of fathers argue about a recent baseball trade; a cluster of mothers talk about Mrs. Foster's trouble with her teenage daughter Barbara and generally about family troubles and when and when not to seek professional help.

It's all pretty typical.

When the intermission is over, everyone files back into the auditorium for the second half of the talent show. They get to see tutu'ed Becky Finley do her *Nutcracker* ballet number that was televised statewide last month. Becky is a little scrawny girl but acts like she's devoting her life to art. She keeps her face in a pucker as she minces and does pointy things in the air with her toes. Talk about stuck-up. No one really cares for Becky and her dancing, but they all applaud like mad to show how cultured they are.

A couple of solo songs follow, the usual Broadway stuff, *Cats, Annie.* There's an MTV dance done by a dozen kids with silly grins. The chorus sings about the Lord. The band again fills the auditorium with the miserable racket of beginners puffing and tootling away. Mr. Moskowitz takes a big bow, as if he has done something brave and wonderful, and waves a hand for the band to stand up for louder applause. People clap because Johnny or Lorraine is so cute up there, and also because they're glad *that's* over.

After the last number—a song in a reedy nasal whine by Cathy Carmichael, who's in the sixth grade and wearing a dress that shows she's getting breasts—Mr. Sykes comes onstage and says a few words about how all our children are remarkable and we should be proud. The men and women of the future, he says.

Everyone heads home, the kids flushed and chattering. Mrs. Bender, Mrs. Strapelli, Mrs. Showalter, Mrs. Worth, and Mrs. Davis clean up from the bake sale. They put the unsold cookies in boxes, empty the coffeepot, and count the money.

"Where did Mrs. Palmer go?" someone asks.

"Oh, was she here?" someone else says.

Mrs. Strapelli never quite gets the opportunity to find out more about Mrs. Bender and Steve Wanamaker and does Mr. Bender know yet. Oh if only she could be a fly on the wall.

The PTA has made $341.26. That includes a few raffle tickets. They haven't reimbursed Mr. Popovic yet for the paper plates, cups, napkins, and plastic spoons and forks. Mrs. Showalter, the treasurer, will make a full report at the next meeting, which is Wednesday the fifth. Put it on your calendar, girls.

Night falls on Lincoln Elementary.

George has gone home.

A few hours later, a night watchman walks by outside, flashing a light in a window here and there. He notices that there is another car in the parking lot besides his own but doesn't think much of it. There is very little crime in this neighborhood, just some vandalism now and then. He coughs, leaves.

A blank of time in which nothing happens. In the cafeteria kitchen, a faucet drips. A clock clicks every minute as the minute hand changes position incrementally. Moonlight shifts across tables and walls, and then later there is no moonlight, and then later it gradually begins to be day.

Perhaps we doze off.

The body isn't discovered until 9:30 A.M., when pots and pans are banging and Mary Cora Perkins, going into the refrigerator to get a few boxes of meat patties for lunch—cheeseburgers and french fries today, always a favorite—comes running out with a scream and "Oh my God, oh my God!"

Yes, it's Mrs. Palmer. Not a mark on her. She looks fine, actually. The only indications that she is not alive are the color of her skin, extremely pale with a bluish cast, and the fact that her eyes are open and not blinking. Half open. A lock of hair fallen over one eye. She seems engrossed. What does she see, that is so interesting, from the other side?

She is bent, between prone and sitting, her hands behind her, her feet together. A peculiar position. Almost as if her wrists and ankles were bound before, and perhaps the two knots connected, pulled taut, tied. As if, in other words, she was trussed. And then someone came back later—the murderer—after she lost consciousness from the cold, and removed all the rope. Except that there are no impressions of rope on her unfeeling flesh. Unless he— the murderer—used something like a cloth or strip of rubber between rope and skin, to keep the wrists and ankles free of clues.

This is pure conjecture.

Doors to walk-in refrigerators cannot be locked on the outside, by state law, but you still need the use of your hands and arms to work the handle. To leave. It is quite frigid in here after a while. We find ourselves wishing for a coat, a hat, gloves. For a sweater under the coat.

But wait, if Mrs. Palmer was tied up, what kept her from screaming for help after the criminal left? Screams would have carried even through that thick, well-sealed door. Unless she was gagged, too. And then the murderer, when he returned to untie and take away the rope when she was unconscious, also removed the gag. Are there creases from a gag at the corners of her cold, open mouth? We can't see any.

The only evidence of a culprit and foul play is the faint smell in the refrigerator room of . . . cigar, stale sweat, and hops. But it is too faint, apparently, to be noticed in the excitement, because no one notices it, and by the time the police arrive, it is dissipated. With the door open, too. No one dares close it now, though the ventilating damage to the clue has been done.

The police ask questions and make notes in notebooks—calmly, matter-of-factly, despite the sobbing and exclamations all around them, as if this sort of thing is not an enormity, a crime against nature and reason, but something that does unfortunately happen from time to time, even in the most peaceful, safest communities. It's called accidental death and has a code number.

Well, there are still a few puzzling things about this. How Mrs. Palmer happened to lose consciousness in the walk-in refrigerator. No sign that she fell and hit her head. No bump on the head (looking through the hair). No contusions. As far as anyone knows, she didn't have epilepsy. A heart attack? The coroner will check all that out.

But what was she doing in there anyhow? There was milk, plenty of milk, in the small refrigerator by the dessert case. She didn't have to use the walk-in.

The police talk also to the principal, who tells them how appalled, shocked, dumbfounded, and devastated he is by this tragedy. He knew the woman, Jane Palmer, well, quite well. She was a decent, caring soul. The best teacher at Lincoln. Everyone adored her.

He will call for an investigation immediately into the kitchen equipment, its safety. Perhaps the door stuck.

He can't say more—please excuse him—he is too broken up.

Before the police depart, the chief or sheriff, whatever he is, puts a gentle hand on Mr. Sykes's arm and says that they can take comfort at least in the fact that Mrs. Palmer did not suffer much pain. Death from hypothermia is like falling asleep. You get numb, slip away, and then it's over.

Mr. Sykes notifies the superintendent. They talk about notifying the school lawyer. And the insurance company. There is a lot of notifying to do. The newspaper, too. And don't forget the next of kin. We can't forget the next of kin.

At one point in the day, between phone calls, when no one is looking, Mr. Sykes takes out the green toy telephone and in a low voice reports briefly, succinctly, to Mrs. Zimmerman.

He feels relief that it is over.

At the funeral that weekend, he says a few words. How very sad it is, how very shocking. How we are all mortal and should therefore attempt to live lives of virtue and help others, as Jane Palmer did, practically a saint, may she rest in peace.

Most of the school is there. Some of the children squirm, joke, even giggle behind their hands, because they don't know what a funeral is—they haven't found out about death yet—and perhaps, too, because they don't really think of teachers as human beings. Teachers are something like turtles, only bigger, more tedious, and in power. If Mrs. Palmer were present, she would smile forgivingly, having spent almost twenty years with children of this age.

Also present is Roger, twenty years old, unshaven and unwashed. At him she would not smile forgivingly, we are afraid, because he has been her cross and curse. The son—an only son—she sometimes wanted to throttle blue and keep throttling, and he probably would have deserved it. He's a big kid, but clearly immature. Sullen, pouty, no doubt angry that his Mexican trip or carouse was cut short. Maybe he is even thinking that his mother died on purpose to cut it short. Teenagers can be amazingly self-centered. But this is not news.

Cathy Carmichael is in tears, inconsolable, no one knows why. Maybe it has less to do with Mrs. Palmer and more to do with growing up.

The Zimmermans are there, all in formal black, as if they were members of the family. They are odd, closemouthed people. Butter wouldn't melt. Hmm, little Christopher is missing. He was in Mrs. Palmer's class, wasn't he? Must be at home with the measles or something.

Sic transit. Pity. Way of all flesh.

Who are those two in the back? Those two men.

You won't believe it, they're the FBI.

Here in Wenderoth? You're kidding.

No, honest.

Well, they do say her death was strange, suspicious. No fingerprints on the refrigerator door, for example, not even her own. As if they had been wiped clean.

One of the kitchen workers could have done that. They're not too bright.

But on the inside, too?

Well, but if Mrs. Palmer didn't leave the refrigerator, there wouldn't have to be fingerprints on the inside handle, would there?

What bothers me is that even if this was a murder made to look like an accident—which is pretty far-fetched, since Mrs. Palmer didn't have an enemy in the world and there's no motive—what does the FBI have to do with it? The FBI is only interested when state lines are crossed. Are you trying to tell me that our Mrs. Palmer was bumped off by the Ku Klux Klan, the Mafia, or Colombian drug lords?

People file past the body before the lid is put on. Her eyes and mouth have been closed, thank goodness. And she doesn't look so uncomfortably cold. The skin is more natural. She seems at rest. The mortician may charge his captive audience an arm and a leg, but he does do a decent job, making this whole experience less difficult on the nerves.

The drive to the cemetery in East Carlyle is like any other drive to any other cemetery.

Birdsong and fresh air. A lot of grass. As Mrs. Palmer is put into the ground, a clergyman intones, but you can hardly hear him. Roger clenches his fists, mutters, and stares into space. Cathy Carmichael practically faints and has to be led away. Her mousy cousin, Kaelin Zimmerman, puts an arm around her as they walk to the cars. Mr. Sykes makes the comment that this cemetery is quite beautiful and he may come here sometimes on a Sunday, why not, to rejuvenate his spirit.

At some remove, behind a tree, Calvin Hornwood says to his colleague, Calvin Pliscou—two Calvins, but no particular significance in that:

"We'll need a list of all her students."

"This year, or past years, too?"

"Start with this year. A child may have said too much, and Jane Palmer may have begun putting two and two together."

Again came the smell of hot metal, so strong it made your eyes tear. Christopher was getting accustomed to it, becoming a seasoned traveler. Maybe, when he grew up, he would spend all his time exploring the universe's seven different kinds of deep. Then in his declining years he would be an old salt, with gray hair like his grandfather and incredible tales to tell about narrow escapes on the treacherous Seas of If, Isn't, and What.

The little window over the tub fogged up as it usually did. Not that there was ever that much to see while they were in transit. A spark in the darkness, a glimmering spiral, intersecting curves, a billowing in profile, a horizon line with something like city lights and a touch of filigree. It wasn't interesting. Gramps said the reason for this disappointment was that the view went against common sense and no mortal mind could hope to get a hold on it. Gramps directed Christopher's attention instead to the showerhead, which served as a kind of steering wheel, though the real steering, he said, was paramental, done by your upsilon and omicron. "It's like using a pencil," he explained, "to help when you have to add a lot of numbers. The *pencil* isn't the adder. If you had to, you could grit your teeth and do without it."

There was a nice vibration around them, a warm hum, as on an airplane. Christopher had been on a plane twice, when the family went to visit Dad's brother in Cleveland. He and Kaelin had looked out at the clouds while Brian wore a radio headset and read a magazine about clothes.

A sudden bump.

"Already?" Christopher asked.

"Dropping in on Emily," said Gramps. "Just for a minute. It's on our way."

"Emily my grandmother?"

"She hasn't seen you yet, you know. I always drop in when I can. Emily's lonely right now, needs cheering, because I'm away at the war. She's got a long wait: I won't be back for four years. She doesn't know that. That's between you and me, Christopher. You see, I was wounded and in a hospital. Couldn't get back, couldn't walk. But if we tell her that, she'll only worry."

"I didn't know you were in a war, Gramps."

"It didn't have a lot to recommend it," he said under his breath. "You should avoid wars if you can, my boy."

They opened the door and walked into a hallway that had blue-white wallpaper with little maroon dots.

"Who's there?" called a voice with an edge to it, like an oboe.

They went downstairs, and Gramps made the introductions.

She had an angular jaw, just like her photograph, but she was much younger and fuller than in her photograph. The eyes were bright and lively, not watery-pale. Christopher's grandmother got down on her knees and gave him a muscular hug.

"You take after my father," she said, looking him over. "That straw hair, and the mouth. Pleased to meet you, Christopher." Another look, a lovely smile, then a pointing finger. "Milk and cookies for you."

"We can't stay long, Emily," said Gramps. "Debra's after us."

She clucked. "What a pity. You'd think our poor daughter would mellow, wouldn't you."

Christopher wasn't hungry, having just had a breakfast that included three times the amount of bacon he was used to. But the cookies were oatmeal raisin cookies, which he loved. He sat at the kitchen table.

"You look so old, Cesar!" said Emily.

Christopher's ears pricked up at "Cesar," but Gramps shot him a private psi-scowl that said: Don't ever call me that if you know what's good for you. And if you're smart, little pip-squeak, you'll forget you even heard it.

"I'm getting on, dear," he said to Emily with a shrug. "The way of all flesh."

Actually, in this kitchen now, Gramps was younger than Christopher had ever seen him. His face glowed—or maybe the light of love was just reflected from his Emily. Or maybe it was both things, a glowing love and a reflecting love, at the same time.

Husband and wife sat and chatted with cozy half sentences, nods, and allusions while Christopher consumed two cookies, drank a glass of milk, and went after the oatmeal crumbs with a wet fingertip.

Then something unexpected happened—something spooky, like a thundercloud gathering out of nowhere and the world falling silent. Emily put her veined ivory hand on Christopher's little hand and said in a voice that was sweet and sad:

"Christopher."

"Yes?"

"You know, the end of life."

"Yes?"

"It is not so terrible, when it comes. Also, it is not half as final as people think."

At first Christopher thought she meant that he shouldn't feel bad about her being dead in his time, or maybe that he shouldn't worry about his grandfather's remark—getting on, the way of all flesh—and the obvious fact that the old man, whether he sat quietly on the porch of an institution in Florida or went zigzagging through time and space with his grandson, didn't have all that many years left.

But then a shiver went down Christopher's ten-year-old spine, and it wasn't from the cold milk. Emily meant *him*, Christopher, not his grandparents.

The end of life.

She was preparing him.

Consoling him.

Christopher hated when the curtain to the future was parted. It was like talking on a telephone line that had an echo. You couldn't concentrate on what you were doing at the moment. Images from next week or next month kept getting in the way and tripping you up.

He shuddered and quickly put this doom omen out of his mind. Completely out. If he was going to die young, he didn't want to know about it.

He made himself forget. He knew how to do that.

After a good-bye hug from Emily and another cookie offered but refused (he was stuffed, still burping hickory), they went back upstairs to the bathroom.

"Uh, Gramps?"

"Yes?"

"Could I use the bathroom before we go?"

"Sure. Oh, you want me to step out. Privacy, okay. You're not going to smell it up, are you?"

"No, just number one."

"Go ahead, go ahead." Gramps waited in the hall, looking at his watch.

It occurred to Christopher, as he tinkled alone, that this was probably the most convenient room in the house to travel in, if you had to choose. Traveling in a bedroom gave you a soft bed to sleep in at night, true, but a tent and sleeping bag weren't so bad. The worst part of camping, he had always thought, was being forced to use outhouses that smelled awful and had huge spiders, or, when there wasn't an outhouse, having to squat behind a bush and keep your fingers crossed there wasn't any poison ivy around or hornets.

Their next stop was 1888, the city of Paris. Workmen were climbing in and out of a maze of metal struts with their pulleys and ladders. To see them you had to wipe the sweaty window with your hand or sleeve. Gramps said that this structure, when it was finished, would be three hundred meters high. Impressive for the time. It had lots of triangles, rhombuses, trapezoids, each shape dependent on a person's vantage point. Gramps started to tell him other things about the big Erector-set tower, but there was a sudden, impatient knock at the door, and a rough voice said:

"Dépêche-toi!"

So they had to focus on the tiles, focus to the point of unfocus, grab a passing string, and take off again on the wide, foaming Sea of Was.

In 2674 B.C. they stopped on a sun-drenched plain, and the window now—since there weren't bathrooms as such in 2674 B.C., and in general no kind of indoor plumbing—was merely an opening in a tent, though the window remained a window on the inside. That way, the tiles were not disturbed. Christopher saw workmen cursing in a cloud of dust among thick quivering ropes. "Cheops," said Gramps. "It will be one hundred and forty-seven meters high. Impressive for the time."

"Gramps," said Christopher, "you don't have to give me a whole tour of history. We had this in school. We did Egypt last year."

In passing we note, regarding what eventually will be one of the Seven Wonders of the Ancient World, though it doesn't look like much now, that a tetragonal pyramid has *three*-sided sides, a *four*-sided base, and *five* faces in all, if you think of it not as a building on the ground but a polyhedron floating freely in the air of Platonic abstraction.

"This isn't history in a classroom," said Gramps, peeved, "this is history in the making, as you watch. It is unfolding before your very eyes."

Christopher sighed. He understood. His grandfather, concerned about the boy's missing so much school, was trying to turn their adventure into a field trip.

Sometimes the best way to deal with adults was to sit back and wait for them to get out of their system whatever was bothering them.

At the next stop, a jump of more than ten thousand years, the window above the tub was an opening in rock. Since no workmen were present, Gramps and Christopher left the bathroom and found themselves in an alcove in a cave. It was pretty dark—not much light filtered in from outside, where it seemed to be raining—so Gramps had to use his flashlight.

"Look at that," he said, making echoes, pointing to a wall with antelope and bison pictures on it. Anemic stick-figure hunters ran after the animals, brandishing clumsy bows and arrows and spears.

Christopher didn't tell him that Mrs. Palmer had covered this a month ago. He didn't say anything.

The cave smelled like an outhouse, and there was scuttling in the corners, probably rats.

"All right, all right," said Gramps, finally realizing that the educational material was not being well received. "We proceed straight to our destination."

They returned to the bathroom in silence.

For their destination Christopher was expecting something picturesque and awesome—maybe dinosaurs grazing or at battle, with anvil-headed dun-and-white pterodactyls watching like vultures overhead, and with an erupting volcano or two in the background. What he saw instead was a bleak, rocky shore. Boulders with ribbons of scum on them at the waterline. There was the sickly, bitter stink of rotten eggs. A haze. The air was clammy, too cold and too warm at the same time.

Gramps showed him how to breathe through his nose, using a little upsilon in the septum to filter out most of the hydrogen sulfide, and also how to tweak some of the carbon dioxide and carbon monoxide molecules into a coupled pair of oxygen atoms. This way, when you took a walk, you wouldn't get a headache and your heart wouldn't do flip-flops.

Not that there was anywhere to walk. It was nothing but stones and boulders, stones and boulders—no sand, not a grain of sand between the sea and the gray cliffs about half a kilometer behind them. You couldn't see the cliffs very well because of the haze. Christopher found he had to be extremely careful where he put his feet: this was prime ankle-twisting and toe-stubbing terrain. One climbed and scrabbled more than walked. Christopher stayed away from the scum, which was extremely slippery and smelled like dead fish.

The bathroom, wedged between two boulders, looked like a boulder itself on the outside. Gramps, grunting, arranged a few rocks to make it even more a part of the landscape.

"Not that this will fool a probe from your mother," he said, "but a remote scan—it might fool a remote scan."

Christopher got up on a high boulder, looked around, and made a face.

"I know, it's not great," said Gramps. "A good place to hide, however. I'm thinking this should serve for about two weeks."

"Two weeks?"

"Then we'll have to move on. So they don't triangulate on us and use glue."

Christopher was appalled. "Two weeks? But there's nothing to do here, Gramps."

There was an occasional slap of water on stone. A leisurely, unenergetic slap.

Nothing moving, not even a breeze.

And Gramps hadn't packed any entertainment, no Nintendo, VCR, TV, or answer box, economizing on space since the bathroom was so small.

"Listen, Christopher," said Gramps. "It's hard for young people to have nothing happening. I know that. But we can't have action all the time. It's not the way the world works. Sometimes we have to have . . ." Gramps stopped to think of what we had to have. "I don't know, character development. Or description. Or just . . . a fallow period. So a person can be alone with his thoughts. Or maybe build something that takes time and care. Or maybe just rest. This is an opportunity for you to catch up on your adverbs."

Christopher rolled his eyes, put his head in his hands, and let his tongue hang.

Time moved very slowly over the next few days.

It moved like the gray water, that is to say, not moving much at all. It was hard to fill the hours. And if you didn't try to fill them, time moved even more slowly, as if it were a beast of burden with something else on its mind. Christopher got so bored that the boredom actually became a taste and then started to throb painfully like a toothache.

He played word games with Gramps. Geography. Ghost.

He got into political arguments with Gramps.

He went for walks, or walk-climbs, among the endless boring stones and boulders.

He practiced throwing, with and without his arms. He threw until his shoulders and elbows were sore and his hindbrain even sorer.

He examined the shore scum under an upsilon-enhanced magnifying glass. Nothing interesting: prokaryotic glob, no nuclei to speak of, no pseudopodia, hardly even DNA, just stuff lying there and taking its sweet time evolving.

He went swimming, but had to stop that because another kind of slime, pale red, got into his hair and stank even worse than the shore scum, and it was a lot of trouble unpacking the tub each time—with Gramps complaining—so he could take a shower to get it all out.

"Don't use up the soap," Gramps would mutter. "And make sure you scrub the tub afterward. Pee-yoo."

Christopher daydreamed.

He did his adverbs. In desperation he even went on to gerunds.

The only change in the weather was that sometimes it was more overcast than at other times, though even when it was less overcast, you couldn't really see sun or clouds because of the haze.

Sometimes there was a rumble in the distance. Not much of a rumble, though.

At night there was a constant light show—shooting stars—but

through the haze the show was too dim and blurred to be exciting or even just pretty. Christopher hoped that a meteor would hit close to them, but no such luck.

He tried building a snowman out of stones and stone stickum, but Gramps said not to: it might interfere with causality, whatever causality was, if the figure survived to historical times, and in any case it would certainly make them more visible to Christopher's mother, which they didn't want, did they?

Christopher asked Gramps to tell him about his war years. To tell him about when he was a boy, what it was like in the days before they had postage stamps and the internal combustion engine. Gramps wasn't a good storyteller. He kept digressing and making side comments, as if talking to himself and forgetting Christopher was there. And the things he chose to talk about were usually very dull.

Gramps's main theme was women and older men. "Women like older men, my boy," he would say, "because older men have good manners and are respectful. You treat a woman right, she treats you right. It's as simple as that. Human decency."

Or, "Women like older men not because older men have money—though money doesn't hurt, of course—it never hurts. It's because older men have experience. That's the reason. You can rely on older men. They know what to do in a situation. They're not going to make the kind of stupid, mortifying blunders young men make because they don't know any better. Experience, experience."

Or, "Women like older men because older men are in good shape physically. Yes, don't laugh. I'm serious. The ones that weren't in good shape all died off by now. Nature selected them out, you might say. Look at my muscle tone." A sleeve rolled up, revealing a stringy arm with three liver spots on it.

On the eighth day, Christopher, fed up with the sight of boulders in all directions, got up early—Gramps was snoring—and set out on the long, difficult trek to the cliffs. The only thing mildly interesting about the cliffs was their color, a reddish brownish gray, and probably the only reason this was interesting was that it provided a little relief from the whitish grayish gray that had been surrounding Christopher and Gramps for a whole week now in the form of stones and boulders. It provided relief also from the dark, flinty gray of the water, which was somehow even more boring than the stones and boulders—maybe because you expected something from a body of water but this one just lay there, slapping the shore once in a while and without conviction.

Christopher was so miserably bored, he began to think that being scooped out might not be so bad after all. He was in a foul mood.

Stepping from boulder to stone and stone to boulder, he twisted an ankle.

He banged a shin.

He twisted his other ankle.

He bit his lip and used the F word.

He used the F word louder.

With a groan he sat on a boulder halfway to the cliffs, maybe not even halfway, and wiped the clammy sweat off his forehead. His eye happened to fall on something at his feet: a flat, very thin object caught between two stones. It was shiny. It looked like a credit card or a postcard.

It was a postcard.

From his sister. Christopher recognized the handwriting. The picture on the card was the old courthouse in Harrisburg, Pennsylvania. The hasty message was short and to the point. It read:

"Mother's closing in, run! Kaelin."

Ruby Star

*i*n K'i-kit-toy (or Tik'it-oy) the triangles are all scalene and the curves relentlessly hyperbolic. It gives you the impression that the buildings will fall at any moment. Or that they are actually falling, but frozen momentarily in their fall. Or that they have in fact already fallen, but then somehow half bounced back, for a moment. Panda Ray would like this place: the architecture's impossible, breath-catching balance between immobility and motion. It would make him chuckle his old Dravidian chuckle.

We are in another galaxy, galaxy number—we were told the number but have forgotten it. There are so many galaxies. Millions, hundreds of millions, maybe billions. The universe is a big place.

Christopher? He is *not* having a good time here in K'i-kit-toy (or Tik'it-oy), *n*th city of an *n*th nation on an *n*th continent on an *n*th planet of an *n*th sun. The boy is homesick. He misses his pebble puzzle, his walks in the field off Green Street, and he misses Buzz-in-the-closet.

He can't get used to wearing these translating headphones all the time. They're heavy, and they bump into things when you turn.

He can't stand the noise. The people here call it music. It's everywhere. No beat to it, no tune, and so loud: jackhammer Muzak, sometimes with a shrieky-shrill feedback problem. All through the night, too. Around the clock. The K'i-kit-toyans (or Tik'it-oyans) have difficulty themselves—you constantly see them leaning toward each other, cupping their ears—but they don't mind the inconvenience of not always hearing the first time. They take pride in it, saying that this is part of city living. Christopher wonders if they would go insane in silence. Or if they use silence—special silent rooms—to torture prisoners in the local prison or to loosen the tongues of spies.

Gramps doesn't want to leave. He has found a native woman here he wants to "make time with," as he puts it, winking. Ruby Star is her name, though of course not in her native language. She has big red lips, deep dark eyes, and her body is embarrassing. It looks as if it were put together from different kinds of tropical fruit, all very ripe. It is hard to know what she sees in a dried-up old geezer from Earth.

She is nice enough to Christopher, giving him a little present every time she comes up to the apartment before she and Gramps go out on their date. Gramps has almost used up his supply of Old Spice, and his bow tie is getting frayed at one edge.

The presents are gadget toys that have no purpose or function Christopher can figure out, even when he consults the answer box—which is not the kind of answer box they have at home, the one from the future that Mother doesn't like them to use too much. Well, of course it isn't the same, how could it be, it's an *alien* answer box.

For example, when Christopher gets a four-inch windup soldier from Ruby Star (it looks like a soldier, but who knows what it really is), he winds it up, turning the key, and nothing happens: the soldier doesn't march or shoot or shout orders, it just stands there. When he asks the answer box if the toy is broken, the answer box says, "Broken."

"How do I fix it?" asks Christopher.

"No, no," says the answer box, "it's supposed to be broken."

"It was made broken?"

"Rephrase that," says the answer box.

"The toy was built," Christopher tries to rephrase, "in such a way that it wouldn't work from the beginning?"

"But it does work," says the answer box.

"You just said it was broken."

"Broken, yes, broken is how it works."

"I don't understand."

"What don't you understand?" asks the answer box—and so on. It's an answer box, obviously, that doesn't provide answers that are useful if you are so unlucky as to come from another galaxy.

Christopher could ask Ruby Star about these gadgets, but he doesn't. She makes him uncomfortable—partly because of her tropical-fruit body and partly because he's a little resentful: she has been taking up so much of Gramps's time lately that Christopher doesn't have anyone to talk to. The K'i-kit-toyans (or Tik'it-oyans) don't like to talk to children, and their own children are nervous and stay out of sight. Peeking out sometimes from curtained windows, one eye at a time.

Christopher, also, hasn't seen any pets.

(The B'i-kit-oyans are not people, they're animals. It's not always easy to tell the difference, since they go on two legs, wear clothes, and don't have much fur. But though animals, they're not domesticated, not pets. If you make the mistake of scratching one behind the ears, it becomes mortally offended. They are a very touchy genus.)

It was on an Ocher Tuesday that Christopher approached his grandfather, who was engrossed in a book of etiquette, a thick book, like an unabridged dictionary.

"Gramps," he said.

"Hmm?"

"Could you put down that book for a minute?"

The old man frowned, took off his translating goggles, and looked up. He shook his head, shook the book. "They have so many rules," he said. "It's incredible. Hundreds of rules. Contingencies. In this case, in that case, in the other case. What a complicated social life."

"Gramps," said Christopher, "don't you think we've been here long enough?"

Gramps looked at him blankly.

"We've been here more than two weeks," said Christopher.

"Two weeks," said Gramps, "is not such a long time."

"But won't Mother get a bead on us?"

"Who?"

"Mother."

"Oh, your mother." Gramps scratched his chin. "I suppose she might. . . . On the other hand, there *are* a couple of quasars between us and her. Causes a lot of interference, a quasar does."

"Let's move on, Gramps. My throat hurts from talking loud all the time."

"Mine, too. Crazy custom, this music. You get used to it, though."

"Why do we have to get used to it, Gramps? Let's just go."

"What?"

"I said, let's just go."

Gramps put the book down and drummed his fingers on the arm of his chair, which was kind of a cross between a club chair and a Wassily chair, an unsettling combination. He drummed, then winced, and with his left hand kneaded the fingers of his right. "Arthritis acting up. Ow. Other than that, I feel tip-top."

"Gramps," said Christopher. "I don't like it here."

"You don't, huh?" The old man studied his grandson. "Christopher, I've been meaning to tell you. I'm not that old yet, you know. Old maybe, but still with some frisk. Well. I was thinking of staying here awhile. Miss Star is quite a beauty, isn't she? And she's taken a shine to me. I'm sure you've noticed. She doesn't hide her feelings, bless her. She likes you, too, though they don't go in much for children here. Can't say I blame them. Kids are trouble, trouble the universe over. Look at my daughter."

"Gramps, are you thinking of getting married? To an alien?"

"Listen, my boy, I'll tell you something. This alien business. It's narrow-minded, for one thing. I mean, who an alien is all depends on your point of view, doesn't it? Of course it does. *We're* aliens to *them*. And then . . . you probably won't understand this, being so young, but—" Thinking how to put it. "The difference between men and women, Christopher, is so great, so very great, fundamentally, I mean, that the question of what species a person happens to belong to, or whether his DNA is left-handed or right-handed, that difference, why, it's a drop in the bucket. That's all it is, a drop in the bucket. Hardly figures in the overall picture."

Christopher looked hard at Gramps. Was the old man finally becoming senile? Or was it simply the effect that big red lips, dark eyes, and a tropical-fruit body had on the male brain, on all male brains, regardless of age, after puberty? Would Christopher, too, in time be reduced to this? It was humiliating, and at the same time sad, the power hormones had over the seat of reason.

"But Mother," he reminded his grandfather, trying to remain patient and use simple words, "Mother is honing in on us. If we stay here much longer, she's sure to find us. We have to keep moving. You know that. You said so yourself, Gramps."

78

Gramps put a finger to his nose, squinted, nodded, and smiled. "I've been thinking about your mother, too. I can still think, my boy. I'm not a vegetable yet. Not yet. I have an idea, a way we can shake her for good. If it works. A little guile. We let her catch you."

"*Catch* me?"

"Yes, but not you, Christopher, not you. Another you. We pull another you out of the Sea of If and put him in your place and make Debra think it's you."

Christopher thought for a moment. "But that wouldn't be fair to *him,* would it?"

"What?"

"To him."

"Him?"

"The other me. The Christopher we put in my place. He'd get scooped out and be like Brian."

Gramps sighed. "Christopher, my boy, you have to be a little philosophical. In some of the other If worlds, your mother does catch you. That's a fact. And there are an infinite number of such worlds, that is, an infinite number of Christophers who get caught, just as there are an infinite number of Christophers who don't. So you have to look at it this way. The overall picture. We'd only be adding one to an infinity of Christophers who get caught. One plus infinity is the same as infinity. Doesn't really matter whether you add that one or not, now does it?"

This didn't sound at all like the Gramps he knew. Christopher felt ashamed.

"Come on, Gramps. It sure does matter to the Christopher we let Mother catch."

Gramps, annoyed, said, "All right, if you look at it that way, true. But let me tell you, Christopher, it's a dog-eat-dog world out there. Sometimes a person has to climb down off his pedestal of virtue and be practical. I've been around a long time and I know what I'm talking about. A person, you know, has an obligation to himself, too. It's called self-preservation, saving his own skin. Charity begins in the home."

Christopher was so disgusted that he turned and walked away.

"You can't always be worrying about the other guy!" Gramps called after him.

But the other guy in this case—thought Christopher—was not

another guy at all, it was another Christopher, another himself. How could Gramps not see that?

As Gramps, grumbling, put his nose back into the endless, intricate chapter on K'i-kit-toyan (or Tik'it-oyan) courtship—an old man blinded to right and wrong by the evil influence of Ruby Star—Christopher went down the scalene hall toward the bathroom, keeping a careful hand on the wall because the angles and planes were still so disorienting. Even after two weeks it was easy to become dizzy, stagger, and crack your head or knee.

He locked the bathroom door behind him.

Several times now he had seen Gramps catch a cosmic string and use the showerhead to steer. He had even helped once or twice, while Gramps took a bite of a sandwich or had to scratch an itch. Traveling wasn't all that difficult. The main thing to watch out for, when you grabbed ahold or swung from one string to another like Tarzan, was the whiplash, the "tail of the snake," as Gramps called it. If you weren't alert, it could flick unexpectedly and send you rocketing in a wrong direction, into a wrong Sea. The strings contained tremendous energy, since they were at the bottom of everything and were tucked and coiled into all those funny dimensions.

He sat on the edge of the tub and considered the rose tiles. Began focusing on them, until they swam, the pentagonal suns and stars and wheels turning and alternating. . . .

He remembered how his grandfather took care of him when in the third grade he got the measles and had to spend a whole week in bed. Gramps came up all those stairs to his room next to the attic and read to him from some magazine on America's heritage, an article about railroads in the West. It began boring and grew twice as boring, but Christopher had loved hearing Gramps's thin, husky voice when his hot head throbbed and the room rotated. He had loved feeling Gramps's cool hand on his forehead. Or when Gramps propped him up so he could sip a little water.

With his upsilon and omicron Christopher looked for a cosmic string, saw one, reached out, but hesitated.

He remembered walking into a room once when Gramps was talking to someone. It was an argument, but a friendly argument, the kind in which you disagree but enjoy continuing with the disagreement, maybe to see where the thing leads, like playing tennis and no longer caring who wins because the rally has become so interesting or so much fun. Except that Gramps was by himself.

There was no one else in the room, and no telephone or talkie.

Christopher had tiptoed out, unnoticed, a lump in his throat.

If he took off now and took the bathroom with him, what would Gramps do? Gramps would be stranded in this nth city of an nth nation on an nth continent on an nth planet of an nth sun in a galaxy whose number we have forgotten, a galaxy among billions.

He would probably never see his grandfather again.

Gramps would come into the bathroom at some point, maybe an hour later, and see that the tiles were all yellow and scalene, and realize that his grandson had deserted him.

Probably Gramps wouldn't mind so much at first, infatuated as he was with his Ruby Star. But what would happen when he ran out of Old Spice? What would happen when Ruby Star finally cast her eye elsewhere, "taking a shine" to some other old man from some other distant planet? Who knows, maybe that was her heartless hobby, going through octogenarians from abroad as if they were Kleenex. Maybe she made jokes about them to her mother, who sat all day in a kitchen that smelled of broccoli. A mother who had fat jiggly arms, a hairy chin, and laughed like a donkey.

What would poor Gramps do when Ruby Star spurned him?

No, impossible, Christopher couldn't walk out on the old man. Gramps needed him—and he needed Gramps, too. If he traveled by himself, he would get lost, he would end up in an awful place from which there was no return. Or he would go where Mother would have no difficulty finding him, and then it would be all over, Gramps stranded millions of light-years from home and Christopher scooped out.

They needed each other. They had to stick together.

Christopher felt like crying. He whimpered a little, but the sound—not completely covered by the jackhammer Muzak—embarrassed him, so he stopped.

A Normal Girl

It took Kaelin every bit of her self-control not to start the car for Harve. The old Chevy wouldn't turn over. It made an *rrr-rrr* sound, as if the battery was breathing its last. Harve groaned, said, "Damn," said, "Oh, come on," and kept turning the ignition key.

Rrr-rrr.

It's very important, she told herself, to let him take care of things. To let him take charge. He was the man. If she started the car for him, then little by little she'd be doing more things, then everything, for him, and he'd never mature, and it would be bad for their relationship.

Kaelin gripped her hands together in her lap and tried to smile. They would be late to the Halloween dance, her first dance. She didn't count the socials she had gone to with her girlfriends, where everyone sat around and gossiped and giggled and looked at the few gawky boys huddled at the far end of the room. This was her first real date; it was not just going out for ice cream after school, though ice cream with Harve was wonderful.

"Oh, damn," said Harve. "I think I flooded the motor."

Tonight, at the dance, in the bright, decorated gym, Harve would take her out on the floor in front of everyone, she in her good blue dress and new shoes, and he would put an arm around her, and they would dance. Kaelin didn't know a lot about dancing. Neither did Harve. But she had explained to him that if you went slow enough, it didn't matter, no one would be able to tell. As long as

you didn't actually trip over the other person's foot—and you
wouldn't if you were careful to keep your feet always in contact with
the floor.

A slow shuffle side to side. One-two, one-two.

"What if it's a fast dance?" Harve had asked.

"Then we just go have a soda, or sit and make conversation."

She read books on etiquette and advice columns. She read Ann
Landers and Dr. Joyce Brothers. She had instructed Harve that
when they danced, he wasn't supposed to put both arms around her,
the way some people did. "That's like making out in public."

They had had their first kiss a week ago. A brush of the lips only,
in his car, when he dropped her off at the corner of Carter and Wilson Streets. That was a week ago, but Kaelin could still feel the kiss.
It thrilled her, warmed her every time she thought of it, feeling it
again. And she loved the way Harve smelled: lime aftershave and
talcum powder.

The car stank of gasoline.

"We'll have to wait awhile," he said. "I think I flooded it."

It would be so easy to make a spark catch in the place it needed
to catch inside the engine, in that rounded metal pocket over the
drum-thing. She wouldn't even have to concentrate a lot. She could
do it while she was talking to him, in the middle of a sentence. No
one would know. But she would know.

And that was no good, because more than anything she wanted
to be a normal girl and live a normal life.

When a car got a flat tire, a normal girl waited for the man to
fix it. She waited patiently, her hands folded. She didn't do anything extrasensory or supernatural. She had faith in her man. She
relied on his big arms and male know-how.

Kaelin smoothed her blue dress and looked down at the shoes
she had bought to match the dress, for the dance. Dark blue with
black buckles. Mother had okayed the purchase, after a pause with
raised eyebrow and sardonic half smile.

If Kaelin could manage to be a normal girl, she would get married in a few years and live in her husband's house, in another town
with any luck, maybe even another state, and only have to talk to
her mother once a week or once a month, over the phone. She could
get Harve to be ambitious—he wasn't ambitious now, but he was
young and forming, it would be easy to make him ambitious, if he
loved her—so that he wouldn't dream of staying in the small town

he was born in and grew up in. In another town, in another state, if Kaelin cried a little at night sometimes, she wouldn't have to worry about Mother overhearing.

The far hearing didn't work well beyond a mile or two, unless you were out in the middle of a desert. There were too many different sounds in the world, and after a point they muddied together.

"Here goes," said Harve, and this time the old Chevy did start, though with so much shuddering and smoke, for a moment it didn't seem like it would make it. Then the car settled into a reasonable rhythm, with an occasional cough but not too bad a cough, and Kaelin breathed a sigh of relief. They wouldn't be very late.

"Good girl," said Harve, patting the top of the dashboard as he pulled out. He had wide, honest hands.

They were not late at all, it turned out, at the gym. The DJ was talking to Mr. Dunst, and Mr. Wanamaker was helping a couple of kids attach a papier-mâché Frankenstein head to a basketball backboard—holding a stepladder for them. Miss Gillespie came over and complimented Kaelin on her hair and dress, though Kaelin hadn't done anything to her hair except brush it a lot, and the dress was really shabby compared with what some of the other girls were wearing. Andrea, Claire. It was Miss Gillespie being charitable again. She was the kind who liked to rub your nose in your inferiority, with a beatific smile like Mother Teresa. Everybody hated her, but they didn't dare admit it openly, and maybe not even to themselves, Miss Gillespie was so sweet. She had been a nun before she went into public education. In class she mentioned the Lord every other sentence.

"Neat," said Harve, looking at the decorations: skulls, witches, pumpkin heads, black cats.

Kaelin had him escort her down the hall and wait while she went to the ladies' room. In the hall with her he walked on the outside, that is, on the side away from the wall. When they went to the principal's office to fetch something for Mrs. Stevenson, a list Mrs. Stevenson forgot and needed, Harve stepped ahead as he was supposed to and opened the door. It was all according to the book. Whenever Kaelin told him that etiquette required something, he did it without hesitation or complaint.

He's so chivalrous, she thought, and felt a little weak inside, from a rush of love.

They danced to all the slow music, but unfortunately there

wasn't much of that, so they spent most of the time standing to the side, watching others and pretending they were socializing. A few people did talk to them, but not for long. The people moved on, heading for something more exciting, whatever it was. Kaelin didn't mind. She wasn't going to be any belle of the ball in this life. She would marry, have one or two children, and never say or do anything remarkable.

Of the adults, besides the teachers and parents who were there to chaperon, there were two men. The men acted a little like security guards, the burly off-duty policemen who in the evening patrolled the halls and parking lots to keep down rowdy behavior and vandalism. At dances sometimes a couple of boys got drunk, bringing in booze secretly, or else they would be drunk to begin with, come to the dance drunk, and then there would be a lot of trouble afterward. Mr. Sykes lecturing them all at assembly, threatening to take away privileges, to cancel the senior trip at the ski resort, and so on.

The two men were watchful yet apart, in the way of security guards, but they were much better dressed than security guards. They wore dark suits and shiny dress shoes. One of them looked like the bland Jehovah's Witness who had come through their neighborhood, door to door, about a week ago, polite and smiling. The other looked like Clark Kent: a clean, square chin and black hair slicked down.

Toward the end of the evening there was a slow dance, to a beautiful song about young love sung by Whitney Houston. Harve took Kaelin out on the dance floor, and after a while, as they shuffled together, he held her closer than he ever had before. He held her to his big strong chest. She knew she shouldn't, but she let her head rest on his shoulder, as if she were tired, and then he put his cheek to her cheek. The embrace felt so natural. It also made Kaelin a little numb and dizzy, as if she had taken a whiff of epoxy glue or of that gas the dentist used when a few years ago he removed the cord between her two front teeth because her molars were coming in and there wasn't room for all of them in her mouth.

Everyone clapped, and the Great Pumpkin, who was really Mr. Dunst, came around and handed everyone a candy cane out of a burlap bag, like Santa Claus. "Happy Halloween," he said from inside his big orange head. It was dopey but funny.

When Harve went to help move something for the cleaning up,

the Clark Kent man came over to her and asked nicely if she was a Zimmerman. Kaelin Zimmerman?

Yes, she was, she said.

The man asked her if Christopher was still sick.

Sick?

Her brother hadn't been in school for two weeks now, the man explained.

Oh yes, Christopher was getting over the chicken pox, Kaelin said.

The man thought it was the measles. Someone had said measles.

No, chicken pox, Kaelin said. The doctor had quarantined him. It might be another week.

Which doctor was that, the man asked, but just then Harve came back and the man smiled, nodded, and retreated.

"Dr. Hill," Kaelin called after the man, lest it seem that she was trying to hide something. Dr. Hill was not part of the family, but he was under their control, like Mr. Davies, Mrs. McCarthy, Mr. Gasparino, and Mr. Sykes. He would corroborate the story—any story—if anyone came snooping.

After enough days passed, *if* they passed and Christopher didn't return to school (scooped out), the chicken pox would have to be replaced with something else, Kaelin supposed. Lord knows what Mother would do. Kaelin had never seen her so angry, and with each day that passed and they didn't find Christopher and Gramps, the anger grew worse, like a thundercloud that keeps gathering and gathering, until the sky overhead is unbelievably heavy, inky, and charged.

Harve took her arm and led her out to the parking lot, opening all the doors for her, the car door, too, as if she were a queen. A beautiful moon was out, and wispy white clouds sailed slowly, majestically across a great expanse of bright, twinkling stars.

Such a romantic night, with that moon. He would kiss her tonight, for sure. And it would be more than a quick brush of lips on lips after ice cream. Kaelin was a little afraid, but also felt a singing inside her, she was so happy.

The car this time did not go *rrr-rrr* at all, as if the machine didn't have the heart to stand in the way of young love. Harve patted the dashboard and said, "Good girl." He had a wonderfully simple sense of humor. What a simple, honest soul he was. She loved everything about him, his name, the color of his hair, and he looked so handsome now in the moonlight, almost like a movie star, Keanu Reeves.

When they stopped on her street, across from her house, they sat for a moment in silence. Kaelin's heart hammered, but she didn't slow it down, she didn't want to do anything atypical, especially not in this so traditional, American moment.

Harve was screwing up his courage. He turned to her.

"Kaelin," he said.

"Yes?" She was breathless.

"Listen, I don't know . . . I thought . . ." He took something from his jacket pocket and held it out to her. "We like each other, and I thought . . ."

She took it. It was a ring.

"A friendship ring," he said.

He wanted to go steady with her.

She put the ring on. It was silver. Much too loose, but she closed her hand so it wouldn't wobble or fall off.

"If you want to go with me," he said awkwardly, "I'd like that."

Her answer was to put her arms around him and kiss him on the mouth.

He couldn't say anything for a moment, overwhelmed by the kiss, by her kissing him. Their faces were so close that the rest of the world didn't exist, there were only the two of them, the young man and the young woman. Kaelin thought: This is just like out of a book. This is a teenage romance.

"Great," Harve breathed in her face, smelling of Coca-Cola, "great."

He kissed her, but it didn't last too long and he didn't try to put his tongue in her mouth or anything like that. The kiss was just right. Harve was such a gentleman. Kaelin thought: I am so lucky. A dance, and two full kisses. This is all working out perfectly.

But the perfection was ruined when she said good night to her date, her official boyfriend now, and got out of the car and saw those two men who at the Halloween dance had been standing and watching like security guards. They were in a car more than a block away, its lights off, parked under a tree, and the Jehovah's Witness one was looking right at her through night-vision binoculars.

Kaelin was careful not to let her eyes rest on the men for more than half a second, because if she did, they might suspect that she could see them even at that distance and although they were in deep shadow, no part of their car exposed in the moonlight. She waved good night to Harve and went up the walk until the high hedge cut her off from the snooping men.

Behind her, Harve's car went *rrr-rrr, rrr-rrr,* and she heard a thought from one of the men, probably the Jehovah's Witness, and in the thought caught not only his name, Calvin Pliscou, but the name also of his divorced wife, Mary Beth.

The thought was: We're wasting our time.

Did Mother know about those men? She probably did. And it was probably making her twice as furious, if such a thing was possible. The old house loomed high over Kaelin, black against the starry sky. It was like a haunted house, just right for Halloween, with that odd satellite dish at the top resembling, in moonlit silhouette, a crooked scaffold that lacked only a noose.

Mother was no doubt at her monitor, her bank of monitors and speakers, and would sit there through the night, and then all day, searching the event waves for Christopher's little footprint, little fingerprint, little voiceprint. Mother would sit there as cold and heartless as an iceberg, her eyes not missing a single rill or eddy in the stream of information. It was only a matter of time.

Poor Christopher. Poor, dear, doomed Christopher.

As Kaelin went up the steps to the front door, she felt the loose ring on her finger, Harve's ring. She began twisting the ring, and then twisting her fingers, as if they were knobs, the left hand, the right hand. Would this nightmare ever be over?

What a Traitor Looks Like

It is cold, below freezing. Snowflakes are coming down slowly, separate flakes, a flake here, a flake there. Although they are coming down slowly, the flakes are still too fast and erratic in the air (and too small) for us to make out their intricate, lovely symmetries, each symmetry unique.

Harve has invited Kaelin to the Thanksgiving football game. She will wear her red sweater and gray coat but hasn't decided yet on which wool cap, the black or the blue-and-green. Black goes better, but that cap is awfully worn. It used to be Brian's before he took more of an interest in clothes and grooming and joined the debating team.

She looks out the window of her room at the swirling snowflakes. She misses her little brother. Foolish but brave Christopher.

She decides she will send him another postcard, telling him that she and Harve are now going steady, telling him also to please be careful. Gramps means well but can't be relied upon to do the sensible thing. The old man, since Grandma passed away, doesn't have all his marbles. Look at the way they stayed too long at that last place. It was so close. Mother was ready to pounce. They came within a hair of getting caught.

Kaelin realizes that this is futile, that Christopher will eventually be caught and probably sooner rather than later. But she can't help helping or at least doing what she can. So before she sends the card, she will spy on Mother again and give Christopher an update on the enemy's movements.

Mother is in her war room, surrounded by maps, blinking lights, computers, and with the answer box at her elbow. She wears a headset. Her eyes dart from screen to screen. She will not notice the tiny spider on the wall by the door, above and behind her: the lifelike eight-legged plastic-and-rubber robotoid peering over her shoulder and reporting back to Kaelin.

"She's lost the scent," the spider informs Kaelin.

Kaelin is tremendously relieved. Maybe Christopher will escape the monster after all. Somehow. Miracles do happen. But she shouldn't allow herself to hope: she will only be more heartbroken later, when the worst comes to pass and her brother returns to school and the teachers all remark on how well-adjusted he has suddenly become.

The postcard depicts a historical roundhouse, faded redbrick, in the railroad yard of Altoona, Pennsylvania. Kaelin writes a quick message—and here, in case anyone is interested, is how she plans to send it.

First, go down to the kitchen and unplug the toaster. It must be a pop-up toaster, not the kind that has a door and broils as well as toasts. Clean out all loose crumbs. Whistle into the slot you will be using to mail your card or letter. A low whistle—don't worry about resonance, fundamental, overtones: as long as the sound is low, soothing, and uninterrupted. Five seconds is good. Now place the toaster in the freezer. This is the only difficult part, making room in your freezer. Nowadays many freezers in refrigerators, even if you go to the trouble of taking out all the frozen fish, steaks, peas, and orange-juice concentrate, simply won't accommodate a pop-up toaster. Chill for forty-five minutes. Time may vary slightly, according to the make of toaster and the make of freezer. The coils should glow an unmistakable blue. Remove toaster, insert your letter, making sure the address faces the *outside,* and shake gently with intent and omicron. If the card or letter is not dispatched, check to see that all the coils are unbroken and that the address is correct and complete. You may have left out an apartment number or a zip code.

Kaelin had to hurry, because Harve was picking her up at ten. She put the toaster in the freezer—with no one around to ask, "What in God's name are you doing, Kaelin?"—glanced at her watch, and tiptoe-ran back upstairs to brush her hair and finish dressing. In forty-five minutes it would be five to ten. She could mail the postcard right before she went out the door.

Harve liked football, but Kaelin didn't particularly. She would learn to like it. She brushed her hair and thought about football. Football, baseball, and basketball went with American, inconspicuous, and normal.

Harve and she would get married, and every morning they would drink coffee and read the papers. He would rake leaves; she would iron shirts. Their little son would play with blocks; their little daughter would have a dollhouse. Their dog would be named Spot or Rex and have no metal in him. There would be a goldfish in a goldfish bowl, with a little green seaweed at the bottom cheerfully waving back and forth.

At five to ten Kaelin was back in the kitchen, wearing her cap (the black one after all, because the blue-and-green really didn't match) and holding her gloves, scarf, and postcard to Christopher. But the refrigerator, when she approached it, morphed into Mother, who plucked the postcard from her fingers.

"Hmm. Not for the mailbox, apparently," said Debra Zimmerman. "Who can we be writing to?" She looked at it. "Christopher, of course. Well, I am not surprised." She saw the address and said, lips tightening, "The future. He's in the future." She turned it over and read: "Harve gave me a ring. We're going steady. Be more careful. Mother almost had you on that planet. Love, your Kaelin."

Kaelin was paralyzed. She was a sparrow confronted suddenly, up close, out of nowhere, by a giant jade-eyed cat. By death, noiseless, wise, all-powerful, irresistible, and fascinating. Would she be scooped out on the spot, or would they hold a family council first? A part of her, detached, observing, like a scientist, posed the cold question.

"I can't say, Kaelin, that I'm disappointed in you," Mother went on, tapping her chin once, twice, with a point of the rectangular card. "It was plain where your sympathies lay." Another tap. A slow shake of the head. A cruel smile. "Our poor, timid, drab Kaelin leading the double life of a secret agent."

Mother had never liked her.

Kaelin wondered what it would feel like when her soul was taken from her body. Did it hurt? Or was it simply like turning off the lights? She tried to say a prayer in her mind, but couldn't think of a prayer. She couldn't take her eyes off her mother's face.

"You have been very bad, my dear," said Mother with a tsk-tsk. "Aiding and abetting, mutiny, treason. When our family can't afford such things, as you well know. Such luxuries. When our family simply can't allow them."

I won't do it again, Kaelin wanted to cry out. I swear! And she meant it, she meant it with her whole heart. She wouldn't do it again ever.

A car beeped outside: Harve, on time.

"Your date," said Mother.

Mother and daughter watched each other in silence.

"You have been very bad," said Mother. "And yet, Kaelin, I must confess that you have also been most helpful." She pointed at the address on the postcard. "It would have taken us longer, I don't know how much longer, to find your brother, and at a time when his absence from school has become . . . awkward."

"Mother—"

Mother held up her hand sharply: Not a word out of you.

The car beeped again, a short beep, polite Harve not wanting to sound impatient or annoy anyone with his horn.

"And I believe, Kaelin, that you will not do anything like this again. I hear it in your uninteresting head, I see it in your uninteresting face."

Oh I won't, I won't! Please spare me! Let me live!

"So I think, my dear, that we will merely ground you for this. I think that neutralization is not necessary in your case."

Kaelin almost fell, her relief was so intense. I'm not going to die, she thought.

"You are grounded for a week. But in the future, you will stay home more. Where we can keep an eye on you, you understand."

Kaelin almost wept, she was so grateful to be allowed to live.

"You will stop seeing this Harve boy. You will stop indulging in adolescent fantasies. You belong with the family, my dear, and nowhere else. Surely that is obvious, given what you are. What we are."

Kaelin nodded again and again, an eager dog, a faithful puppet.

There was a timid knock now at the front door.

She went and opened it and told Harve, in one breath, that she couldn't go to the Thanksgiving football game with him, she was grounded. Also, she said—speaking so fast that her words stumbled together and she had to go back and repeat them—she couldn't go steady with him anymore, she was sorry about that, but her mother said she was too young, and her mother in general didn't approve of young people going steady, so here's your ring back, Harve, and thanks for everything, really.

Harve, holding the ring, didn't know what to say. His eyes stricken.

"Good-bye," gulped Kaelin, and closed the door in his face.

Behind her, her mother's voice: "No meals and no television for a week, young lady. Go to your room."

Kaelin went up to her room. She would do whatever her mother said from now on, to the letter. She wanted to live. She couldn't have Harve? Well, that was a small, such a small, price to pay. A teenage boy, nice but nothing that special. And even if that special, too bad. She would stop loving him. Love only made people do and think perilous things. No more peril for Kaelin. Never again.

And little Christopher? Better to lose a brother than to lose herself. Christopher had committed suicide, anyway, with his defiance. It was only a matter of time. Only a matter of minutes, now that they knew where he was. Why should she be scooped out with him? Why did boys have to be so defiant?

It was better to survive. Survival was better than anything.

In her room Kaelin took off her coat and sweater, put away her cap and scarf, folded the scarf before setting it in the drawer. Big, stupid tears ran down her cheeks. They would pass. It was just biology, stupid girl's tears. She took a deep breath, and after a while the tears stopped. She dried her face. She looked in her mirror and saw a wan, colorless face, a little swollen from crying. Mother was right: drab and uninteresting Kaelin.

That was fine.

Outside, a sad car on the street went *rrr-rrr, rrr-rrr*.

Meanwhile, downstairs, Mother looked at the postcard to Christopher with eyes of flint, and she summoned Father.

Monty Zimmerman appeared, squinting, holding a newspaper, his suspenders down. "Yes, dear?"

Without a word, Mother handed him the postcard.

"Oh, my," he said, and fingered his mustache. "The future." He had dyed his hair that morning, in the sink. It was the color of licorice. But the mustache and eyebrows hadn't been dyed, so they looked weirdly pale in contrast.

"He's in a protected sector," said Mother, "so we'll have to use a more primitive method. The most primitive method. Otherwise we set off alarms."

"You mean—"

"Yes."

"Oh, my."

Father put down the newspaper, pulled up his suspenders, and ran a shaky hand through his hair, which made his fingers gray. His mouth twitched at the left corner.

Twitch, twitch, went his mouth.

"Now?" he asked.

"Of course now."

"On Thanksgiving?"

"It's not *our* holiday. What is the matter with you? Have you gone soft in the head, Monty? What does Thanksgiving have to do with it?"

"And the school? What do we tell them?"

Mother gave Father a withering look. "We tell them," she said, "that the child had an unusual allergic reaction to Dr. Hill's medication and was found dead in his bed. He just stopped breathing, poor thing. It happens."

Father nodded, stood for a moment, sighed. "An allergic reaction . . . A shame we can't just scoop him out." This was muttered more to himself than spoken aloud. No point in aggravating Mother more. "But we can't, we can't, not there. . . . Setting off alarms . . . Too bad, though . . ."

Muttering, sighing, he went and got a pair of leather gloves and, in the basement, from the Peg-Board over the workbench, a small coil of piano wire.

We are in an amusement park, in what used to be Delaware. Delaware no longer exists, and amusement parks now are called fun cities. Fun cities are really more than amusement parks: they're a combination of carnival, therapy center, consumer marketing laboratory, and a couple of other things that you, being from the past, wouldn't possibly understand. Gramps has taken Christopher here because the boy is becoming difficult from boredom, loneliness, and the strain of being constantly in an unfamiliar place. They've exhausted the grammar book. Christopher refuses to look at another predicate nominative, objective complement, or correlative conjunction. He needs a little R and R. He's only ten.

There are lots of rides. Rides on different levels and at different speeds. There is a purple neon catenary. A floating giant yellow goose. A train that lurches nervously up and down like a sewing machine that's coming apart as you watch.

There is a lot of junk food and band music. Shows, displays, demos.

Gramps is not paying attention. He is interested in those women who are hardly wearing anything. You can't get a full sentence out of him; his neck cranes, his words trail off. Christopher thinks it's funny, but at the same time he is annoyed. Annoyed not so much at Gramps as in general.

Christopher is in a bad mood. The creepy feeling he has been having on and off lately is mostly on now. He doesn't want to feel this creepy feeling, but it's there, insistent, like a splinter under the skin. The feeling—it's as if you're in a horror movie, where nothing has happened yet but the deep organ has started playing. Gradually it goes up the scale, and you know that soon, any minute, a half-decomposed corpse with a grin and no eyelids will pop out of a closet or bathtub and come at you, wielding an ax. Christopher doesn't want to be in a horror movie, doesn't want to go through some awful scene of screams, slime, and spurting blood.

There is a Tunnel of Horror. On the outside, loudspeaker moans and manic laughter. Christopher will skip the Tunnel of Horror.

Clowns on every corner hand out samples to passersby. The samples are interactive gadgets, which reminds us a little of Ruby Star and her presents for Christopher whenever she came for Gramps. Except these gadgets work, and they are truly amazing. There is a ring that talks with you so well, so intelligently, you can't believe it's all done by microchip, you think there has to be a remote and that someone at the other end is laughing at you. There is a cube that shows real pictures from your mind. A pen that squeals when you misspell a word with it or fail to put in a comma. A comb that, in addition to combing, dances Spanish dances when you clap—energized from the static electricity.

Christopher loves gadgets. He stops at every clown and doesn't refuse one handout, until his pockets are bulging. The boy shows a definite bent in the direction of science and engineering.

This fun city seems to have, on its staff, almost as many physicians and lawyers as there are visitors. Before they let you on a roller coaster, they take your pulse and blood pressure and give you waivers to sign. They are particularly anxious at the sight of Gramps, who has a lot of wrinkles and the only gray head in the crowd. People in the future evidently prefer not to age biologically, or at least not to show it in public.

"Having a good time?" Gramps asked. They were sitting on a bench by a gourmet ice-cream stand.

"Okay," said Christopher, working on a chocolate fudge mousse cone with jimmies.

Gramps patted Christopher's knee. "You're blue. You miss home."

"I guess," said Christopher.

They sat and looked out over Rehoboth Bay, except in the future it was no longer Rehoboth Bay. The pleasant breeze smelled of blossoms and ozone. On the ground at Christopher's feet lay a melting scoop of cashew brickle ice cream someone had dropped, and a row of ants stretched from the ice cream to a crack in the dry earth. If you focused on the red-brown ants and the forked crack in the earth, you could be in any century.

"But I can't go home, ever," said Christopher.

"We'll figure something out, my boy," said Gramps, but his eye was on a woman who had enormous pink bull's-eye breasts that bounced as she walked past them. "Holy cow," he whispered.

After the ice cream, grandfather and grandson rode on a loop thing that had peculiar gravity and three different seat belts for each person. Christopher liked that one. They went to an arcade and shot at video aliens with violet laser rifles. Every time you hit an alien, it cursed and shook its fist at you. Christopher didn't find that interesting; it was too much like the games·at home. They rafted down a bubbly waterfall that followed a spiral which didn't appear to be either logarithmic or Archimedean. They ate souvlaki, popcorn, pistachios, fried clams, and Szechuan steamed dumplings. Christopher wanted to do the gravity loop again; Gramps said go ahead but, if Christopher didn't mind, he would sit this one out. His stomach was starting to do loops of its own. People wouldn't like it, he was sure, if he brought everything up in midair. Sour rain with chunks, my boy.

A nurse came and gave Gramps a pill and a soda that had a poppy-seed taste, which helped his stomach.

So they started separating. Meet you back at this kiosk in half an hour. Meet you back at the orange pavilion, by the giant kielbasa, in an hour. There were no undesirables in evidence—no kidnapping con men or sweaty-handed peverts—and plenty of alert staff were stationed at intervals, keeping an eye on things, so the child was safe. And if Christopher took a wrong turn and got lost somehow, he had a beeper location gizmo in his shirt pocket and could home in on Gramps that way.

Not a thing in the world to worry about.

And Gramps, for his part, could now check out the girlie booths, unencumbered by a kid. (For even in the open-minded, anything-goes future the presence of juveniles in girlie booths is frowned upon, and rightly so.)

This, anyway, was how Christopher Zimmerman ended up alone in the Hall of Digital Mirrors.

The images in that fun-house maze were created not by glass with a silvered or amalgam backing but by a highly high-tech array of hologram pixels, the clever convergence, computer-mediated, of coherent light. In the long-ago kind of fun-house mirror maze—a maze with actual, physical mirrors—people would put out their hands to keep from bumping noses or heads, and in no time the grease from fingers and palms accumulated on the glass, and then you could tell immediately where the real doorway was. With so-called digital mirrors, however, there was no glass, no grease, and the reflections remained as sharp and clean as life. A wrong turn didn't mean a bumped nose but a corridor that led nowhere: a dead end or else back where you started.

Christopher looked at his watch: he had to meet Gramps at the gate to the Putting Green in twenty minutes. Was there time to do this maze? Probably not. He set his alarm for fifteen minutes. He would just take a peek, not really get into it.

He saw long, shaded corridors. At the end of one, third to the left, was a little kid facing him. Christopher took a step; the kid took a step. It was himself.

It gave him a chill. The kid didn't seem like a reflection at all—he seemed like something out of a dream that had walked, impossibly, into the real world.

Half the corridors were straight, half curved. Sunlight streamed in through windows in different places and at different angles. Christopher could see parts of some of the windows, but many were out of view, just around a corner or a bend. The corridors were all still. It was like being in an empty church. He sensed that this maze was a really tricky one, advanced, not for beginners or children. He had to try it. He would try it tomorrow and tell Gramps it might take him an hour, maybe even two hours.

He turned and made for the entrance, but stopped halfway, because to his surprise there were several doors to the outside, though he had thought there was only one. In all of them, you could see a clown dancing. The same clown doing the same dance. So they couldn't all be real. One door led out; the others were reflections of it.

Christopher proceeded slowly, carefully, looking hard for clues as he walked. He breathed a sigh of relief as he exited the Hall of Digital Mirrors, but somehow, instead of stepping onto the concourse and into the noise, the concourse dissolved and he was in a corridor, and there was not even a door in sight.

Up ahead, another person was walking. Christopher, suddenly afraid of being alone in this place, ran after the person, but the person, without turning around, started running, too. Maybe he had heard Christopher's footsteps and thought someone was after him. Christopher stopped; the kid stopped—it was only a kid. It was Christopher himself, his reflection seen from behind.

"It's time," said Christopher's watch. "It's time."

Christopher pushed a button on his wrist to make it stop saying, "It's time." He took out the beeper gizmo, which told him, with two short beeps, that Gramps was directly to his right—but that didn't help much, since there was a wall to his right. Gramps might be half a kilometer away, through all kinds of walls and buildings as the crow flew.

After trying a few turns and a few corridors, Christopher called out. "Hello?"

Nothing, not even echoes, which you might have expected in a hall of mirrors.

"Is anybody there?" he called.

"Hey!

"I'm lost!

"Help!"

Complete and perfect silence.

Part of Christopher said there was no reason to panic: there had to be a listening device somewhere in here, and people were probably on their way to rescue the poor scared child because they didn't want a lawsuit.

Another part of Christopher, however, noticed that the creepy feeling was growing, swelling, a clear sign that something was going to happen soon. Something bad.

To him.

He thought maybe he should use his upsilon and omicron to escape, to break free of the maze while there was time, even though Gramps had told him this was a protected sector, rigged with a special futuristic alarm system, and the police here were really hard on nonhumans who used powers. Christopher didn't want to get Gramps in trouble. The man was over eighty, too old to sit in jail.

Creating a scene, besides, would be sure to draw Mother.

He ran down one corridor after another, past windows filled

with sunlight but nothing more—no outside to them, only light—and turned left, right, right, left, on the chance that he might blunder out of this by pure luck. Running around a corner, he ran smack into Gramps.

"Oof," said Gramps.

"Gramps!" cried Christopher.

Except that the oof had been in the wrong voice. And Gramps was too big in the shoulders.

The man pulled off his rubber face—the face of Gramps exactly, complete with sunken cheeks and the large wen on the forehead above the left eyebrow—and Christopher screamed, seeing black hair, very black hair, instead of gray, and a face that was at once extremely contorted and extremely familiar.

"Father!" exclaimed Christopher.

Monty Zimmerman snarled, baring his teeth like a wolf. It wasn't a personal snarl, not meant against Christopher, not vicious or even angry—it was simply the kind of grimacing that karate experts use to charge up their bodies and prepare their minds when they have to accomplish something difficult and dangerous, such as chopping through a concrete block with a naked hand.

By the time Christopher recovered from his shock enough to begin to understand why Father was here—and Christopher was not a slow child, as Mrs. Palmer could tell you if she were alive—it was too late, the piano wire was around his neck and jerking spastically, closing off air and blood.

The whole thing took less than half a minute. A most upsetting scene to watch, this, but fortunately there were no witnesses to be upset. No one had to look as poor little Christopher did that grim dance that goes back to prehistoric times, a dance as old as humanity, older—the first dance, before there were such things as proms, parties, or dance music, or any music at all, even primitive drums. It was a two-step but bore no resemblance to Kaelin and Harve's two-step at the gym; it was much faster and more complex, a frantic, flurrying, syncopated kick-step, almost as if the body were attempting the impossible: to leave itself. The dance had the infectious rhythm of a fly caught in a web, of a fish pulled from the brine and dropped onto a wooden deck, of a rat thrown into fire—or of anyone in the family of man, past, present, future, who is garroted. We omit the usual description of lolling purple tongue, bugged eyes, and blood-flecked saliva. This is a sweet, innocent, ten-year-old boy with straw-colored hair and freckled cheeks, and it seems wrong, it seems just too cruel, to dwell on the ugliness of his last moments, giving him such a hideous, frightening mask for the rest of eternity. Therefore we look the other way until the final kicks—thump, pause, thump—end.

Exit Monty, panting, by a back way.

About an hour of motionlessness then, with the exception of the liquid-crystal numbers on Christopher's watch, which blink and change regularly, indifferent to the cold wrist they are strapped to, indifferent to the fact that it is growing colder, and the skin less resilient, and the joint less flexible.

An agitated Gramps is already at a local security station giving the police a description of the missing boy, when the body is discovered. The police immediately call up on their screens, from the hidden camera at the door, the faces of all those who entered the Hall of Digital Mirrors prior to the approximate time of the crime, and they find that the last to enter—and the only one to enter after the victim—was Gramps himself. It's unmistakably Gramps: the gray hair, sunken cheeks, and that odd marble-bump on his forehead. (In the future, people don't know what wens are.)

Gramps protested, naturally, with a babbling stutter, "I—I wasn't there. No, I was at—an exhibit. One of those—you know, uh, girlie things, peep shows. The Fleshpot."

"Did anyone see you there?" asked a phlegmatic inspector.

"I beg your pardon?" It was hard for Gramps to concentrate. He still couldn't believe Christopher had been murdered. Who could have done—and to a small child—and why? There were no psychos running loose in the future; all psychotic genes had been carefully sifted out and discarded. The future had some awful problems, but that, thank goodness, was not one of them.

"Did anyone see you there?" the inspector asked again, slowly. Time was on his side. He had his man.

"See me there?" said Gramps.

"At the Fleshpot."

"At the Fleshpot."

"Yes, you are quite recognizable, Mr."—a glance at the ID—"Mr. Cesar Porter. If someone saw you, they would remember you."

Gramps tried to think. Did anyone see him there? Well, probably not. It was dark, with lots of curtains and veils and shadows for anonymity. Not being seen by others was one of the points—

wasn't it?—of voyeurism. A little innocent healthy male voyeur-ism. He felt not innocent, however, but guilty. He should have been with the child. A child, taken from his home, was entirely the adult taker's responsibility. But who, who, who could have anticipated—?

"Probably not," muttered Gramps.

The inspector nodded.

The future had an efficient judicial and penal system. It was a well-oiled mechanism. There were no long waits, a minimum of red tape, and never a miscarriage. Gramps was represented by two attorneys. One stressed the lack of a motive; the other argued a fail-ing mind, degenerative senile dementia due to arteriosclerosis—and this was supported by the testimony of an eminent geriatric physician flown in from Maryland or what used to be Maryland. The prosecution made short work of both defenses, and the judge agreed, gaveling with his gavel twice, two loud, resonant raps that filled the courtroom like gunfire and made Gramps jump.

There was no jury, which also saved time and made justice that much less obstructable.

Gramps was sentenced, escorted by huge roboguards to a copter, and flown to a facility where he was escorted, processed, escorted again, lectured to, and finally put into a humming Flash Gordon cylinder and with a thrown switch and a crackle beamed down to a self-contained prison deep in the earth. A prison embedded in dense porphyry-obsidian rock five kilometers beneath an impene-trably black ocean bed.

The transport beam, note, is one-way only and, by the immutable laws of conservation and thermodynamics, absolutely irreversible.

Also note the four-meter-thick bdellium shield installed around the spherical prison like the shell around a filbert: it will annul and frustrate any long-range activity of a paranormal nature. In other words, Gramps cannot leave the premises with his upsilon and omicron—or communicate, using his upsilon and omicron, with another of his nonhuman ilk on the surface—or ever hope to be ex-tricated by said ilk likewise exercising, illegally, said upsilon and omicron.

The bdellium shield, moreover, and this is very clever, has a counteractive-reflective effect—like rays of light bounced and fo-cused parabolically—on the site of the exercise of any upsilon and omicron *within* its precinct, so that a split second after such unlawful exercise, the exerciser is zapped out of existence by a bolt of his own petard, as it were.

Gramps had better not even brush his teeth using his upsilon and omicron.

The most he can do, in the event that despair drives him over the edge of sanity and into violent, foaming suicide, is use his prohibited ability to set off a fusion reaction that in less than a split second will turn the entire contents of the prison, himself included, into pure energy. But even that, even that, will accomplish no more—at the tremendous depth we are talking of here—than an undramatic, forgettable blip on a seismologist's graph in Baku, maybe, or Djakarta.

The prison has no warden, no guards, and no staff. The authorities do not care if everyone in it perishes. There are only twenty-three cells altogether, and only seven of them are presently occupied. (The future has pretty much done to crime what we have done to smallpox.)

When a prisoner expires, the cell heats up, cremates the body, disposes of the ashes and unburned bits, and straightens, repaints, and air-freshens itself for the next occupant. Some cells have been waiting more than a hundred years for a new occupant. Crime is really down.

Gramps is not thinking of escape. Nor is he shuddering with the psychological agony of being buried alive in kilometers of rock. His head is bowed, his face in his hands. He groans. He moans. He still cannot believe that Christopher has been murdered, that Christopher—his only pal, not counting Emily and Panda Ray, and they don't really count, not being creatures of flesh and blood—he still cannot believe that little Christopher, his dear little Christopher, is no more.

Don't Underestimate Gramps

The cell is like a bathroom. Other than the cot, the only furniture—if you can call a sink and a toilet furniture—is a sink and a toilet. And the dimensions of the cell are quite small, not much bigger than the dimensions of the bathroom in Gramps's house, the one he used for his flight from incarceration in that life-care community: golf, tennis, and blood-pressure stations at the edge of the Okaloacoochee Slough. Golden Years.

Perhaps it is his karma to be incarcerated. Perhaps he should just submit and not fight it.

Gramps is despondent. He stares at the floor a lot. He shakes his head. Sometimes he talks—to himself, to Emily. He's not sure if she can hear him where he is.

He doesn't dare talk to Christopher. Shameful, how he let that child down.

"Ah," he breathes, "if I ever get out of this . . ."

Which is absurd in two respects. First of all, he won't ever get out of this, it's impossible. He might as well be in a black hole, stuck as he is more than halfway into the earth's crust, actually closer to the semimolten mantle than he is to the surface and the air and the sight of birds flying.

Secondly, even if he *could* get out of this somehow, that wouldn't bring Christopher back to life, would it?

Would it?

Upsilon and omicron (assuming there is a way—except there

isn't—to sidestep the bdellium concave mirror effect) can work veritable miracles, but alas, resurrection is not one of them.

Impossibility, then, on top of impossibility; impossibility taken to an impossible power.

He shakes his head.

"If I get out of this," he promises Emily, "I'll never look at a woman again."

He'll take cold showers if he has to.

There is no shower in this cell. He has to make do with a sponge and the sink, using an acrid, pinkish liquid soap from a built-in soap dispenser.

In a dream one night, he was having a conversation with his beloved wife of many years. She looked worn-out and didn't seem to be listening. He was talking about random, deranged killers who appeared out of the blue and against whom there was no protection. She interrupted him finally, impatient.

"Cesar, it wasn't a random, deranged killer, it was family."

"What?"

"Sometimes you are quite obtuse." It was not like Emily to be short with him. He began to pay attention, even though this was only a dream. "Don't you see, it has Debra written all over it," Emily continued. "Our hard, unforgiving daughter. Don't you remember the time she got back at that Gallagher girl who stole her boyfriend—David, I think it was, David Heim or Hein. The one who wore bow ties and laughed too much? Debra waited until summer camp was over and then gave Betsy Gallagher cancer in her senior year."

"We don't know that."

"Of course we do. A healthy sixteen-year-old coming down with vaginal cancer like that, with no family history? And do you think it was an accident that poor David got gored in Pamplona the next summer—that thing where tourists run in the streets with the bulls—and the doctors couldn't save his genitals?"

"Emily."

"Don't Emily me. That's Debra's style. It's always been. As if she were some kind of Mafia don, and anyone who crossed her couldn't go unpunished or else her honor would suffer. The woman is a monster, she has no heart."

Gramps sighed. "Were we bad parents?"

Emily came over, gave him a sad hug, then started to fade. "We were all right, Cesar," she said, attenuating. "Hitler's parents were probably all right, too. It doesn't have to do with the parents."

"So you think Debra did it, killed the boy?"

". . ."

Gramps spent the next several nights—not that "night" had much significance five kilometers under the bottom of our planet's deepest oceanic trench—tossing and turning. He felt responsible for the evil his daughter had done, for the evil that had befallen his grandson, for the great injustice and pity of it all. He felt responsible and, feeling responsible, he decided to do something. He couldn't just sit there. He had to try to make things right.

"I'm sure you'll think of a solution, dear," Emily whispered into his ear at one point between troubled dreams, and she kissed him on his sunken cheek, for encouragement. "You always do."

One morning—not that "morning" had much significance, either, in this rock-locked prison of the far future—Gramps woke and his eyes fell, as they always did, on the toilet. It struck him how much the cell resembled a bathroom. It was essentially a bathroom with a cot. He remembered all the time he had spent in his own bathroom, retiling it. It had taken months, almost a year. Measuring, cutting those rose tiles. Murder on the knees.

Now, if one could tile the concrete walls of this bathroom, that is, of this cell . . .

But how could one tile without a tile cutter? Without tiles?

He shook his head and sighed.

Of course, it didn't have to be tiles, did it? It could be anything on the walls that made the same pattern, the pattern with golden ratios in it and shifting fivefold symmetry. With one, two, and the square root of five all joined together in their intricate, intimate fractal dance of stars and suns.

It didn't have to be tiles; it could be, for example, paper. Paper cut according to a stencil or from a template—a kite template, a dart template—and then pasted carefully, one after the other, on the wall. Positioned exactly and pressed into place.

The only paper he had, however, was toilet paper.

And the only thing that might work as an adhesive was the liquid soap. (For brushing your teeth a powder was dispensed, not a paste.)

Also, there were no scissors to cut the toilet paper with. There were no sharp objects in general. Nothing in his pockets: the police had taken his ID, bills, change, and emery board.

Curious, he tried tearing some toilet paper, using an edge of the sink, then an edge of his cot, and learned that it was impossible to tear toilet paper that way and get a straight line, even if you were very patient. Maybe the grain was too rough, or maybe there was no real grain. He tried folding and making a sharp crease, and found that if he separated the paper at the crease, using his thumbnails, working slowly and a little at a time, he could make a reasonably straight cut, if you didn't look too close. Seen from a distance, it was straight enough.

But how to fashion a template from which to produce the necessary toilet-paper "tiles"? The special cartwheeling kites and darts were built on the golden section, built from triangles found in a regular pentagon after you drew in the diagonals, but to get those triangles you needed to construct a pentagon, and to construct a pentagon you needed to construct a line segment that was in extreme-and-mean proportion to another—and to accomplish that you needed, at the very least, according to Euclid, whose authority rests on many centuries and is corroborated by more mathematicians than you can count, a compass, a straightedge, and a pencil.

Gramps tried unraveling a thread from one of his socks to make a string-compass. It didn't work very well; you really couldn't do precision compassing with it. Particularly as the arthritis in his fingers made it hard for him to keep the thread taut as it pivoted. And his plastic green toothbrush was not of much use as a straightedge.

And what would he make the template *from*? There was nothing to use, no large piece of wood or cardboard, and nothing, besides, with which to cut and mold that nothing. It was hopeless.

He puttered gamely for a while, experimenting with several pieces of toilet paper pressed together with soap, experimenting with several sock threads twisted together to make a cord, and so on—all in the venerable tradition of convicts who have little raw material at their disposal but all the time in the world.

He had to make sure that it was hopeless, and after a few weeks of puttering he concluded that, yes, it was hopeless, all right, to do the geometrical construction he needed to do: hopeless, with a homemade sock-cord compass, crooked toothbrush, and fingernail marks on toilet paper instead of pencil on real paper.

Did we mention that his food—warm mush—was served in a bowl-like depression in a corner of the floor, from no discernible opening? The mush appeared regularly, and he had to eat it either with his fingers or else like a dog, head down and on all fours. There were no utensils, no aluminum fork or spoon you could bend into a useful tool.

Not that there was any lock to pick on any door. There was no lock, because there was no door.

Even if there had been a door—to a hallway, say—the fact remained that there was nowhere to go in this spherical bubble set deep in the dense, hard bowels of Mother Earth.

The geometrical construction itself would have been child's play. There are a few ways to obtain the golden section. Here is one of them, in five ridiculously easy steps.

1) Make one.
2) Add one.
3) Go up one.
4) Go out one.
5) Half that.

1) *Make one.* An arbitrary length. You set your compass—which Gramps in his cell unfortunately doesn't have—to any length you like, mark it off on your basic horizontal line, and call that "one." If you're doing this at home and want to label points, which is not a bad idea, call the first compass pivot point A.

2) *Add one.* With the compass at the same setting, that is, open to the same angle—that is, untouched—you put the pivot point now on the mark you just made in step 1 and mark off again on the horizontal line. Call this second point B. Since you've added one to one, line AB is two in length. What could be simpler?

3) *Go up one.* Make a perpendicular at point B. It doesn't matter what the compass setting is, so you can conveniently keep it the same. (If you are unable to make a perpendicular to a line at any point using a compass and straightedge, don't be embarrassed; consulting a high-school geometry book will take you ten minutes, no more. This is not rocket science.) On the perpendicular now mark a length of one up from B, and that point you call C.

4) *Go out one.* With your straightedge connect A and C and continue for a piece, imagining another infinite line. Note that ABC

is a right triangle and that according to Pythagoras, one of the first great geniuses to walk the earth, the length of hypotenuse AC squared is equal to AB squared plus BC squared. In other words, with nothing but a one and a two we have arrived most straightforwardly at the square root of five. Are there any questions? No? Put the pivot of your compass at C and along the continuation of the hypotenuse mark yet another one, and call that point D. AD is therefore the square root of five (AC) plus one (CD).

5) *Half that.* Bisect AD. For this you'll need to open your compass a little. Don't be nervous: bisecting a line is essentially the same thing as making a perpendicular. (Feel free to consult the geometry book on this if you need to. No one will laugh. You're among friends here.) Call the halfway point E. AE is half of AD and thus has a length of the square root of five plus one all divided by two. This length is in golden ratio to your original "one." For it, Americans use the Greek letter phi; the Brits, probably for the same reason that they say dustbin instead of garbage can, use tau. It doesn't matter.

From here it is but a hop, skip, and a jump to our exciting goal. Set the compass back at one (making its opening coincide with BC, if you like) and now draw two arcs above the hypotenuse line, one arc from A, the other from E. Call their point of intersection F and with your straightedge draw triangle AEF.

Note the following. The two small angles of this triangle are equal and 36 degrees; the large angle at the top—AFE—is 108 degrees, which happens to be not only three times 36 but also, behold, the interior angle of a regular pentagon. Except that we don't need a pentagon now, because with one and phi, drawing arcs from different ends and connecting their intersections, we will have our dart and our kite in no time.

Arc of one up from F and of phi northwesterly from E, intersect at G, and there's the dart: AFGE, with sides (clockwise from A) of one, one, phi, phi.

Arc of phi northwesterly from A, and likewise roughly west of G, intersect at H, and there's the kite: AHGF, with sides (clockwise from A) of phi, phi, one, one.

This is what was denied Gramps for lack of the basic tools and supplies, which he could not jury-rig or improvise satisfactorily. There is only so much a man in his eighties can do with toilet paper.

And yet.

A thought came to Gramps as he lay on his cot and stared with numb despair at the rough concrete ceiling. A memory more than a thought. An early memory, very early, from when he was in elementary school, and that's a hell of a long time ago. Something a kid showed him once, a little trick that he had completely forgotten until now. Childhood is filled with little tricks. Spinning a top. Snapping your fingers. Making fart sounds with a cupped hand in your armpit. Folding paper to turn it into an airplane, a noisemaker, a cootie catcher.

There was more than one way to skin this particular geometrical cat.

Great and wondrous are the mysteries of the universe.

He smiled.

What he remembered was that if you made a knot—the simplest knot possible—in a strip of paper (sides parallel) and were careful to keep all the parts of that strip flat, and if, tightening the knot, you then creased neatly all the bends and snipped off the two pieces that stuck out—you obtained a perfect pentagon.

Gramps went and tried this with a length of toilet paper. The wide strip, eleven and a half centimeters to be exact, required about a meter to make the knot. Whenever the flimsy toilet paper buckled or folded inappropriately, he unbuckled and unfolded, smoothing out. Then he tightened the whole thing, creased, and sure enough: not only a pentagon but one with most of its diagonals showing, that is, the greater part of a pentagram, since the toilet paper was so thin, you could see the edges under it as well. He didn't need to tear off the strips protruding, didn't need to finish the pentagon or pentagram; what caught his eye were the two isosceles triangles at the top, over the golden trapezoid.

Every angle 36 degrees or a multiple thereof. One triangle was 36, 36, and 108 (see above, the very AEF of our construction); the other was 36 and two 72s.

You could think of it as a one-three-one triangle and a two-one-two triangle: each totaling five, because five times 36 is 180, and every triangle in the world—on a flat plane, that is—totals 180 degrees, which is half a circle.

If the pentagon's long diagonal that supports both isosceles triangles is thought of as a mirror, that is, if you add a mirror image to each triangle on the other side of that line, you find that the doubled one-three-one triangle is your dart, the doubled two-one-two triangle your kite.

No compass and straightedge needed, therefore, and no templates, just a little patience and some meticulous and repetitive folding and creasing and tearing.

The floor of Gramps's cell soon filled with bits, shreds, scraps, and crumples of toilet paper, some dry, some soaked with liquid soap.

Too much soap, he learned, was no good: it dissolved the paper.

He discovered also that the soap worked better if it was thickened first with the gray dental powder.

The cell maintenance machinery apparently didn't mind how often the toilet was flushed, or how often the soap and powder were used, not to mention the toilet paper. There was an endless supply of these items.

But in a closed prison such as this one, you would expect recycling.

Gramps sang as he worked. He was not disheartened by the countless frustrations. A dart that tore in the wrong place after hours of preparation. A kite that fell off the wall after it was painstakingly positioned. Fingers, knuckles, wrists that hurt like the devil, there being no aspirin.

The difficulty of old bones reaching high places, standing precariously on the frame of the cot and stretching, stretching.

Or finding that a section of the wall wasn't right, wasn't precise enough, the angles too noticeably off, and thus having to do that section all over again.

Gramps sang.

He sang "Old Folks at Home."

He sang "Danny Boy."

He was pleased with the color, too. If the pale gray-pink was not a pretty rose, it was not altogether out of the ballpark of rose, either.

"But what are you going to do," asked Emily, "when you have to catch hold of a cosmic string? What if there isn't one right nearby? You won't have time to wait, with that damned bdellium parabolic zapper activated the instant you use your upsilon and omicron."

"True," said Gramps. "But we do have a chance, my dear, we do have a chance. If it doesn't work, at least I get to go down swinging. Better that than sitting here shaking my head. Worlds better."

"Do be careful, Cesar."

Time passed, and the walls of the cell gradually covered with the same remarkable tessellation as was Gramps's traveling bathroom. The same rhombs and pentagons, the same asterisks and wriggling zigzag rays outward, the same local isomorphism. The symmetries dizzyingly alternating, the similarities tantalizingly dissimilar. The graceful repetitions blending into unexpected counterpoints or surprising interruptions, which themselves in turn were repeated regularly and gracefully . . .

The cell smelled of soap.

Gramps was happy. One way or another, he was leaving. Soon, maybe tomorrow, he would thumb his nose at the warm mush in the bowl-like depression in the corner of the floor. If he was lucky and caught a string, he would soon be sinking his teeth into a crunchy apple. Into a carrot. A green salad, a thick T-bone steak, a baked potato.

But more important, much more important, if he was lucky—and he hoped he would be lucky—he would soon be on his way to the rescue, just like the cavalry in the movies, or the marines, or the caped superhero with a steely eye, a set jaw, and terrific muscles.

This was one time his daughter was *not* going to have her way.

We are back at the Hall of Digital Mirrors. Gramps materializes in a corridor. More precisely, his traveling prison cell materializes with him inside it. He has been traveling the Sea of If and is here to pick up an alternate Christopher before the boy's father gets to the boy first with the Gramps mask and the piano wire.

So it appears that Gramps did catch a cosmic string in the nick of time after all and avoided being vaporized by a bdellium-backfiring zap. It appears that he indeed escaped the escape-proof prison embedded in kilometers of rock far below our feet.

On the other hand, maybe not.

In the Sea of If, which is a real Sea and not the product of your imagination or mine, an infinite number of Grampses caught a string in the nick of time—and an infinite number didn't. Is this the same Gramps we recently saw in his cell singing happily as he stuck pink toilet-paper darts and kites one by one to the wall? That is the question.

The answer: We can't be a hundred percent sure.

Christopher died. That was a great tragedy. But it's possible that Gramps died, too, trying to reach this alternate Hall of Digital Mirrors in order to save him—making a double, compound tragedy like *Romeo and Juliet.* Life is full of toupees that slip, pots that boil over, cells that turn malignant. And one misfortune, unfortunately, doesn't rule out another.

We mustn't dwell on the darkness, however. We must think positively, otherwise there's no point in going on. Even if this Gramps is an alternate Gramps, we will have to make do with him; just as he will be making do with an alternate Christopher.

Observe that the traveling prison cell now has a door and a window. Gramps installed those en route, knowing he wouldn't be able to use his upsilon and omicron once he arrived at the fun city in what a thousand years ago was Delaware. That is, he would be able to use them, yes, but not without setting off alarms, because this part of the future is a protected sector—as has been mentioned—and the authorities don't cotton to nonhumans.

Gramps knows he has to keep a low profile here.

But he has to keep a low profile in general, considering that there are an infinite number of Mothers out there trying to hunt down their respective disobedient Christophers.

Using the door, he stepped out into the corridor.

Christopher came running around a corner. He ran smack into Gramps.

"Oof," said Gramps.

"Gramps!" cried Christopher. "You found me!"

Gramps gave the boy a big hug, a desperate, tight hug, which the boy found a little peculiar. They had been apart not several months but only about an hour, from his point of view.

The real Gramps in this place—which is not to suggest that our Gramps is not real—let us say, rather, the Gramps who belongs to this alternate line—is presently absorbed in watching whatever it is one watches at the Fleshpot, so there should be no untoward entrance of him now complicating the situation. It wouldn't do to have two angry Grampses in a tug-of-war, each pulling at an arm of a bewildered Christopher.

"This place is creepy," said Christopher.

Even as he said it, they saw a Gramps and Christopher huddled together at the far end of the corridor. A digital reflection, clearly, but it made Gramps jump a little: he was expecting duplications not from mirrors but from the tricky Sea of If. After all, if he had embarked on that Sea, so had an infinite number of other Grampses, all with the same idea.

"Come on, let's get out of here," he said to Christopher.

"What's wrong?"

"I'll tell you later. No time to explain now. Hurry."

"Stop! Not that way!" cried someone. It was an old man who

looked and sounded a lot like Gramps: the spindly legs that hobbled even as he ran, the high wheezing, the wen over the left eyebrow.

"Damn," said Gramps.

"He's coming around the corner," gasped the old man. "I saw him. Monty's coming. Go this way instead. Hurry."

Christopher was confused, finding himself between two Grampses, neither of whom appeared to be an image. "Do you mean my father?" he asked, because how many people have the name Monty?

They followed the advice of Gramps Sub One and ran into a side corridor, where another traveling prison cell stood.

"In, in," urged Gramps Sub One.

On their heels was a Gramps Sub Two, who said, "What's going on here? What happened to the boy? Is he all right?"

"Shh," hissed Gramps.

"It's Monty," whispered Gramps Sub One in explanation, pointing back.

"Monty?" said Gramps Sub Two. "Ah, wait a minute, I see. You're *anticipating* him. That means he must have—"

"Watch what you say in front of Christopher," cautioned Gramps. "He doesn't know."

"And what's this?" asked Gramps Sub Two, seeing the traveling cell. He apparently didn't share the prison experience of Gramps and Gramps Sub One. Perhaps his story was that he didn't go to a police station to report the missing child but looked around instead, and saw a crowd gathered and emergency flashing lights in front of the Hall of Digital Mirrors. Then he heard the news—perhaps even saw the body as it was being taken out—and ran back to the traveling bathroom to sail the Sea of If.

"In, in," said Gramps Sub One, and they piled in with Christopher and closed the door.

There was not much room in the cell. One Gramps sat on the toilet, one sat with Christopher on the cot, and one stood, leaning against the sink.

"Aha," said Gramps Sub Two, noticing the wallpaper and nodding.

They took off as quickly as they could. If Monty found traveling prison cells and multiple Grampses in the Hall of Digital Mirrors, he'd report back to Mother, and then the opposition, too, would use the Sea of If. Things would grow so complicated then, it would be impossible to disentangle them, like a fishing line snarled into an enormous ball of knots.

"Where do we go?" asked Gramps.

"What a mess," muttered Gramps Sub One, shaking his head.

"What did Father do?" inquired Christopher, beginning in a puzzled way to figure things out.

"Never mind," said Gramps, Gramps Sub One, and Gramps Sub Two all in hasty unison. The unison was funny—but logical, too. The same person can reasonably be expected to say the same thing in the same circumstances.

Just before they grabbed a cosmic string and heave-hoed, they looked out the window and saw—or some of them looked and saw—people at the other end of the corridor. It was hard to tell from this distance who was a reflection and who wasn't. Or who was a real Gramps and who was Monty Zimmerman wearing a Gramps mask. It might have been all of the above, a combination.

With a frightened Christopher Prime or Double Prime thrown in.

For such is the nature of the Sea of If: Once its waters are muddied, after a point the muddying proceeds as if of itself, like a chain reaction. The pattern of branching events, accelerating, degenerates into such noise, a person can't hear himself think. Alternate causes contaminate alternate effects, making for linked loops and vicious circles within circles that are even more vicious.

As they traveled, the window fogging up the way it usually did, there was time to take stock and hold a council of war. (Gramps observed that in the traveling prison cell of Gramps Sub One the bowl-like depression in the floor was in a different corner, closer to the cot. But this was an insignificant detail, and he put it out of his mind.)

"What now?" said Gramps Sub Two.

"Maybe the first question," said Gramps Sub One, "is who—which of us—takes charge of the child. Of his future protection. Which of us will be his grandfather, I mean, when push comes to shove and the dust settles."

"When the dust settles," opined Gramps, "he should be returned to his original Gramps."

"Returned, you mean, to the line from which we took him," said Gramps Sub Two.

"Unless *that* Gramps . . . ," said Gramps, thinking.

". . . has also taken to the Sea of If," said Gramps Sub One, continuing the thought.

". . . and appropriated another Christopher in another line," said Gramps Sub Two, finishing the thought.

"What a mess," sighed Gramps, and they all shook their heads and thought of a deck of cards shuffled and reshuffled, irretrievably mixing suits.

"Did Father take me back," asked Christopher, "and you're trying to undo it?"

"Not exactly," said Gramps Sub One, patting him on the knee.

The other two Grampses had experienced the same patting impulse, but Gramps Sub One beat them to it. It was obvious that each considered himself Gramps and regarded the other two as Sub One and Sub Two: that is, not completely authentic. Copies, to put it crudely.

"Did Father scoop me out in another line? Is that it?" Christopher pictured himself walking through the fun city with a vacant smile on his face. He shuddered. "And you just saved me from that?"

"Close enough, close enough," said Gramps, patting the boy's head.

"Don't think about it," said Gramps Sub Two. "Let's not get morbid, my boy." And he gave Christopher a friendly little punch in the arm.

The Grampses were competing, being territorial about Christopher. "How childish," Emily would have said. Or, in this case, maybe a whole chorus of disapproving Emilys.

A concussion shook the traveling prison cell, knocking everyone to the floor and also knocking loose a few gray-pink darts and kites from the wall over the toilet.

"What in holy hell was that?" said one of the Grampses.

Christopher was at the window first, wiping it with a sleeve. He gasped when he saw another window, distant but growing nearer, in the strangely glowing void. In that window Mother stood behind the business end of what looked like a howitzer.

"It's Mother!" he shouted. "And she has a cannon!"

"Evasive action!" cried Gramps Sub One, assuming command—maybe because it was his cell and he considered himself the captain of it. After that there was a lot of grabbing of strings and cursing under breaths and panting.

They switched with a sickening lurch to the Sea of Was, then took a sharp turn through the Sea of Where, and in a wild spray of ether tacked back to the Sea of Will Be, where there was now a storm.

"Have we shaken her?" asked a Gramps, gritting his teeth and holding on to the sink with both hands.

Christopher looked again. Coming through the spume and squiggles were two enemy windows, two Mothers on their tail now—no, three Mothers. No, *four*. Three had howitzers and the fourth had something different, meaner looking. In each pursuing window each Mother was so impassive, so stone-faced, she seemed more a statue than a living person. Christopher wanted to hide under the cot but didn't: he couldn't, not with all his grandfathers present.

Booms, concussions.

One Gramps held a handkerchief to a cut on his head.

"We can't shake them," said another. "They have a lock on us."

"Monty no doubt found an abandoned prison cell or bathroom in the Hall of Digital Mirrors, or both, and told Debra. She put two and two together."

"What is she using?"

"Something from the Fxn armory, I'm sure. Who cares?"

"Firing on her own flesh and blood."

"Watch out!"

A hole was blown in a wall near the ceiling. Everyone was covered with dust and bits of concrete. Two Grampses coughed and spat. The prison cell began to list badly.

"She wants to kill us!" said Christopher. "Is that . . . is that what happened at the fun city, in the maze of mirrors? Did Father try to kill me? Or did he do it, did he actually kill me?"

"We have no choice, men. We'll have to—"

"—pull alee—"

"—ashore—"

"—all hands—"

"—to Panda Ray."

"What Sea is Panda Ray in?" asked Christopher.

"Not a Sea," said Gramps, working a string like a hawser and wincing because of his arthritis.

"Not even the Sea of Is?"

The old man shook his head. Christopher had never seen him look so old and tired. "Think of it," said Gramps, or it might have been Gramps Sub One, but who cared, "as a harbor."

When they landed and stepped out, they stepped out of what was a broom closet, although it contained no broom: only a much-used rag mop, a bucket, a deep sink, and, on the floor, a few bottles of some kind of cleaning fluid.

They stepped out into a hall, a quiet and large hall. Its wooden floor was waxed and polished to a high sheen; on either side were tall doors with glass in them. Although the lights weren't on in the rooms, Christopher could see that they were classrooms. A hint of blackboard, a silhouette of lectern.

"Gramps," he said, walking beside one of his grandfathers.

"What?" said the old man, who was limping a little.

"Mother can't follow us here?"

"No. It's the only place she can't go."

"Then . . . why didn't we come here before? Why didn't we come here in the first place?"

"Because Panda Ray is always the last resort."

"Why, if he's a friend? Isn't he a friend?"

They went down stone stairs. Christopher ran his hand along the cool banister.

"Yes, a friend," said Gramps. "But you see, my boy, when Panda Ray solves your problem, whatever the solution is, that's the solution you have to live with. Live with, I mean, for the rest of your life. There's no going back, no bargaining, no choice."

"Didn't he pull you out of the Sea of Isn't?"

"Yes, Christopher, but he pulled me out *his* way. That's the price—it's always his way, when he helps. I was different, before. I don't regret it. But I was different, not what I am now. I was changed by the pulling out. You understand? Panda Ray is a prince, absolutely, but help like his you don't ask for unless you have nowhere else to turn."

They emerged into a courtyard, a quadrangle, massive church-like buildings high on all four sides. A lot of narrow windows, a lot of gray stone and ivy, a lot of arches with Latin carved over them. They went toward the arch opposite.

"We like to stay the way we are," Gramps continued, more to

himself than to Christopher. "We never like to give that up. Only as a last resort."

"What is this place?" Christopher asked as they passed through a great dim vaulted hall with echoes and then went up a flight of wide, worn steps.

"Panda Ray calls it Cambridge," said another Gramps.

"Sometimes he calls it Oxford," said another.

"Which is it?" asked Christopher.

"Neither. Both. It's his style. You'll see."

They knocked on a door and opened it. Inside was a room with carpets and lamps and stuffed club chairs. It was like a reading room in an old-fashioned library or like a lobby in an old-fashioned hotel. There was the smell of leather, tobacco, last week's newspapers, and maybe a touch of British surrey cologne.

Panda Ray, sitting in one of the chairs, laughed when he saw the three Grampses and Christopher. It was a bubbly, liquid, musical laugh. "Ah," he said, "you are three. How very amu-sing."

Christopher saw that Panda Ray was short, round, and extremely brown, brown almost to the point of black. The man was like a berry, roasted.

"Ah, and this is Christopher, yiss?" said Panda Ray, smiling.

"Will I be changed, too?" asked Christopher.

This amused Panda Ray more than anything. He seemed practically to melt with merriment. His body shook with inner laughter. He held out a brown hand with stubby brown fingers.

"Sit, sit," he said. "We do not stand on cere-mony here. Ah, Christopher, how wise you are for your years. First thing, you bring up change. Sit, sit."

They sat, pulling up club chairs to make a circle. Five equidistant points, therefore: the vertices of a five-pointed star. If you looked at the person to your immediate right and then turned toward the person to your immediate left, the angle of total turn would have been 108 degrees: or 36, from where you sat, between each other person in a chair. Subtended arcs.

"My mother wants to kill me," Christopher told Panda Ray.

Panda Ray nodded, as if you had told him that in cities streets have cars and curbs and there are often traffic lights at the intersections. "Fam-ilies," he said, nodding. "It is that way, yiss. Sometimes the parents kill the chil-dren, sometimes the chil-dren kill the parents. Look at Cain and Adam."

Christopher wrinkled his brow. "Cain and Abel, don't you mean?"

"Abel? What Abel?"

"Cain killed his brother Abel."

"Oh no no no. There was no Abel, no brother. Cain was an only child. He killed his father, Adam."

"The Bible says he killed his brother, Abel."

Panda Ray shook his round head and fluttered his dark eyes. "Oh no no no. He killed Adam so that he could marry Eve, his mother. She was very, very beauti-ful, you see. Eve was more beauti-ful than anyone who came after, she was the most beauti-ful person, because the Creator, he made her first, you see. Direct-ly. The original person."

"God made Adam first," said Christopher, "and then he made Eve out of Adam's rib."

Panda Ray laughed up and down the Pythagorean scale. "Where did you hear this?"

"The Bible," said Christopher. "In Sunday school."

"No no," said Panda Ray. His Dravidian eyes crinkled with fun as he wagged his finger. "It is all wrong. Your Bible makes up dif-ferent stories. What hap-pened was this. I will tell you. The Creator he made Eve. Then, later, he made Adam to pun-ish her, to hum-ble her, you see, because she was con-ceited because of her great beaut-y. She thought she was as beauti-ful as the Creator, yiss. That was her sin. That was the reason she dis-obeyed and ate the Apple of Beaut-y. So the Creator he made a man, a lesser creature, to rule over her, and made it that she would love this man-person des-pite herself. That is why women are so angry to this day. They are ruled by a lesser creature, a hus-band, that has no beaut-y."

Christopher thought that Panda Ray was a real character. He reminded him a little of Uncle Ernie in Cleveland, who smoked cigars and always had an off-color joke to tell—about private parts—which you never completely understood, mainly because his voice would drop below audibility at the dirtiest places.

"The boy wants to go home," said one of the Grampses. "He's only ten."

"Ten is a very interest-ing num-ber," said Panda Ray.

"Do you think it's possible?" asked the Gramps that sat to the first Gramps's right and Christopher's left. "Can he go home without Debra neutralizing him or worse?"

"It is possible," said Panda Ray.

There was a silence, and everyone looked at Christopher. "You'll be changed," came a psi-thought from one of the Grampses or maybe from all three at once. And Christopher understood that this being changed meant more, a great deal more, than a different color for his hair or a different shape for his nose. He would have to give up some of his Christopherness, possibly a large percentage of it.

It was like being blindfolded and walking the plank, a pirate's saber point poking-pushing at your back and with hungry sharks waiting for you in the choppy water below. Christopher felt cold and shivery.

"You will have to take the Sea of Isn't," said Panda Ray. "It will make you a little dizzy. Things do not stay the same, you see. No. You will think maybe they cannot make up their mind what they are, how they should be. They cannot decide. The tree says, 'Do I look better with my boughs this way or with my boughs that way? And the bark, tell me please, is the bark right?' " He chuckled. "It is very amu-sing."

"But you'll be with me, Gramps, won't you?" asked Christopher, though he didn't know which Gramps was Gramps. Maybe all three would go with him. More company, that way.

"No no no," said Panda Ray. "Alone, Christopher. You must go alone."

The pirate plank over the Sea of Isn't was high, narrow, and slippery, and Christopher had no choice, he saw that now—he saw it in the identical faces of his three weary grandfathers. They shook their heads in unison, left, right, left, right, as if watching a very sad, very slow tennis match.

When you went to Panda Ray, he saved you his way, not your way. His way. That was the price.

2

Part Two

It is an astonishing fact that, in spiral phyllotaxis, the numbers
of contact parastichies are usually two adjacent numbers of the
Fibonacci series.

—C. W. WARDLAW

Assailed by the smell of cooked celery, he held on to Panda Ray's hand, held tight.

Have I begun changing already? he wondered.

The floor buckled and rolled under their feet, as if they were on the back of a giant worm. The buckling and rolling reminded Christopher of one of the rides in that fun city of the future: a ribbed canvas walkway with moving humps. High swells in the canvas came from behind and tried to knock you down.

He looked back at the television set but couldn't see it now. The television through which they had entered the Sea of Isn't. That jumping test pattern with the funny lines. Irregular lines but not so irregular, and crosshatched. Panda Ray had muttered something like, "Almond bars," but it wasn't almond bars, of course. Anyway, they had stepped right through the pattern, from the reading room with all the club chairs, just like Alice getting up on the mantelpiece and climbing through the mirror—except that the TV screen had been close to the ground instead and they had had to stoop low.

Going through the set made Christopher feel there was too much electricity accumulated in his joints. If he wasn't careful, painful sparks might come out of his fingers and toes.

"Go with the motion," advised Panda Ray. "Fighting it will make you dizzy, yiss."

Which motion?

"The flow of all things," said Panda Ray.

Christopher saw himself in a passing mirror. He was definitely different—assuming the mirror was a real mirror and not a trick mirror or something else. His freckles were gone. His nose was longer and pointier. Also, he had a bigger Adam's apple, which bobbed comically when he swallowed.

They went down wide steps that gave off smoke, like a person or animal breathing in cold weather. In the open door of a classroom—no, it wasn't a classroom, it was a bedroom—Mr. Osborne held up a sign. He sat in his bed, grimacing from the effort to sit up, clearly weak from Asiatic flu. The sign read: NO ADVERB HOMEWORK TODAY. When Christopher and Panda Ray continued on, the poor teacher shut his eyes and fell back on his Donald Duck pillow.

Christopher mused: Mr. Osborne seemed the last person in the world to have a Donald Duck pillow. The man was always so dignified, dry, and down-to-business. But this, he reminded himself, was the Sea of Isn't, wasn't it?

Pure omicron, Gramps had said.

In the hall, they went by the lavatories. Cathy Carmichael stood at the entrance to the boys' lavatory, one foot actually inside. She was ill at ease. Christopher saw that this was not because of her proximity to the forbidden urinals but because her body was so grossly out of whack and off balance: her new breasts, enormous in her sweater, must have weighed a ton. Shaped like torpedoes, too.

From another galaxy, Ruby Star's mother brayed.

"Hi, Chris," said Cathy in a low voice, her head lowered.

"Hi, Cathy," said Christopher, not looking at her, feeling her mortification.

The worn marble steps led out to the quadrangle, where the grass was all on fire, smoldering, though, as the Bible says, not consumed by the fire. Still green though on fire.

Christopher felt dizzy, as if he had a fever. Could he have caught something from Mr. Osborne's sign?

"This way," said Panda Ray.

"That way," said Panda Ray.

The Dravidian was rounder and browner than ever, a purple-raisin brown, and his eyes twinkled with amusement, with delight. Change was his element.

"The fluxion of a fluent," he purred. "The fluxion of a fluent."

They took a walkway to a driveway and the driveway to a street. At the bus stop, a dog was lifting its leg. The dog was none other than Buzz, but it wasn't the Buzz Christopher knew. This Buzz was made not of metal, carpeting, and microprocessors but of living tissue, except that unfortunately the living tissue was no longer living: the dog was a zombie. It had bald patches and black nails, some of them missing; it smelled of decay and old bowel movements.

Buzz didn't wag his tail. He cast a cold, dull eye on his master and growled deep in his throat. He lifted a lip, showing a discolored undead tooth. Keep your distance, said the tooth. Christopher felt a pang for having neglected his friend so much. For going on walks lately in the field off Green Street, where the wind was so sweet, and completely forgetting the dog, leaving him in the dark closet upstairs.

An occasional thump of the tail in the dark closet, a thump no one heard. Once an hour, a lonely thump. Could you blame Buzz for being angry?

The bus pulled up, a double-decker with ads on it for mouthwash and shirt studs. Brands Christopher had never heard of. But he reminded himself that this wasn't the United States of America. The engine alternated between a straining *rrr-rrr* and bursts of jackhammer Muzak.

As they boarded, the sky opened and there was a downpour. Christopher was startled by the loud banging on the bus windows and roof, from the rain. At first he thought it was unusually big hailstones, but then he saw that there were pieces of metal falling here and there in the flapping sheets of rainwater, large silvery hunks of metal. They were flashlights and toasters. One pedestrian had been beaned and was sitting on the sidewalk, holding his head, his mouth mouthing ouch.

"I will take you to your house," said Panda Ray.

The drenched street stank of boiled asparagus as the two-story bus careened around a corner that hadn't been there before.

What house?

"You will become ac-clima-ted," said Panda Ray.

They went around a big circle-square with gray statues on horseback and an imposing granite dancing clown in the middle.

"Where are the pigeons?" asked Christopher, thinking of Trafalgar. He was so dizzy now that his stomach began doing loops, and he was afraid that a little more of this and he would bring up sour chunks. The passengers would be disgusted and poke at him with their ferruled walking sticks.

"Your house," answered Panda Ray. "The house where you live."

Christopher didn't understand but gathered, from this, that he would be staying here for a while—wherever here was in the Sea of Isn't—seeing as accommodations had been arranged already. He hoped the house would be a little more stationary, a little more realistic.

Taking deep breaths didn't help much.

The bus went along a hedgerow. Starlings flew—if they were starlings.

"How long will I be here?" asked Christopher.

They went over a bridge, the bus creaking.

They bore through the night, as if the night were a tunnel. Unless it really was a tunnel. No stars.

"When you are ac-clima-ted," answered Panda Ray, still holding Christopher's hand in his brown hand, "you can leave your house. If you leave before you are ac-clima-ted, you may fall down."

The vertigo became so great, in waves, that Christopher sometimes thought they were not in a bus at all but in a dirigible gondola, with an enemy typhoon at eleven o'clock and bearing down fast.

The clouds laughing ho ho.

Did he have a fever? Was he delirious? There was no Gramps to come up the stairs and put a cool hand on his forehead; to prop him up for a little sip of water; to read to him in a thin, husky voice about the boring railroads of the nation's past.

"Your mother, she will not murder you," said Panda Ray with a sweet, motherly smile, although the cabin of their blimp was filled with the awful stench of cucumber gone bad.

"Where are we?" asked Christopher.

The ocean below sparkled in the sun. No landmarks, no arrows on it saying THIS WAY or THAT WAY.

"When I am changed," asked Christopher in a voice not his own, "will I be better than I am now, or worse?"

Panda Ray laughed. He was very amused.

"Will I see Buzz again?" asked Christopher. "And Gramps, where is Gramps now?"

"Good-bye, Christopher," said Panda Ray in answer, kindly.

"Good-bye?"

"Yiss. We are almost there."

Christopher looked out the window. The turnpike exit signs flew past. The cabbie's hands gripped the steering wheel. They were callused, tobacco-stained hands, the nails horny and yellow. The top joint of one finger on the right hand was missing.

The man smelled of cigars and stale sweat, but you hardly noticed that over the overwhelming reek of brussels sprouts.

They turned into a street between houses that didn't look British in the least. In fact, this neighborhood seemed not only American but Pennsylvanian, and not only Pennsylvanian but central Pennsylvanian. It seemed to bear some resemblance, even, to Wenderoth.

"Good luck, Christopher," said Panda Ray, opening the cab door for him.

The sky was sea green. The big trees were a bluish metal green, like cleaning fluid.

The houses were old and looked defeated, listless. The house before which they had stopped was gray clapboard, with peeling paint and a rusted rooster weather vane. Also on the roof was a big microwave antenna dish.

"This is *my* house," said Christopher.

"Fifty-four Wilson Street," said the cabbie. His LED meter showed a number, but the number was irrational.

"Remem-ber now, don't go out until you get your sea legs," said Panda Ray, helping the boy out and also up the steps.

"That didn't take long at all, did it?" said Christopher, weak and wobbly but glad to be home.

Where was everyone? The place was so quiet. As if he were in a museum or a mausoleum.

Where was Panda Ray and the taxi? Gone?

Gone.

Christopher, somehow, was in his room, in bed. The room swam. It was difficult to keep things in focus. Like Mr. Osborne he grimaced from the effort to sit up. This had to be the Asiatic flu, a bad strain, which he caught from that sign in Cambridge or maybe Oxford.

His dresser was the wrong color, wasn't it? White instead of yellow or yellow instead of white. One of the two.

And the wallpaper. He didn't remember having toast brown butterflies on the wall. Or were they caramel brown bats?

Exhausted, he fell back on his Donald Duck pillow, and that was odd, too, because he didn't have—had never in his life had—a Donald Duck pillow.

The wallpaper? It should have been, let me see, a flower pattern with vertical lines. He was sure of that. Not a hundred percent sure, but pretty sure. Less and less sure, though, as he sank into the accelerating whirlpool of spoiled cabbage and merciful sleep.

A House without Rules

Christopher wakes and finds that the room is turning. Is the room really turning, or is it just that he doesn't have his sea legs yet? But, then, what does he need sea legs for if he has returned in one piece from the dread Sea of Isn't and is safely home? He wishes he could ask someone. He is confused. His head feels stuffed with cotton and bees.

It may be his imagination, but the house seems darker. He stares at the ceiling, a rectangle of gray that is slowly revolving counterclockwise.

No, not counterclockwise, clockwise.

Maybe both.

What has Panda Ray done to him? Gramps said Panda Ray was a friend, but Gramps, you know, has not been working with a full deck since Emily passed away. Sometimes he makes sense and is in touch, but sometimes he doesn't and he isn't. When he talks into the air, for example, and then waits for the air to respond.

Christopher's fingers. They're longer than they used to be, the pads are flatter, and the knuckles and wristbones are so large, it almost looks as if he has tumors under the skin. He has ugly hands now, the hands of a stranger.

The hands of a bully.

He should ask Kaelin about this.

In a dream, Christopher goes to his closet to see if Buzz is there. Buzz is there, all right, but it's still the evil zombie Buzz, not the all-patient, loyal, always grateful companion of his youth fondly made of iron scraps, carpeting, and diodes. Buzz snarls when the closet door opens.

Christopher shuts the door, rests his forehead on it, and thinks, Time I woke up from this bad dream.

The room continues to turn. When he gets his sea legs, will it stop turning? Or will it go on turning for the rest of his life? Could this vertigo be part of the permanent change Panda Ray has made?

But why is he standing by the closet and not lying in his bed? He thought he had waked from the dream. Apparently he hasn't, not yet. Except he doesn't really feel that he is dreaming. Maybe he's finished dreaming now. He tries the closet door again.

Buzz growls, and there's a zombie dog smell in there, too. Vile, like the spit-wet insides of an old balloon after it has popped.

He closes the door, his heart thumping.

"I'm dreaming," he tells himself.

But if he's dreaming, he should be in bed, not standing here with his eyes open.

He tries to get back into his bed, but now the bed is revolving along with the ceiling—or in the opposite direction, or possibly in both directions at once—and he's afraid he might miss the bed and hit the floor instead, and then the bed could roll over him and crush him with a squush and a crunch, like a black water bug under a shoe.

He feels that he is inside a giant clock, its cogwheels all pinching and plucking at him as they turn in tandem and also perpendicularly to each other.

He gropes for the door—the door to the stairs, not the closet door, though since both are moving, he's not sure which is which. He definitely doesn't want to open the closet door again. A third time, and he might be bitten. An infection from a zombie dog bite is bound to be nasty, too, requiring more than a simple dab of Mercurochrome and a Band-Aid. Gangrene would set in instantly, and before they could get him to a doctor, he would swell up to twice his size, turn purple, choke, twitch, die, and become a zombie himself, a zombie boy: an unliving Christopher.

Was that better or not than being scooped out?

And what would his teachers think when he sat in class, flies buzzing around him and blind earthworms writhing on the floor around him and on his desk?

Christopher grabbed the doorknob as it went past, took a quick peek through the door using a little upsilon to make sure Buzz wasn't on the other side; then he opened it and found himself on the landing, which had such an awful tilt to it that he got down on all fours immediately to keep from falling over the banister and plunging three flights.

Which would have made Mother furious. One of the rules of the house was Absolutely No Flying.

Christopher remembered being smacked hard, when he was four or five, a stinging smack across his face for flying at a birthday party. His own birthday party? His sister's? Brian's? He remembered chocolate cake all over his mouth and the big tears that dripped through the chocolate and crumbs as he bawled.

He crawled on all fours down to Kaelin's room. Her light was on.

Did her light mean it was night? But how could it be night now, if he had waked up in the morning only minutes ago? He should have taken a look out the window, to see what time of day it was.

He was still so dizzy, his head stuffed with oakum and ants.

He tapped quietly and entered.

Kaelin was sitting in bed, reading a paperback and smoking a cigarette. She wore a robe. She had an angry, unKaelinish pout on her face: nothing at all mousy about the pout.

"You're smoking," said Christopher.

"So?" She flicked an ash on the blanket, where there were other ashes and some twisted cigarette butts. There were also a few cigarette burns in the plaid wool blanket, little round holes rimmed with black.

Christopher stared at her. Something was wrong with his sister. Physically. Her shape. The body was out of whack, but not out of whack like Cathy Carmichael's. It wasn't breasts, it was her belly.

"You're pregnant," said Christopher in a whisper.

Kaelin looked at him with a humorless smile. "You have a problem with that, little brother?" she said, quite loud. Her voice was throaty, maybe because of the smoking.

"Mother will hear," he said.

"We don't have to worry about Mother anymore," Kaelin said. "Where have you been?"

"Are you marrying Harve?" Christopher asked.

"Harve?" She put down the paperback and looked at him as if he had a screw loose.

"Your boyfriend."

Kaelin shook her head, as if he belonged in the loony bin.

Christopher noticed now that the shaking of her head, and the way her lips moved when she spoke, and the way her fingers went when she flicked the cigarette—that all her movements were slower, just a shade slower, than natural. Like one of those clever but primitive animations where the creatures were made of clay.

"I have lots of boyfriends," she said. "But you're asking me who the father is, right? I have no idea, little brother. Harve hasn't been around in quite a while. He was nice but what a drip. Anyway, I'm not marrying anybody. Why should I?"

She took a long drag on her cigarette and blew out rings—pink rings, blue rings, and a large one that turned, as it expanded, into an unflattering caricature of Mother.

Christopher sat on the floor because of his vertigo and tried to think. It was difficult to think.

"Why don't we have to worry about Mother?" he asked, wondering what Panda Ray had done to Mother.

"Go and see for yourself," Kaelin said, picking up the paperback again.

"Is this the Sea of Isn't we're in?" he asked.

"I don't know what the fuck you're talking about," she said, reading. The paperback was a worn, torn, grimy, thick book. It was *The Rise and Fall of the Third Reich* and had a black swastika on the cover. It smelled like phlegm.

"What about Brian?" he asked.

"What about him?"

"Is he here?"

"He's in college, Indiana. Where have you been, little brother?"

"Was I away a long time? Was it years?" Maybe time passed differently from one Sea to another. What grade would he be in now? Would he have to do remedial work to catch up? Or would they put him back a grade, to sit with kids even smaller than he was? It would be odd to be the biggest kid in the class.

Kaelin was reading and smoking, not interested in Christopher's problem, whatever his problem was. He couldn't have said himself exactly what it was. But one thing was clear: she wasn't there anymore for him. His sister probably didn't even love him anymore. It didn't look like it.

After Gramps, Kaelin had been his most important ally.

Would Gramps be home and back to one person again? Christopher dreaded finding out. He dreaded finding a bad Gramps. Though a bad Gramps was hard to imagine.

"Is Gramps at home?" he asked his sister.

"He's dead," she said, not looking up, turning a page.

"Dead?"

"That's right. We buried him in July. August. July or August. The poor bastard didn't make it to Golden Years, did he. Where have you been, little brother?"

Christopher couldn't think of anything to ask after that, so he got up, steadied himself, and left. The stairs were turning, too, but not as fast as his room. They were churning more than turning. Maybe he was getting his sea legs. He started down, but saw that the light was on in Brian's room.

Had Kaelin lied about Brian being away in college?

Christopher peered in and saw not Brian at Brian's desk but Father. Father was working on his stamp collection, had a big album open and a loupe in one hand.

What was Father doing in the middle of the day? Why was he here working on his stamp collection and not at the office? Why did he have that unFatherly ear-to-ear grin on his face?

"Hello, Father," said Christopher.

Monty Zimmerman didn't answer. He had been slowed down more than Kaelin, much more. Perhaps the effect had to do with age. The older you were, it seemed, the slower you were. His skin was definitely the color of clay. Or maybe of sandstone, or maybe of soapstone, or maybe of shale.

"Can you hear me, Father?" asked Christopher. "What's going on here?"

Monty Zimmerman blinked. It took a whole minute for him to complete the blink. There was a gleam in his eye. The gleam seemed to be saying that yes, he could hear Christopher fine.

"Did Gramps really die while I was away?" asked Christopher, because Kaelin might not have been telling the truth. This new, pregnant, profane Kaelin in a robe.

Everything was so different.

Somewhere in the house, a toilet flushed. Who was using the toilet? Could there be another member of the family? A brother or sister Christopher had never met? Because wasn't anything and everything possible in the Sea of Isn't—assuming this was the Sea of Isn't and not another Sea, an even more treacherous Sea, one that Gramps had never mentioned because it slipped his aging mind?

"Won't Mother be angry?" asked Christopher.

Because Mother didn't like to see Father working on his stamp collection. She always said, "Why don't you *do* something, dear?" Or, "The knives could use some sharpening, if you have nothing better to do." Or, "It aggravates me, I can't tell you, seeing you sitting there like that for hours."

Now Christopher understood the huge grin on his father's rough-hewn, immobile face: Mother was indeed out of the picture.

It was hard to believe. How had Panda Ray managed such a thing? Mother, after all.

He left. He continued down the stairs. He put an ear to his mother's door. Silence. No static on the transceiver, no words exchanged with Mrs. Fxn, no scraping of a chair or clearing of a throat.

A wave of dizziness made him kneel, but it passed. He got up.

He held his breath and opened the door. Mother wasn't in. There was a tiny robot spider spy in a corner of the ceiling, but the thing was deaf and blind, rusted through. There were cobwebs around it, attached to it, hanging from it.

The curtains were heavy with dust. The semicircular lace cover on the end table by the bed was dark gray, practically charcoal, with dust. Mother had not been in here for a very long time.

Her instrument panel was dead, not a single light across the console on. Evidently the bdellium dish wasn't working. Either that, or the subether was still. Though the subether was never still, filled with voices from unimaginable distances.

On the other hand, if this was all taking place in the Sea of Isn't, the subether might be still, the countless voices all still.

Christopher found his mother on the front porch. She was seated on the white swing, but the swing wasn't moving. That is, it was moving just as the rest of the porch was moving, but not moving as a swing moves. In that respect, it was motionless, though moving. Christopher held on to the doorjamb to keep from falling. His head was stuffed with gypsum and gnats.

"Mother," he said.

She wore no jacket or coat, didn't even have a shawl around her shoulders, although it was below freezing. Through the porch screen you could see that the trees were covered with ice and rime and clumps of frozen snow. Christopher's breath came out in white puffs.

"Mother," he said, making a puff. Two puffs, one for each syllable.

She was stone, all stone, except perhaps around the eyes, where it was a little more like dried mud than stone. And maybe—yes—there was a trace of smoke that issued from her nostrils now and then. The barest wisp.

The expression on her face, he thought, was anger mixed with surprise. Indignation mixed with perplexity. But a stern, unyielding, displeased countenance. In that respect Mother was very much still Mother.

In her lap lay a crossword book, open to a puzzle half filled in. The pencil in her hand was poised over a long vertical word that began with the letters C, A, T and had a P in it toward the end. But the pencil point was motionless—motionless, that is, relative to the porch, which was revolving slowly.

Could she hear him? And what if she could? What did it matter?

Christopher searched his mother's pockets for the key to the credenza in the living room, where she kept the answer box from the future. He found the key in the third pocket.

It took him time to negotiate his way from porch to hall, from hall to foyer, from foyer to laundry room. But what was the laundry room doing up here? The washing machine and drier were supposed to be in the cellar. But apparently not, if they were here. From the laundry room he made it to the hall and finally to the living room.

Uncle Martin smiled and winked from his portrait above the fireplace.

"This is still a dream," Christopher thought, because not only did they not have an Uncle Martin, at least not as far as he could remember, but they also had no fireplace.

No, wait, they did have a fireplace. He forgot.

They didn't, they didn't. What was he thinking of?

The answer box, when he took it out, seemed the same.

"Testing, one, two, three," Christopher said into it.

"I'm working," said the answer box.

"Great," said Christopher. "Is this the Sea of Isn't?"

"No," said the answer box.

"Then where am I?"

"Yes," said the answer box.

A pause.

"Yes doesn't answer my question," said Christopher cautiously. He waited, but the box was silent.

"Why aren't you saying anything?" he asked it.

"You haven't asked a question," replied the answer box.

"But I did. I asked you where I was, and you said yes."

Silence. No answer.

"You didn't answer my question," said Christopher, feeling cold, trying again. "Why didn't you answer my question?"

"But I did," said the answer box.

"You didn't," insisted Christopher. "Yes is no answer to where am I."

Another silence. The answer box just sat there, fuzzy green felt speaker in a gunmetal frame.

Christopher gave up. The answer box was useless. He muttered the F word. He was becoming more comfortable with the F word.

He put the box back in the credenza and locked the credenza. He had no problem putting the key in the keyhole this time, even though the hole was moving. Maybe he was getting his sea legs at last, learning to go with the flow of all things, as Panda Ray had said.

But why did he need to lock the credenza?

He didn't need to lock the credenza.

Mother always kept it locked, she insisted on that, but Mother wasn't in charge anymore, was she? She was encased in rock, or maybe she was rock herself, through and through.

Christopher unlocked the credenza, his heart racing, and dropped the key with a little thud into the wastebasket. He looked around.

Nothing happened.

Uncle Martin winked again.

Christopher went to the kitchen to pour himself a glass of milk. Maybe milk would help his stomach. The refrigerator was on the wrong wall, but so what.

The milk was cold yet tasted more like chalk than milk. It made his nausea worse instead of better. He drank some water from the tap to get rid of the chalk taste in his mouth, but the water, though clear, had an even stronger chalk taste. Bitter, sour chalk.

He didn't wash the glass and didn't put it carefully in the drainer. Instead, he left the glass carelessly on the counter, dirty.

Fuck Mother, he thought.

He was free. He could do whatever he wanted. He could do whatever he liked. Whatever he wished. Whatever occurred to him, whatever entered his head.

If only he wasn't so dizzy, his stomach hurting in waves and with each wave making loopier loops. Would he ever get his sea legs? This was a nasty joke played by Panda Ray, the British liar-sadist. Gramps had warned him.

Christopher's head was stuffed with bunting and horseflies, caulking and crows, but he fought down his nausea and gamely, bravely explored the house.

Everything was moving, sometimes with a sudden dip or a sudden rise, but he was growing accustomed to the dips and rises.

There was coal, of all things, in the cellar and hardly any light. On a slope of coal lay a broken doll with one eye missing.

In the dining room there was no table, and the captain's clock atop the sideboard was chuckling, wheezing, unable to catch its breath, as if it had stolen an enormous sum of money and gotten away with it, hee hee.

Christopher looked for his special pebbles under the sink, then in the flowerpot under the back steps. Outside, the sun beat cruelly, burning his ears even though he was exposed to it less than a minute. What a fierce sun. He also checked the bookshelf in his room. No pebbles there, no pebbles anywhere. Not one pebble.

It made him feel like crying, he had worked so long and hard on them.

He said, "Shit."

He climbed into the lazy merry-go-round of his bed and woke only once in the night, to go to the bathroom and vomit. The vomit burned his throat and the inside of his nose. Not much in the way of chunks in the toilet bowl, but the color was disturbing: bright red, like red paint or moving-picture blood. Maybe he should see a doctor.

Boys Will Be Boys

We are back at Lincoln Elementary. The school looks much the same. A little dingier. We notice that the C in the LINCOLN on the front of the building has half fallen out of position. It now spells U instead, dropped and hanging uncertainly, awkwardly, between the N and O. There is more trash in the bushes than before. Plastic soda bottles, notebook paper, an occasional beer can, an occasional pencil, the frozen-eyed head of a doll. Just the head. A window has been broken and taped. Wisps of vapor rise from the grass. And the whole building, playground included, and chain-link fences, and parking lot—everything is revolving slowly.

The tiles on the walls inside are not a pastel terra-cota anymore but grayish brown, taupe. Possibly that is the reason the light seems weaker. Unless there is some temporary problem at the power plant. Instead of the smell of apples, beaverboard, and disinfectant, the smell of gym lockers and rancid milk assails our nostrils. We pass room 16 and think of Mrs. Palmer, what a devoted teacher she was.

The black-and-white factory clock on the wall tells us that school is almost ready to begin. Two minutes to nine.

In the band room, among old battered horns, sits Mr. Moskowitz, cleaning his glasses. He is not making much progress. He is mostly limestone. This doesn't seem to bother him.

In the boiler room, among bandaged conduits, dented ducts, and strange echoes, sits George, Mrs. Palmer's potbellied executioner.

He is mostly magnetite and in the midst of repairing a vacuum cleaner. At the rate he is going, it will take him a hundred years.

In his office, Mr. DiVincenzo sighs as he opens a file, but no one can hear the sigh's hushed, melancholy reverberation through the cold caverns of his lungs. He is feldspar.

In the main office, Betty frowns at a computer screen, whose cursor keeps flashing in the same spot, while in the principal's office Mr. Sykes is casting a critical eye on his manicured fingernails. They are schist and serpentine, respectively, those two, and going nowhere.

In the hall stands Mrs. Davis, ready for the little darlings. But how will she tell Johnny not to push or Larry to tie his shoe or Becky not to forget to see Mrs. Bloch today, how, if she can't even open her mouth? She is practically all gneiss. A problem.

The bell rings. Where are the children? The children are late. Possibly the buses went slower this morning, on account of all the fender benders. Let us hope the buses went slower. They carry a precious cargo, after all.

Traffic is usually not that bad out here in the sticks of Wenderoth and Quail Ridge, but even a seasoned, alert, and careful motorist can have trouble staying on the road if the road constantly slides away from him or makes right-angle turns in places it never made right-angle turns before.

The mist coming out of the ground doesn't help, either.

We wait half an hour, an hour, an hour and a half. We wait two hours. Time passes slowly in an empty school hall. Finally we hear the buses. But the children, when they come in—curiously, there aren't that many of them. Another flu making the rounds? A field trip? A religious holiday? We haven't checked the calendar. Betty could tell us, but she's busy, still hunched and frowning at the computer screen, deep in whatever thought she's stuck in.

Among the children is little Christopher Zimmerman. He's been home sick for such a long time. More than three weeks, isn't it? Yes, more than three weeks. Look how thin and pale he is. He's lost his freckles. Is it our imagination, or is his hair darker, too? Illness does change children. Christopher seems somehow more angular. Also more indrawn.

What did he have, you ask? Measles or chicken pox, we forget which. Or maybe scarlet fever. Someone said it was touch and go there for a while. It's no picnic, is it, bringing up children.

They go to their classrooms, but obviously there won't be much teaching taking place today.

Calvin Hardwood, FBI agent, he of the 1950s Clark Kent hair and glasses, has stationed himself at a corner and watches the children carefully, intently, as they pass. He notes that today there is little laughter, little chatter. Well, but the weather is so dismal, raining on and off. The sky is like the belly of a dead fish, with greens and grays and that long, blurry, watery band of swollen white down the middle.

The agent talks into his walkie-talkie.

What is the FBI looking for here at Lincoln? This question has been asked before, but we ask it again. What danger threatens the safety of our nation? And what can that national danger possibly have to do with these innocent little middle-class boys and girls?

True, some of them are not so little. And not so innocent, either. Take Billy Bethany, younger brother of Jack Bethany, who is in high school now but in detention or suspended more than half the time. He will end up, everyone says, in the state pen for armed robbery.

Like his brother, Billy is big and broad. Even though he's only in the fifth grade, you can see the football player in him. He's gap-toothed, has high cheekbones and a frog-wide, cruel smile. His hands are heavy ham hands. Everyone dreads those hands—even Stupid Loomis, who is Billy's sidekick, henchman, minion, and groveler. Stupid Loomis gets punched in the arm frequently: his arms bear at least as many bruises as the arms of the smaller boys who have the misfortune to cross the path of Billy and Stupid in the cafeteria, in the hall, on the playground, or waiting for the bus.

So far Christopher has escaped the painful black-and-blue arm initiation—probably because he is unusually small, like a kindergartner. Even the worst bullies have some code of honor when it comes to size. But Christopher appears to have grown a couple of inches during his illness, and his new gauntness, too, gives him an older look. Stupid Loomis has made a note of this with a sinister nod. Today Christopher, poor thing, is fair game.

No, there is not so much innocence in this school as we first thought. Angela, for example. Her goody-goody behavior is an underhanded role she assumes cold-bloodedly at the expense of her classmates. Have you noticed the way she always brings her virtue to the teacher's attention immediately after another child has fallen from grace? Jimmy Barnes can't spell *junction*. Angela shakes her curly head when he haltingly puts a *k* after the *n*. She shakes her head precisely to catch the teacher's eye. She will not raise her hand, oh no. With her curls alone she will get Mr. Mortimer to call on her—and when he does call, she will make a surprised double blink, hesitate, be embarrassed, and show the greatest reluctance as she delivers, in a sweet, shy voice, the coup de grâce to suffering Jimmy.

Or Becky Finley, the already famous ballet dancer. Only ten years old and thin as a rail, but she could give her mother lessons in snobbery, and that is saying something.

Or our poor Cathy Carmichael, who has taken to wearing tight sweaters and wiggling her buttocks when she walks. Her blush in class is no blush of innocence. As stony Mrs. Gray puts rows of multiplied fractions on the board, Cathy is imagining a nocturnal scene in which she takes off her clothes, *all* her clothes, even her underpants, in the company of David Holz or dreamy Mr. Wanamaker. Or a scene in which he takes off her clothes, *all* her clothes, even her underpants, though she tells him no, no, no and pummels his hairy chest with feeble fists.

Billy the Bully leers at her, and Stupid Loomis laughs a hoarse, coarse laugh: Boobs, boobs. Cathy scorns them, of course, but is extremely pleased with this tribute to her feminine power.

Even little Christopher, unless our eyes deceive us, has something disconcertingly adult-unclean about him. The satisfied look of a criminal who is planning a heist or a prison break or a rubout.

Rain beats on the windowpanes, vapor rises, and the teachers stand (or sit) powerless in their excess of substance, weight, and ossification.

The children therefore are unsupervised, alas, unsupervised from K through 6.

The classrooms do not hold them long. They filter out, first on the pretext of going to the bathroom, then brazenly, getting up and leaving in the middle of an explanation of how Paul Revere saved us or why the Liberty Bell has a crack in it.

But to tell the truth, we would lose patience ourselves in such classrooms. The pauses between instructional words are intolerably long, excruciating, as marble tongues and lips move imperceptibly to form the next syllable. If indeed there is any movement at all. The next syllable may never come. We cannot breathe; we need air.

The children gather in small groups in the halls and outside.

By the Dumpster, between rain puddles, we find Jimmy, Felice Dewey, the Harrison twins, and little Christopher.

"I'd love to hit Angela Dean over the head with a brick," said Jimmy, morose.

"I know what you mean," said Carole Harrison.

"Yeah," said Felice.

"Why don't we do it?" said Lori Harrison, who was a little taller than her sister and had darker hair. "Why don't we just do it? All get bricks and hit her over the head."

"Not worth going to jail for," said Jimmy.

They nodded, picturing Angela on the ground in the rain like a broken doll, eyes open at an odd angle and unblinking.

"I hate brownnosers," said Felice, fingering a scab on her elbow. "I hate their guts."

"Yeah," said Carole.

The Dumpster and the puddles were revolving slowly, but, then, so was everything else.

Ken French joined the group, said a few words about pussy, his stepfather, the family car, and fell silent. Together the children stood and watched the drizzle and the mist.

"Lousy day," said Jimmy.

"Yeah," said Christopher.

"I hate Mr. Dunst," said Felice. "And Miss Gillespie gives me a pain. I can't stand her buckteeth."

They nodded.

Ken said something more about pussy, and a drunken bird flew by overhead at a sickening tilt. A starling, probably. The drizzle stopped, but the mist kept rising. The sun tried to shine in the bloated sky but couldn't get through and after a while gave up.

Billy the Bully and Stupid Loomis approached. Jimmy said, "Oh no" under his breath and looked around for an exit, but there was no place to run or duck into, and it was too late now, anyway.

"How's everyone doin'?" asked Stupid.

"Who's this?" said Billy, looking at Christopher.

"It's Chris Zimmerman," said Stupid. "Remember him? Pee Wee."

"Oh yeah," said Billy. "Pee Wee."

"We have to go," said the girls, and they left, leaving Jimmy, Ken, and Christopher the way relatives all leave when it's time for the patient to be put on the gurney, strapped down, and wheeled to the operating room.

Billy cracked his knuckles one by one. He had enormous hands, enormous knuckles. His knuckles were like a row of rocks, a mountain range.

"All right, men, up with those sleeves," said Stupid.

Jimmy and Ken were pale and looked ill as they rolled the sleeve of their right arm all the way up to the shoulder. Billy grinned a big frog-grin and punched each boy in the meaty triceps-deltoid area of the upper arm. He administered the punches like a doctor giving injections. Businesslike, precise, knuckles first.

"You, too, Pee Wee," Stupid said to Christopher. "Up with that sleeve. We got to toughen those muscles, make a man out of you."

Jimmy and Ken were rolling down their sleeves and trying not to show pain while Christopher reluctantly unbuttoned the button at his wrist and started rolling up a sleeve.

"Not that arm," said Stupid. "Your right arm."

When Jimmy and Ken walked away, not looking anyone in the eye and not looking back, Christopher found himself alone by the Dumpster with Billy the Bully and Stupid Loomis.

He rolled up the sleeve of his skinny right arm. White gooseflesh.

"All the way up," said Stupid. "Come on, come on."

Christopher shut his eyes and braced himself for pain, but the punch, when it landed, was much worse than he expected. The pain went into his body so deep and was so intense, he couldn't help twisting and making a little moan, no matter how unmanly that was. His whole arm was paralyzed. He knew he would have an ugly, angry, hard purple knot from this, and a soreness that would last for weeks.

He also knew that every time he went to school, from now on, he would live in fear of the next encounter with Billy the Bully, the next rolling up of the sleeve and punch, knuckles first, deep into the arm. There would be knuckle-punches on top of knots and bruises, too, inevitably, and they would hurt deeper and double. The pain would be unbearable.

Christopher looked at Billy and Stupid as they ambled off, Stupid laughing, Billy jiggling his head slightly at a tilt as if he were a pirate captain who had the power of life and death over his crew. What a cruel joke, Christopher thought. The first day of his freedom from Mother, and he falls under another cloud of oppression.

He groaned. He felt like crying.

But why put up with it?

There was no need to put up with it.

There was no need to put up with anything anymore. Was there? No. No need.

Sic semper tyrannis, he thought. Although he was only in the fifth grade, he had read a biography of Abraham Lincoln—after whom the school was named. It was a biography written not for fifth graders but for adults. All Mother's children were intelligent. *Sic semper tyrannis,* Christopher thought, setting his little jaw.

And as steam rose and flies buzzed noisily around the Dumpster in the noonday heat beneath the bloated summer sun, he squinted at Billy's departing, jiggling head, looked inside it, and saw, among other things, a nerve that went from the brain all the way down the neck and toward the heart muscles.

He fiddled with the nerve—nothing to it—and in no time Billy was breathing funny and staggering. Pulling at his collar and shirt, as if his clothes were suddenly too tight. Thump-thump-thump went the heart, taking too many steps, tripping over itself in its hurry, and then there was a pause, no thumps at all, the confused pump-organ undecided whether or not it should continue.

Billy sank to his knees and swayed. Stupid Loomis pulled at his arm and shouted something like, "What's the matter, Billy? What's the matter?"

Should I finish him off? thought Christopher.

And then he thought, Why not? Billy Bethany had nothing to offer society, except maybe in the field of football. But there wasn't much chance of that, even; he would probably end up a thug like his brother Jack, never making it to a college team, a varsity letter, the pick, the NFL. He didn't have anywhere near the intelligence.

So Christopher cut the nerve in two—it was easier than snapping your fingers—and thought, not without a touch of pride, My first murder. As if murdering were a rite of passage, like a tattoo or inhaling a cigarette in an alley.

While Stupid ran calling for help in a high voice and Billy lay sprawled and still, facedown in the mud, Christopher buttoned his sleeve and went back inside. He chose the south entrance so he wouldn't have to go past that dorky FBI man with the walkie-talkie and the teeth that were too even and too white.

No point in taking chances.

It was a good thing, too, that the south entrance was moving in his direction and not away, because of the wind that came up out of the southwest, the wind and the sleet. Christopher grimaced, clutched his collar tight around his neck to keep out the little pieces of ice, and trotted quickly to shelter.

Kevin Cornwood said to Kevin Pliscou—two Kevins, but no particular significance in that—"I think this is an incident."

"An incident?"

"They have shown their presence."

"So you don't believe it was a heart attack."

Cornwood smiled a flinty, humorless smile. You couldn't see his eyes too well because his lenses were so thick. "An eleven-year-old kid dropping dead like that on the playground, with no warning?"

Pliscou twisted his face skeptically. He had the nondescript, polite looks of a Jehovah's Witness going from door to door in a suburb. "It does happen, Kev, now and then. That Allentown high school basketball player, in the middle of a game? A kid walks around with a heart defect, and no one knows until he collapses. Or else it's just one of those things, a mystery."

"Maybe," said Cornwood, who bore an uncanny resemblance to the old comic-book Clark Kent: the square jaw, broad shoulders, the straight-wavy blue-black hair. "We'll see what the autopsy says. Meanwhile . . ." He paced the floor, having to adjust his direction a little each time he stopped and turned, since the floor was revolving slowly. "Meanwhile, I say we treat it as a murder. Committed by one of *them*."

"Another child."

"That's my guess. William Bethany apparently beat up on kids. He was the class bully. One day—yesterday—he picked the wrong kid. Or, you might say, the wrong species." A humorless laugh.

Kevin Pliscou sighed and looked out the window. Half the baseball diamond was covered with dull water that smoked slightly. An owl was perched on the backstop, coal black against a gray sky.

"You realize," began the Clark Kent Kevin.

"What?" said the Jehovah's Witness Kevin.

"You realize the risk. If this is a bona fide incident, then our investigating . . . Our lives will be in considerable danger, Kev."

"I know." The Jehovah's Witness Kevin put a hand to his jacket, touching a left-side bump made by his shoulder-holstered .45. He did it without thinking. As if the gun were a kind of amulet. In a confrontation with this enemy it would probably be useless. "I knew that when I signed on."

He had no children, and Mary Beth, damn her, was probably in the sack right now with some suntanned Hispanic stud from Club Med. Laughing her deep-throated laugh as the springs squeaked and the headboard rattled.

"We'll be walking point, Kev."

"I know."

"Stepping into the hornets' nest, the viper pit, the lion's den."

"I know."

After their phone call to headquarters five minutes ago, unless it was five minutes from now—hard to tell, with all these clocks on the fritz—the SWAT team would be getting ready, the sharpshooters, the guys with the fancy scopes and monitoring equipment and military firepower. State-of-the-art rifles that were all initials and numbers. The SWAT guys would be waiting for the enemy to show his nonhuman hand.

"Our prime suspects are the kids last seen with Bethany. I got a list from Jason Loomis, his friend. He's a suspect, too, of course. Here's the list."

Kevin took the paper from Kevin and read:

> Jason Loomis
> James Barnes
> Kenneth French
> Christopher Zimmerman
> Felice Dewey
> Carole Harrison
> Lori Harrison

There was a flicker of lightning outside, a rumble of thunder. For some reason the room smelled strongly of livestock, as if there were a cattle pen nearby, or a pig wallow, or both.

"So we question these seven first?"

"Yes. Round them up. We'll do it—let's see, there's a conference room, if I remember correctly, next to the cafeteria."

"Now?"

"Why wait? A lot can happen in five minutes."

"I'll tell Mr. Sykes," said the Pliscou Kevin.

"Forget Sykes," said the Cornwood Kevin. "That asshole spends all day looking at his goddamn fingernails. Betsy will tell you what rooms the kids are in. Get them yourself. I'll set up in the conference room meanwhile."

The Pliscou Kevin went to the main office. Betsy ignored him, riveted to her computer monitor, its cursor pulsing like a vein in an infuriated throat.

He spoke to her. She did not respond.

He looked at his watch. It was a row of flashing 8s, but he didn't seem to mind or even be surprised by that. Finally he walked around Betsy's desk and began looking for a paper showing class schedules and rosters of students. There was no such thing.

There was nothing on any of the bulletin boards, just a few chicken feathers attached with tacks, slowly revolving.

He ran a hand in front of Betsy's eyes, but she didn't blink.

"Nobody home," he muttered to himself.

There was no other way but to go from room to room and call out the names. He did this, opening the doors with his right hand and holding in his left the paper with the suspects.

"Jason Loomis?" he called.

"James Barnes?" he called.

And so on.

One room smelled like dill pickles and the elephant house in the zoo. Another smelled like a lumberyard after a heavy rain. He had no idea which class was accelerated and which remedial. He couldn't even tell the jocks from the brains. He didn't know very much about the world of school, having had no children of his own. Mary Beth wasn't interested.

When answering to a name, a child would look up and point a questioning finger at himself or herself, meaning, "Me?" Each time

Kevin nodded, "Yes, you," and crooked a beckoning finger, "Come."

Which they did at once, pale faced, because even in the most surly, recalcitrant hearts the Federal Bureau of Investigation commands respect and maybe awe. Or at least it does in grades K through 6.

The agent gathered five of the suspects in this manner. They followed him in single file, silently, to the conference room next to the cafeteria.

"Can't find Kenneth French or Felice Dewey," he told Kevin Kent.

"They could be home with the flu," Kent said to Witness. "We'll get to them later. All right, boys and girls," he said to the children in a suddenly loud baritone. "Line up against the wall. That wall there."

They lined up, and you could tell they all felt young, small, and weak.

"Do you know what this is?" the Kent Kevin said after a pause, pointing with a stiff, peremptory finger at a brown contraption on the conference table. It had little lights on it, dials, knobs, vent holes, serial numbers, and was plugged into the wall. There was a slot that paper came out of, and other wires connecting the instrument to other things.

The children had no idea what it was.

That is, one did, but he didn't let on.

"It's a lie detector," said Agent Cornwood, emphasizing the word *lie* by making it two syllables, li-ee.

They all looked hard at the infamous polygraph, impressed.

"Now, I'm going to ask you children some questions, and I hope you'll answer truthfully. It's very, very important that you answer truthfully." He looked at them, as if boring with his eyes into their innermost souls. Their mud-smeared, jam-smeared souls. "And then we're going to hook you up, all of you, one by one, to this li-ee detector, and I'll ask you the same questions, the exact same questions." He paused. "Because it's possible, it's very possible, that *one* of you will be ly-ing." He paused dramatically. "The one we're looking for."

The children, breathless, glanced at each other out of the corner of their eyes: Which one was the FBI looking for?

The questions were easy and ordinary at first. What's your name?

How old are you? Where do you live? Did you know William Bethany? What did you think of him?

They had to keep standing against the wall as they answered or others answered. It was clear that the agent regretted that he didn't have a painfully bright light to shine in their faces. He was accustomed to working with a painfully bright light, and in dense, foul, week-old cigar smoke.

"Lori."

"Yes?"

"You have friends."

"Yes?"

"And there are some classmates who are not your friends, isn't that right? Some who don't like you all that much?"

"I . . . guess. Some."

"Some who maybe talk behind your back."

"I guess."

"Do you see them, sometimes, talking behind your back?"

"Well . . ." Lori remembered Elizabeth and Jane at the other end of the room. Their smirks. Their heads together. Looking in her direction now and then. She hated it, the way they looked in her direction. But should she turn them in to the FBI for that? Such revenge seemed extreme.

"Lori," said the big, tall agent.

"Yes?"

"Do you ever listen in when they talk behind your back? Do you listen to what they're thinking? Answer the question, Lori."

Lori didn't know how to answer the question. She didn't really understand the question.

"Do you hear the thoughts inside their skulls, Lori? Answer the question."

She hadn't a clue what the man from the FBI was getting at or what he wanted her to say. If she said the wrong thing, would she go to jail? And would her parents speak to her if she went to jail?

"Do you ever change the thoughts inside their skulls, Lori? Do you make people like you even if they don't?" His face was fierce, his even, white teeth bared, as if he were preparing to bite into something hard.

"I . . . try to be nice to everybody." Except to Miss Gillespie. She hated Miss Gillespie. But that didn't count—did it? Would the bucktoothed former nun point an accusing finger at her out of the

157

lie detector? Would Lori be expelled in shame from Lincoln Elementary, and have to spend the rest of her life working at Burger King while Elizabeth and Jane went off to college and met terrific boys in sweaters?

Her chin trembled. It was all she could do not to burst into tears.

"Jason."

"Yes, sir?"

"William hit you a lot?"

Stupid Loomis squirmed. "Not a lot."

"You ever hit him back, Jason?"

Stupid squirmed, grinned. "He's bigger than me. Was bigger than me. I'd be crazy to hit Billy. I'd get killed." Stupid grinned more, trying to be ingratiating.

"You ever hit him back with your *mind,* Jason?"

An awkward silence. A tense silence.

"Answer the question, Jason."

"With my . . . mind? You mean, did I want to hit him back? I guess I wanted to, sometimes. If he hadn't been so big."

"That's not what I mean at all, Jason. You know what I mean, don't you? Don't you, Jason?"

Stupid didn't. He tried grinning again, at one man, at the other. If they liked him, maybe they'd tell him the right answer and he'd get off whatever hook he was on. He hadn't done anything wrong— had he? He didn't think he had. He wasn't a hundred percent sure.

"Billy was okay," he said. "I'm sorry he died."

As the building turned, sun streamed through the windows, a glaring sunset. The children squinted and winced, not having the courage to raise their hands to shield their eyes without permission. Clark Kent from the fifties smiled; he was glad for the sun in their eyes.

"James."

"Yes, sir?"

"Can you walk through walls? Answer the question, son."

"Walk through walls? No, sir."

"You're not lying to me, are you, James?"

"Lying? No, sir, I wouldn't do that."

"Because it's very important," said the tall black-haired man from Uncle Sam, "it's very important that you tell the truth. All of you." He paced the floor with new energy, as if he were just beginning, as if the night were young. "We have time. We have all the time in the world, gentlemen."

The factory clock on the wall, as if to confirm this, possessed no hands, though it was running. You could tell it was running from the subliminal hum.

"James."

"Yes, sir."

"Can you walk through walls?"

"No, sir."

"You're sure about that, James?"

"I really can't."

The buses had all left, and Carole had to go to the bathroom so bad, she couldn't stand straight.

At a signal from Cornwood, Pliscou stepped forward and slapped Jimmy in the face. The other children gasped and stiffened. Jimmy pressed a hand to his cheek and seemed to shrink into himself, shrink to nearly half his size, until he was closer to the ground even than Christopher. Stricken, he had trouble swallowing. He made a low, odd, pathetic *mmm-mmm.*

"One of you," said Cornwood, "killed William Bethany. One of you stopped his heart on the playground. You thought you could get away with it. You thought people would think it was natural causes. An occlusion, thrombosis, cardiac arrest. You were wrong. You see, we know who you are. What you are. We know all about your abilities. Your powers. Turn yourself in, make a clean breast of it, tell us everything you know, and we'll show leniency. Won't we, Kev?"

"That's right," said Agent Pliscou, nervously touching the bump in his jacket over the left chest. Where also lay, under the .45, his vulnerable, stoppable human heart.

"Turn yourself in now," promised Agent Cornwood, "and Kev and I will take everyone here out to Burger King, and you can have whatever and as much as you like. On us."

Silence.

"A cheeseburger."

Silence.

"A milk shake, fries, ice cream."

The kids eyed each other furtively. Some salivating, too, because it was suppertime—past suppertime, long past, judging by the gibbous moon outside the window. Gibbous or full, it was hard to tell which, the chalky light was so glaring. Maybe full and gibbous both.

No one turned himself or herself in, so the interrogation continued, and the clock went on humming. Hours? Could be.

"Can I please use the ladies' room?" begged Carole Harrison in a pitiful singsong.

She was ignored.

The children were hooked up to the gray-brown lie detector one by one. The others, waiting, had to keep standing in place as the men barked questions and watched the needles twitch and the graph emerge slowly from the machine like a thin tongue, a colorless and endless tongue. The room filled gradually with gray-brown vapor that hung in the air like week-old cigar smoke.

"James."

"Sir?"

"Can you walk through walls?"

"No, sir."

"Can you walk through walls, James? Answer the question."

"I never walked through a wall in my life, sir, and if I tried it, I think I'd hurt my head."

"James."

"I'm telling the truth, sir." But you could see he was beginning to doubt it. Maybe he *was* lying. Maybe he *could* walk through walls.

"Christopher."

"Yes?"

"Did William hit you?"

"Yes."

"Did you stop his heart?"

"How could I do that?"

"Just answer the question, Christopher."

"What was the question again?"

"Did you stop William's heart?"

"No."

"You're sure."

"How could I stop his heart? Do you think I'm a magician?"

"Don't be smart, young man. Answer the question."

"I did answer the question."

"Did you stop his heart or didn't you?"

"I didn't."

"Why are you giving me that look?"

"I'm not giving you any look. I'm just starved."

"Carole."

"What?"

"What number am I thinking of?"

"I don't know."

"What number am I thinking of, Carole?"

"I have to go to the bathroom."

"Answer the question."

"I have to go really bad."

"Answer the question, and you can go."

"Twelve."

"That's not the number."

"Seventeen. A hundred."

"Carole. Stop playing games. We can tell when you're lying. The machine can tell. It's on the graph. What number am I thinking of?"

"I don't know, I don't know."

"You do know, Carole. You do know. I can see it in your eyes. Tell me the number. Let's put an end to this."

"Please, I have to go. I can't hold it anymore."

Cornwood laughed a humorless laugh, the lights from the lie detector playing on his thick black-framed lenses.

The girl started sobbing. Sobbing her heart out. There was a puddle at her feet: urine. The children stared, wrinkled their noses, and looked the other way.

"Carole," moaned Lori, her twin sister, who was crying, too.

Carole, furious, threw her long, loud sobs at the two men as if her sobs were rocks or Molotov cocktails. She had never been so humiliated in her life. Never.

A Visit to the Doctor

On the way to Dr. Hill (in family medicine, but, as the need arose, Hill was also the Wenderoth coroner), Agent Calvert Wormwood said to fellow agent Calvert Pliscou—two Calverts, but such coincidences are without significance—just as two students in a class of thirty may happen to have the same birthday or birthmark—he said, "I suspect the Zimmerman kid."

"Why? The polygraph showed nothing on any of them."

"He wasn't afraid, Calv. He was the only one who wasn't afraid." Wormwood remembered those gray-blue eyes shining with a confidence that didn't belong to a child. Shining also with the pleasure of disobedience. That second kind of shining was common to children. Wormwood had a couple of sons of his own: Ed and Harry. Although he wasn't at home much, he knew the look well. The quiet but sharp glow of defiance in the eyes.

Not a child, but at the same time a child. What was his name? Christopher?

They drove through a flock of owls.

"Damn birds," said Pliscou.

A wing thumped the windshield; a few feathers spiraled in the air.

"Aren't they supposed to be nocturnal?" said Pliscou.

"You're right," said Wormwood.

Hill's office was in a low redbrick medical arts building next to the train station. Not a parking place in sight, because the doctors were all running late, the waiting rooms were all packed, new patients arriving as the hours passed, and no one leaving yet.

As the building turned slowly on its axis, patience hung overhead like smog, a miasma of fatalism.

What was holding up the doctors? Emergencies? No. They were coal and pumice, mostly, the doctors. That was what was holding them up, slowing them down. Open wide and say ah, then stone silence. Or: Bend over please and spread your cheeks, that's right. Then nothing. Or imagine someone looking into your ear for an entire day.

The agents double-parked.

Wormwood elbowed past the patients and receptionist and nurses, flashing his badge. Under the heavy cloud of patience, he alone, it seemed, was not patient. He was on the trail, on the scent.

He entered Dr. Hill's examination room without knocking.

Dr. Hill, fortunately, was more mobile than the other doctors in the building, but conversation with him still had a maple-syrup quality. The man's skin was like dried mud. He exercised care when he spoke, because there were big flaking mud cracks at the corners of his mouth.

"How can I help you, uh—"

"Wormwood. Calvert Wormwood."

"Yes. How can I—"

"You did the autopsy on that sixth grader from Lincoln Elementary. William Bennet."

"Ah."

"Find anything suspicious, Doctor?"

"My report—"

"Any indication of foul play, Doctor?"

Dr. Hill peered over his bifocals at the burly FBI man, who was clean-shaven, clean-cut, and oddly old-fashioned. The horn-rimmed glasses, the lock of blue-black hair that fell over the broad white forehead, curling slightly. The double-breasted suit.

"Foul play, my goodness," said the doctor. "This is not the city, Mr. Wedgewood."

"Wormwood."

"Yes. We are not Philadelphia. Wenderoth hasn't had a murder—"

"Can't you talk a little faster, Doctor?"

"A murder in more than twenty years. Yes. A little Presbyterian adultery now and then, out here in the sticks. Maybe an occasional mishap with a walk-in freezer. Nothing more than that."

"Dr. Hill, could you tell us—"

"The sheriff has nothing to do, poor man."

"The autopsy, Doctor. What did it show?"

"Oh, the autopsy. Heart defect, a bad valve. Poor child. No sign, no warning. It happens now and then. A perfectly healthy child walking around with a time bomb in his ticker. Tsk-tsk. One of those things, Mr. Wedgewood."

"Wormwood."

"Wormwood. Forgive me."

"That's all right."

"And this is your colleague?"

"Calvert Pliscou," said Calvert Pliscou, standing at the door, showing his badge.

"How do you spell that?" inquired the doctor.

"Are you sure it was a bad valve, Doctor?" asked Wormwood.

"Oh, completely shot, yes." The doctor shook his head, and some pieces of ear and jowl fell off. There was already quite a bit of crumbled, dried mud on the floor at his feet—incongruous in a doctor's sterile examination room.

The patient was sitting stoically, shirtless, on the high examination table: Mrs. Showalter in a size D bra. Buddhalike, she, with many folds of midriff fat. Completely unembarrassed, and apparently not even put out by the FBI's intrusion without knocking. But possibly her reaction time was too slow for her to register the intrusion yet, or at least too slow to show her feelings about it. She was mostly asphalt.

"Right atrium," said the doctor. "Infarction." He smiled, and a piece of lower lip dropped to the floor and broke in a puff of brown dust.

"We'd like a copy of your report," said Wormwood.

"Well, ah, I'm afraid—"

"We'd like to see the X rays of the heart."

"The X rays. Actually—"

"We'd like to see the body."

The agent stepped forward and towered above, casting a shadow. Dr. Hill drew back, his smile twisted a little with apprehension. Mrs. Showalter sat motionless. Agent Pliscou considered the woman's impressive breasts and thought of Mary Beth, who was in Mexico now and probably having a ball.

You could hear, through the walls, the whistle of a train either pulling into or pulling out of the station, or possibly both. It was a deep, plaintive call, not unlike a foghorn, *hooo-hooo* or *whooo-whooo,* bringing to mind owls and the full moon.

"We need to make sure, Doctor," said Wormwood, "that there wasn't foul play. That someone didn't stop William Bennet's heart for him. Someone with unusual powers."

"Powers," said Hill.

"Yes, Doctor. There are people in this community, a certain group of people, who are unusual, most unusual. You can't imagine how unusual. They are hiding."

"A religious cult?" said Hill.

"No."

"Terrorists?"

"They have powers," said Wormwood in a whisper, so Mrs. Showalter wouldn't overhear with her asphalt ears.

"Powers," said Hill.

"They are—you might say they are not quite human."

"Oh my," said Hill.

"You might think of them as . . . mutants."

"Mutants with powers. You must admit," said Hill, "Mr.—"

"Wormwood."

"Yes. It does sound like, uh, something out of—"

"*Star Trek* or a comic book."

"Yes. Monsters from Planet X, ha-ha."

"It is no laughing matter, Doctor. These people, they can kill. Kill at a distance."

"My goodness."

"In your practice, Doctor. Have you come across anything very unusual?"

"Unusual. Well, you realize, Mr. Wedgewood," said Hill, "that the human body is full of surprises. Even here in sleepy Wenderoth. Just last week I removed, you won't believe this—"

"There was nothing unusual about William Bennet's heart?"

"Oh, no. I—"

"No improbable blockage? Reversed artery? Severed nerve?" Wormwood advanced, pressing, bearing down.

"No, I assure you, Mr.—"

"Why is it I think you are concealing something from me, Dr. Hill?"

Dr. Hill, stammering, tried to move away. Wormwood blocked him.

"Why is it you do not look me in the eye, Dr. Hill?"

"Really, uh, bad valve, that's all. Mitral. Tricuspid. Right atrium."

"You're covering up, aren't you? For whom?"

The doctor, fear in his baked-mud face, suddenly darted to the left. It wasn't much of a dart, however, because of his substance; the movement hardly even deserved the word *suddenly*. Think of a turtle attempting to sidestep a blow, a slug attempting to parry or feint. He bumped into the sink; the sink got in his way. The room was, after all, revolving, so a person had to keep track of where things were.

Wormwood grasped the doctor's wrist. "Come on, Hill," he said, "make a clean breast of it. Tell us everything. We'll show leniency, won't we, Calv?"

"Sure," said Pliscou.

The doctor whimpered, pulled. His hand came off. He lunged for the door, if you could call it a lunge. Pliscou blocked him easily.

The doctor turned, stumbled, fell. From the angles in his white coat you could tell that his body was badly broken. Irreparably, fatally broken. Like a tumble of concrete blocks covered with a bedsheet. He coughed. He twisted to look up, through his bifocals, from the rubble that was now his body, at the two FBI men. He tried to speak.

"What is it, Hill?" asked Wormwood, bending over.

Dr. Hill shook, shuddered, a gurgle in his throat. They thought he was in pain—but no, he was racked with laughter. The maniacal laughter of despair.

"Chance," he said.

"What?" They put their heads lower and cupped their ears.

"Don't have—"

"Don't have what, Hill?"

He smiled ear to ear—literally ear to ear, since the face cracked apart, split open at the mouth. "You don't have a chance against her," he managed to say somehow, his brown tongue working loose, detaching, fracturing as it detached. He giggled, and in a feeble spray of dust and teeth was no more.

"We killed him," said Pliscou.

"I don't think so," said Wormwood. "I think it was suicide."

"Suicide?"

"I could smell the fear on him, Calv." Wormwood got up, brushed the dirt off his pant legs, jacket, hands. "He was so afraid of *her,* whoever *she* is, that death itself was preferable."

"You mean, you think—"

"A human being, the doctor, in their employ," said Wormwood. "Or in their thrall."

Turning to go, they looked at Mrs. Showalter, who was sitting in the same position on the high examination table, blouseless, fat, her size D bra so full, it seemed swollen to the point of bursting. No, she wasn't in the same position exactly. There was a slight change in the shoulders, the head, one elbow. She looked like she was maybe working up to a scream. At the rate she was going, it would take her at least two weeks.

"Do we just leave her here?" said Pliscou.

"Why not?" said Wormwood.

The two agents stepped over the inert remains of Dr. Hill, which were smoking slightly, and proceeded to the office where appointments were made and records kept.

"We'll get one of the nurses to show us the autopsy report and the X rays, right?" asked Pliscou in the corridor.

"At the moment, Calv, I'm more interested in a list of this guy's patients," said Wormwood, leading the way.

They went through several folders, fingered through a few Rolodexes, looked at two bulletin boards. The bulletin boards held general announcements about billing, health tips—dandruff, your heart—and a cartoon clipping. Not one chicken feather.

The nurses were of little help. Too busy.

The phone rang: a strange gurgling ring, as if it were under water. No one answered it. But maybe it wasn't the phone, maybe it was something else gurgling.

Wormwood's finger went down a row of names in an old appointment book, last month's, and stopped.

"Aha," the agent said.

"What is it?" asked Pliscou, coming over.

"Found what I was looking for."

Pliscou's eyes dropped, followed the tip of Wormwood's finger on the page, and saw the name Zimmerman.

"Zimmerman . . . Christopher Zimmerman?"

"I'm sure. Get your hat, Calv. We're going to pay the Zimmermans a call."

"I don't wear a hat."

"Oh, right."

They had a devil of a time finding their car in the parking lot. The snowplows and sanders hadn't come yet, and there must have been a foot of snow at least. The lot, revolving slowly, looked like a bunch of pillows. A field of pillows, each pillow with its own aerial. Pretty, if you didn't need to get somewhere in a hurry.

The train whistle went *whooo-whooo, whooo-whooo.*

Mighty Mouse

2

The clouds overhead are threatening. They are charcoal gray, more black than gray, and there is an ominous touch of electric green in them. You see a sky this dark, this lowering, and with that weird electric green only before a major thunderstorm, the kind of thunderstorm that penetrates to a person's vitals even when he is safe in his home, in his room, the windows closed and the curtains all drawn.

Yes, you ask, but where is the storm? There is no wind blowing, to speak of. And no matter how hard we listen, there is no deep, distant rumble.

See the rusted weather vane on the roof, in the shape of a humpbacked buzzard? The buzzard does not move. The air is still—and thick, almost too thick to breathe. Why is the air so thick? Is it humidity? Pollution?

We find ourselves again at 54 Winston Street. The house looks a little seedier than the last time we saw it, mildew and ultraviolet radiation having taken their steady toll. The bdellium dish is half eaten by mold or crows, or both. The hedge has yellow spots and brown spots; a survivor of many winters, it appears finally to be giving up the phytopsychic ghost.

A brief rattle of hail. The round, rough pellets of ice have cat's-eye green in them, as if we were near an ocean.

Still no breeze, just the ammonia smell of wet diapers that have been sitting for a week in a diaper pail. The smell puts knives up our nostrils and makes us choke.

Woodworm and Pliscou have parked in front of the Zimmermans' old clapboard house. Silhouetted against the threatening sky, it looks like your classic haunted house at Halloween. It hunches. It rears. It looms.

The two agents—both have the first name Kelvin, but such coincidences happen all the time—look at each other as two soldiers look at each other before a battle: before a perilous engagement that will claim many lives, cutting down many warriors and leaving them strewn on the field like unstrung puppets ere the sun sets.

Woodworm takes off his glasses, wipes them, puts them back on.

"I should go in alone," he said.

"No," said Pliscou, but in his private heart he said, "Yes, yes" and felt tremendous knee-weakening relief. Mary Belle may have left him for some beachcombing Juan or Julio with big muscles, but life was not over yet.

It *would* be over, odds were, if he entered that house, knowing what he knew—not much, but enough—about the enemy. The incredible things they could do, if cornered.

"You stay here, Kelv," said Woodworm, trying to be as resolute as his square jaw and broad shoulders declared him to be. "Listen for me on the walkie-talkie. I'll report every few minutes. If I don't, then assume the worst and call in the National Guard, ha-ha. All right, let's synchronize our watches."

Both men looked at and adjusted the precision timepieces on their wrists. The LED displays showed nothing but a row of flashing 8s, yet somehow Woodworm and Pliscou didn't seem to consider this a problem.

"Here," said Woodworm, taking an envelope from his jacket pocket and giving it to Pliscou.

"What's that?" asked Pliscou.

"A letter to my wife and children."

"Aw gee."

"Just in case, Kelv. You know."

"Yeah."

A clap on the shoulder, a nod, air expelled through the nose, another nod, then Woodworm opens the car door and gets out. Wisps of vapor are rising from the slate walkway to the front door—which is half open, unless shadows are playing tricks. The light certainly is queer, from that awful leaden sky.

The bent buzzard on the roof doesn't move an inch: there is no wind.

Tiny pieces of green ice crunch underfoot.

"Take care," said Pliscou, holding his walkie-talkie white-knuckle tight.

"Right," said Woodworm, also holding his walkie-talkie white-knuckle tight.

Both agents are bathed in cold sweat.

As Woodworm approaches the slowly revolving house, he makes sure his government-issue Colt will come easily out of its shoulder holster if it is needed. "The door is half open," he tells Pliscou over the walkie-talkie.

"Right," says Pliscou, who can see this himself from the car, or at least he thinks he can. The distance between them grows; the street is evidently moving in a slightly different direction, tangential to the house, if that makes sense. Pliscou was never good at geometry. Had his math been better in school, he would have gone into the foreign service, and then Mary Belle, who likes to travel, would not have ditched him, though you can never tell about women.

"Here goes," said Woodworm over the walkie-talkie.

And he knocked on the half-open door.

"Anybody home?" he called.

The half-open door creaked three-quarters open. It was a quite ordinary door. Cracked paint, of an indeterminate color.

"Hello," he called.

"Mr. Zimmerman?" he called.

"Here goes," he muttered into the walkie-talkie, and stepped inside.

It was quite dark. If any lights were on, they were unusually dim—maybe a problem at the power plant, from a raft of electrical storms across the state, the Allegheny Mountains, who knows?

"Hello," he called. "Anybody home?"

The house was silent, like a museum or mausoleum. Deserted? The thought came to Woodworm: The Zimmerman family, alerted that the FBI was onto them, had flown the coop. They could be anywhere now, resettling—under a different assumed name—in another part of the country, in some unsuspecting, quiet little town south of Denver, west of Baton Rouge, north of Durham, east of

Boise. A cancer cell taking root in yet another vital organ of this great land.

He sees a long flight of stairs going up. Dark, polished wood. He decides to start at the bottom of the house.

"Mr. Zimmerman?" he calls. "It's the FBI."

No sense playing his cards close to the vest now. He has come to force their hand. To flush them. If they are still here. They may not be.

He proceeds to the living room or drawing room, stepping carefully.

"What's going on?" asks Pliscou faintly over a growl of static.

"Checking the place out," replies Woodworm into his walkie-talkie. "Just a regular house, so far. The air is thick."

"Thick?"

"Almost like, I don't know, you have to chew and swallow to get it in your lungs . . . Nothing here. Regular furniture, a fireplace—Jesus."

"What?"

"Bats."

Actually only one bat. Brown. Disturbed by the FBI man, it flew around the ceiling in the jumpy-jerky way of bats, then suddenly angled out of the room and was gone. The face in the picture over the mantelpiece winked.

Woodworm proceeded to another room, and to another. So far, so good.

"A washing machine right in the middle of the foyer," he reported. "Seems connected, too."

"A lot of dust," he reported. "Cobwebs. They don't clean."

"Holy shit," he reported when he reached the screened-in porch. "A statue."

"Statue?" asked Pliscou faintly over static.

"A statue of a person, in regular clothes," said Woodworm. "You know, the kind they have in those modern art exhibits. Gives me the willies. This one's a middle-aged woman in a shawl, on a swing seat, very realistic, too, with all the creases in her face. Even a mole with a hair in it. Probably cost thousands of dollars. Incredible, how people choose to spend their money."

Mother in basalt. She looks very angry, though the features are completely frozen. Smoke trickles from her granite ears, hardly noticeable smoke. Can she hear?

Woodworm finds the answer box from the future in the unlocked credenza. "Hello, what's this?" he says.

"What?" asks Pliscou.

"A device of some kind, weird, it must be made by them," says Woodworm.

"This is an answer box," says the answer box.

"Did you hear that, Kelv? The box talks."

"Talks?"

"It says it's an answer box."

"What?" Reception is worsening as house and street turn on different axes, each going its own way like continental plates, only a little faster.

"Strange material. Feels like plastic, but has too much heft for plastic and is too hard."

"Talks?" asked Pliscou from the car.

"All right, if you're an answer box," said Woodworm with a tight smile, "tell me who made you."

"Morton," said the answer box.

"Who's Morton? Mr. Zimmerman?"

"No."

"One of his people, then?"

"No relation. Morton died seven thousand five hundred and eight years from now of his own hand because of backbiting and insufficient government funding. He left two children and nine prototypes."

"That's coming from a box?" came Pliscou's voice over the static, fainter.

"That's right," Woodworm said into his walkie-talkie. "We'll give this baby to the boys in the lab. But first I'm going to check out the rest of the house, Kelv. I don't think anyone's here. Maybe they got wind and flew the coop."

"Be careful."

"Don't worry."

On the second floor he finds another clothed statue, a man at a desk with an inane smile on his face. The statue is bending over a stamp album and holding a loupe. The stamp album is real and the stamps are real. Port-au-Prince, Somalia, nineteenth century.

There is a lot of electronic equipment in an unused bedroom. Difficult to tell for what purpose. It has a funny smell, like the kind of cellophane they don't make anymore. Antique cellophane.

In a corner of the hall, a tiny metal spider hangs at the center of a wire web. Maybe they're art collectors, Woodworm thinks, and the doubt comes to him: Maybe these people are merely eccentric and not *them*. In which case he's made a complete fool of himself, and Pliscou and the others will have a good har-har at him later.

That answer box thing, too: it could be an expensive gadget, nothing more. Some people go to fancy galleries and buy stuff like that.

Though on the other hand it's hard to believe the Zimmermans are that well-off, living in a house so filthy and in such need of repair. The roof must leak: Woodworm sees blotchy water stains on the ceiling and on the green-gray wallpaper.

But sometimes millionaires live in squalor. There are famous examples.

"Uh-oh, someone's home," he tells Pliscou through the walkie-talkie. There is no reply, only static. Light is coming from under a door. He knocks and opens slowly, impressed by how courageous he is being.

"Excuse me," he says. "Mr. Zimmerman?"

It wasn't Mr. Zimmerman, it was a teenage girl sitting in bed and smoking. Pregnant. In her seventh or eighth month.

"You—you're not Kaelin, are you?" he asked, wide-eyed. She didn't look anything like the thin, shy girl at that dance in the gym, the Kaelin Zimmerman in the pathetic blue dress and blue shoes among pumpkins. No, this was your basic hard-bitten delinquent type: a permanent sneer on a coarse face. The kind of face any parent worthy of the name parent would love to slap.

Kaelin looked up slowly—she had been reading a book, a greasy paperback about Nazi Germany—and slowly flicked an ash. "Oh, it's Clark Kent," she drawled.

Was she drinking, too?

"You shouldn't be smoking in bed," said Woodworm. And without even an ashtray. "It's not safe."

"Fucking Boy Scout," said Kaelin lethargically, slurring.

Was the girl on drugs?

"Where are your parents?" asked Woodworm.

Kaelin laughed an ugly laugh. She laughed in monstrous, nightmare slow motion. Her lips were brown.

"Ha," she laughed.

"Ha," she laughed.

The FBI man withdrew and closed the door. He went up the steps to the third floor, which turned out to have only two rooms—and one of those was an attic. Nothing there but the usual things families store in attics and crawl spaces: boxes of old clothes, old china, old books. A bent floor lamp, not unlike the rusted buzzard on the roof. A teddy bear missing half its fur and one eye. A rolled-up rug, taupe.

I have the wrong family, thought Woodworm. Damn.

He checks out the last room. A boy's room: it must be Christopher's.

A sudden rasp of static on the walkie-talkie; a voice too far away to make out—Pliscou trying to get through but failing. Woodworm tells him, "I'll be out in a minute, Kelv." Then he has the urge to guffaw, almost uncontrollable. It's nerves. The relief, he realizes. He's been under a great strain, expecting any second to be turned into a screaming pretzel that pleads for quick oblivion.

Or into something worse.

Something unimaginable.

But apparently that's not going to happen this time around. A false alarm. Maybe fate has decided, unaccountably, to be kind to Kelvin Woodworm; and maybe this reprieve, who knows, will eventually be replaced by the even kinder miracle of a full pardon. Another agent will end up taking the bullet for him, and Woodworm will live to enjoy an honorable retirement, lots of cute, healthy grandchildren piling into his armchair and asking him to tell them again about how he faced the dangerous mutants from Planet X and received a citation for bravery from the president of the United States in the Oval Office.

He saw a row of pebbles on the windowsill.

He heard a low growl from the closet.

A growl? What was in the closet?

"What are you doing in my room?"

Woodworm whirls and sees the kid, the prime suspect confronting him here at the center of the hornets' nest, the viper pit, the dragon's lair. Don't be fooled by the Norman Rockwell face from Middle America, the agent tells himself. Don't be fooled by the blue eyes, sandy hair, snub nose, and Donald Duck T-shirt. By the pint size.

Thunder, as of a jumbo jet taking off for Cleveland in a cloud of sour exhaust.

"Don't act innocent," snarled Woodworm over the rumble-rumble, trying not to choke. "You know why I'm here."

"I don't."

"You murdered Billy Bendix."

"I didn't."

"Yes you did. You stopped his heart because he punched you. You stopped it with a thought because you're not human." Time to lay all the cards on the table.

"I didn't," said Christopher Zimmerman, but his face was hot and his eyes bulged a little, which was always a giveaway when kids weren't telling the truth.

"Don't lie to me."

"I'm not lying."

"Stand still."

"I am standing still."

"You murdered Billy Bendix."

"This—this is my room," said Christopher, stammering, his voice climbing to almost a mouse squeak, "and—and this is my house. Do you have a search warrant?"

"Search warrant? Here's my search warrant, son," said the agent, pulling out his black Colt Magnum. Time to get tough. Time to push and corner.

He grabbed the little boy by the arm and shoved the big gun in his Norman Rockwell face. It wasn't the gun that did it—it was the grabbing, clutching man's fingers, because they happened to clutch and grip hard that tender place on the arm, the right arm, where a few days ago Billy the Bully had punched, digging his knuckles in as flies buzzed around the Dumpster and making an ugly purple knot there under Christopher's skin.

Christopher yelped, "Ow. Ow."

"You okay, Kelv?" the outside Kelv inquired through atmospheric crackling and popping.

Agent Woodworm, alas, is not okay. He has done his duty. He has made the enemy finally show his hand. He has taken the bullet. Or is just about to. God knows, a bullet would be preferable to the manner in which he will now be made to depart from this vale of tears. A bullet would be much less stressful, and oh, so much more dignified. Not that there was any choice. Someone had to walk point for the SWAT team nervously waiting in the vans and helicopters, their lips dry and their fingers flexed sweating on state-of-the-art triggers.

Someone had to flush the monster hiding in Wenderoth.

Christopher looked up through his pain and saw the broad shoulders and square Clark Kent jaw. He thought of he-men, those football-player types with thick necks and bulging biceps and deep throaty laughs and pea brains. They were what was wrong with the world. Those macho bullies always pushing everybody around.

Macho, he thought, and tightened his lips. Goddamn chest hair, he thought, and ground his teeth. Goddamn cocks and balls, he thought, and cursed a curse too terrible to be printed here.

He grew twisted in the face, ugly around the mouth, raccoon dark around the eyes as he reached for some upsilon and omicron, though he knew he shouldn't, don't do it, Christopher, don't, but he was too angry.

The FBI man's hand fell off.

"Stand still," croaked Woodworm, disoriented but beginning to feel the chill of fear. Hackles lifting. What the hell happened to his hand? Where was his hand?

On the floor? What the holy hell was his hand doing on the floor? You dropped a hammer sometimes, a nail file, a pen, maybe a glass with Coke in it. You didn't drop a hand, for Chrissake.

And why wasn't there any blood?

He remembered Dr. Hill on the floor of the examining room, the poor man literally in pieces, dying, and he thought, What's going on? and this was his last coherent thought.

Because little Christopher did a number of things he shouldn't have. First he flew up and punched the agent in the jaw, a Mighty Mouse uppercut. He puffed-cheek-blew all the agent's hair off, making a blue-black blizzard for a second or two in the air behind the agent, and the agent's skull was like a surprised billiard ball. The agent's perfect white teeth? Christopher made them all crack and crumble out by pieces the way you see in Road Runner cartoons after the dynamite. He reversed the agent's ears, turned his nose upside down, turned his eyes inside out. And, in his great anger, he gave the agent breasts, Cathy Carmichael breasts, no, Mrs. Showalter breasts, no, bigger, much bigger, breasts the size of pumpkins, medicine balls, no, parade balloons, huge, ponderous, sky-filling, slow-motion bobbing spheres like moons pulled to earth—which of course broke a great deal of furniture, because

Christopher's room wasn't large enough by half to accommodate all that expanding tit.

The agent was pushed out by it—through the door or perhaps through a wall—and he hung kicking over the stairwell but didn't plunge three flights since most of him now was two giant boobs in Christopher's room, crushing the closet, flattening the bed, splintering the dresser, pouring like swollen dough out of the shattered, demolished window, taking some of the wall with them.

Christopher in the nick of time had flown from the house and up, was hovering now at the height of the crown of an old oak, was watching appalled and fascinated by the consequences of Temper Unchecked. Part of him wishing he could undo, and part of him itching to do more.

And so Kelvin Woodworm of the FBI has fallen after all in the line of duty. A hero. Whether smothered by his own galloping mammary tissue, or killed by the impact of passing quickly or not so quickly through a wall, or by the fact that his heart couldn't possibly supply so much extra flesh with blood and just gave up, overwhelmed, or whether he was killed by the various painful and frightening indignities visited on his face, or by any combination of these things or by all of them at once—it doesn't matter now, does it? The dying is over, and Woodworm, *requiescat in pace,* cannot be hurt or insulted anymore, by anyone.

Agent Pliscou, in the car on the other side of the house, heard the noise—the sound of an icebreaker forcing its way through Arctic floes, the sound of a great tree coming down in a dense Canadian forest. He looked, craning his neck—but it was difficult to see, the sun was in his eyes, a fierce, merciless sun blazing off snow and ice. The entire sky was a shield of white glare.

"Kelv?" he called through the walkie-talkie.

Was that a kid way up there in the trees? No, not in the trees—in the air.

With fumbling fingers Pliscou got out the binoculars and focused.

Christopher Zimmerman, holy shit, floating seventy-eighty feet off the ground. Maybe a hundred.

Pliscou pulled away from the curb carefully, trying not to rev the engine or make the wheels squeal, trying not to draw attention to himself: I'm just here passing through the neighborhood, nice day, minding my own business.

It didn't work. Christopher, using his long vision, must have seen him pulling away and figured out that this was the other agent—because Kelvin Pliscou, holding his breath and crossing his fingers as he drove, never made it to the turn off Winston onto Dekalb much less got to notify the SWAT soldiers. (But their surveillance equipment has alerted them.) His head, without warning, exploded like a ripe pumpkin dashed to pavement.

If you had looked out your window then, parting curtains to see what all the commotion was, you would have observed a car moving slowly off the street and nudging onto the sidewalk between two maples. All the car's windows were bright red on the inside, as if someone had played an elaborate college prank with poster paint.

But no one was looking at the car. On Winston Street all the curtains, revolving slowly, were drawn against the noonday heat.

Hitler Lives

2

Later that day, in the drizzle, the police or soldiers—whatever they were—arrived in their vans and special helicopters. They surrounded the house but at a distance. Sharpshooters took up positions, and a negotiator with a wonderful avuncular baritone spoke to Christopher over a high-quality PA system that gave off wisps of vapor.

Christopher ignored them. He was heartsick about his room. The one place in the world that was his, and now it was ruined, broken beyond repair. And befouled beyond repair, stuffed with dead agent bosom, which was beginning to stink.

"Christopher, we know you're in there," said the voice.

He was sitting in the kitchen, sipping a cold cup of coffee that tasted like liquid chalk.

"Christopher," said the voice, "let's talk. We need to talk. Come out with your hands up. We won't hurt you. You won't be hurt, Christopher, I promise you won't be hurt."

What were the neighbors thinking?

Christopher didn't care what the neighbors were thinking. Stupid people. Everyone in Wenderoth was so dim. Quail Ridge wasn't any better, either, just richer.

They lived among morons. Maybe it was just central Pennsylvania. But humans were probably that way everywhere. Homo sapiens, what a joke.

"Christopher," said the voice, patient but urgent, urgent but patient. An edgy voice going to lengths to sound laid-back.

Christopher walked from room to room, headachy and restless. He didn't know what to do with himself. He couldn't go anywhere now, with the soldiers. And there was no one to talk to. Forget Kaelin.

He went to the porch and stuck his tongue out at his mother on the swing seat, but that didn't make him feel any better.

"I flew today," he told her to her face.

Mother, made of stone, did nothing.

"I guess you're going to scoop me out, huh?" he asked. "Huh?"

Mother, made of stone, said nothing. She only smoked a little at the ears.

This didn't make him feel any better.

Someone out there must have seen him through the screen of the porch, using an infrared scope, because a high-powered, steel-jacketed bullet came whizzing in and bounced off his forehead. Incredible aim—correcting, too, at that distance, for the movement of the street and the movement of the house, which was different, tangential—it had to have been with the help of a computer. The brains of humans were all in their guns.

"Christopher," said the voice. "Turn yourself in, son. We need to sit down and talk. We have questions to ask you."

He rubbed his forehead. A red welt right in the middle, like a caste mark, which brought to mind Panda Ray. Was that raisin brown Dravidian looking down at him now and laughing?

"Christopher," said another voice, not the baritone and not through a loudspeaker but close by. An old woman's voice.

He walked through the house from room to room, looking for an old woman. Uncle Marvin winked at him, maybe, from the portrait over the mantelpiece, but there was no Uncle Marvin in the family, so Christopher ignored the wink.

He saw the ghost finally over the washing machine. White and wavy—a lot of static, interference—seen from another Sea—but he had no trouble recognizing his grandmother.

"Christopher," said Emily sternly, sadly, "you haven't been behaving."

"I know," he said, and felt an uncomfortable weight on him, a weight on his chest that made it hard to breathe. That made him want to sigh.

Somewhere in the house, a toilet flushed.

Christopher walked from room to room, not knowing what to

do with himself. A spider scurried out of his way—a drunken stagger of a scurry, because the thing didn't have the right number of legs. An odd number: nine. A poor design.

"Christopher," boomed the fatherly baritone. "Please, my boy. Please. Turn yourself in. We won't shoot, I promise."

Christopher paced while searchlights stabbed through the windows. How would the neighbors be able to sleep through this? Were they all watching, curtains parted? Were they saying, "Those Zimmermans, I always thought there was something odd about them"?

But who cared what the stupid Homo sapient neighbors were saying or thinking?

Did it make any difference what dogs and cats thought about you on the street? Or what birds thought? Or what ants thought? It didn't make any difference.

"Christopher," boomed the amplified voice of authority, "you can't stay in there forever."

This is so boring, thought Christopher, unable to unload or ease the pressure in his chest. It was sin that had him by the throat and was sitting on his chest, sin along with evil and guilt. All those old-fashioned Sunday-sermon things that turned out to be not as out-of-date as he had thought.

Christopher felt like such a jerk, such a joke, becoming the subject of a Sunday sermon.

"Christopher," said the voice of fathers, principals, doctors, and presidents, "come out with your hands up. Turn yourself in. You can't stay in there forever. We won't shoot, Christopher. We need to talk to you, son. You won't be hurt, I give you my word. My word of honor, Christopher. Christopher."

It was a lot of talking at one time, and suddenly Christopher realized why: the talking was to cover an assault. They were rushing the house now, with their guns. He used his long hearing and heard them coming, soldier boots on the wet lawn, soldier boots on the wet slate. Helmets scraping through the hedge and past the hedge. There were twenty men at least, twenty heroes with square jaws, hairy chests, and balls.

Christopher killed them long-distance. He pushed a few into the earth, burying them alive but not alive for long because you can't breathe soil. He took off a few heads, ruptured a few hearts, cut some soldiers in half at the waist or lengthwise, and one who made it into the house and fumbled for a grenade—Christopher compressed him into a basketball-sized ball, which must have been painful, and lobbed him over the trees.

It was quiet after that, very quiet. Even the voice on the loudspeaker didn't say anything.

"Where is this going to end?" asked Emily's ghost. It hovered, flickering, over the sink while he sat in the kitchen and sipped cold coffee that tasted half like milk of magnesia and half like library paste.

"I don't know," said Christopher, and he added, in his defense, "They started it."

"That's not true."

"The FBI man, he barged into my room with a gun."

"You killed William Bensen."

"He hit me."

"Being hit is no reason to kill someone." Even as a ghost Emily spoke in a sharp voice that cut straight to the heart of the matter.

"He wasn't someone," mumbled Christopher.

"What?"

"Billy wasn't someone. He was no one. They're all no ones, the stupid human people."

Christopher walked from room to room in the empty house and sighed, but the sighing didn't do him any good. He stayed away from the stairwell, where the first agent hung overhead like a rag doll all pulled out of shape. Were bluebottle flies laying eggs already? Or was that buzzing sound from poor Buzz crushed in the closet, maybe shorting out?

No, not in this Sea. He forgot: Buzz had no circuitry in this Sea. Buzz was now a mean, ugly, undead creature who would never wag his tail again or look up with affection when you opened the door.

Christopher felt such a pang of homesickness, he wanted to cry. He couldn't cry.

"Christopher," said the loudspeaker outside, "can you hear me? Can you hear me, Christopher? Those men were not trying to hurt you, son. You have to understand—this is a matter of national security. You are very important to us, Christopher. We are trying to guard you, protect you. There may be others in your family—I don't know if they can hear me—who don't want you to talk to us, Christopher. Who might try to stop you from talking to us. Yes, to stop you. Come out, Christopher. Son. Come out with your hands up and turn yourself in, and we'll talk. We won't hurt you, I promise, sacred word of honor. We have questions to ask you, a lot of questions, that's all, only questions, Christopher. Christopher."

Talk covering another assault. More heroes, more testosterone coming through the drizzle. Again, quick boots across the wet grass and clop-clop on the slippery steps to the front door and the back door, too. Frightening away all the owls perched along the gables and gutters. A lot of disgusted owl-flapping in the air.

Christopher took the men out without any difficulty, too bored now to vary much the method of kill, as in a video game you have mastered long ago and don't care about anymore, playing out of habit rather than desire, hardly paying attention as you rack up point after point. Twenty men, thirty men, forty, fifty. Foolish: soldiers knocked down as fast as tenpins. Next, bam, next, bam.

But then he heard a strange whooshing rip in the sky from the south, coming faster than a locomotive, faster than a jumbo jet or even one of those latest supersonic fighters. Very fast. And Christopher, because he was no dope, understood: just as the lying loudspeaker talk was a diversion for the assault, so the silly assault was really a diversion for the missile. To keep him from noticing until it was too late.

"That's what war does," said Emily. "It just gets more and more so. You'll see."

"Listen to her, my boy," said Gramps, nodding. "Emily knows the world."

He had about two seconds, less than that, before the proximity sensor made the warhead do what warheads are made to do.

The United States government was apparently willing to countenance the loss of all these highly trained soldiers and special agents, plus the combined citizenry of Wenderoth and Quail Ridge and East Carlyle—not consulting them—and maybe a good chunk of the state as well (depending on what was in the warhead) to make sure that the Christopher threat ended here and now.

The human species stopping at nothing to protect itself.

Stupid human species. Because there wouldn't have *been* any threat if they had just left the child alone.

But no, they had to keep pushing, grabbing, hitting, attacking. That was all they knew: the law of the jungle, claw and fang, kill or be killed, eat or be eaten.

The world, Christopher reflected, would be a better place without these erect apes, these carnivorous, cannibalistic, vicious, self-important monkeys who called themselves people. Maybe if you cleared the earth of them, something better and finer and more civilized would take their place in two or three million years.

Cows and sheep might evolve to inherit the earth. Or certain breeds of dog that were good-tempered, intelligent, and noble. Christopher thought of Mrs. Strapelli's black standard poodle, Bessie, who was on a level far above Mrs. Strapelli if you were talking about dignity or soul.

The delicate way Bessie picked up the folded morning newspaper on the stoop.

It would be a purer, cleaner world, no question, without human beings, who not only murdered and tortured one another all the time but also cut down trees and made the landscape ugly. Christopher couldn't imagine evolved poodles cutting down trees, strip-mining, building developments and malls where developments and malls weren't needed, or throwing beer cans and plastic foam cups in the Susquehanna River.

Purge the earth of humans, and the land would heal itself, and the water would be able to filter out all its cancer-causing poisons and become clear and delicious again, and the same for the air.

Otherwise the situation was hopeless: Man the Spoiler would never let any other species replace him, even if it was clearly in the best interests of the planet. Man the Selfish was making the other species go extinct one by one. Soon there would be only people, house pets, livestock, rats, and a few lonely giraffes and elephants in zoos. Maybe an occasional crow or coyote still wild on the outskirts. Not much of a gene pool for the future.

Christopher knew all the proud things said about America, Land of the Free and Home of the Brave, and he was willing to believe it was a lot better here than in other countries, which weren't as democratic, modern, or humanitarian. Mrs. Palmer had told the class the story of the Declaration of Independence, the Constitution, the Green Mountain Boys, the *Monitor* and the *Merrimack,* about Benjamin Franklin's inventions and Thomas Jefferson's visions, but Christopher was thinking more and more, lately, that surely we could do better than this.

The only way to do better, however, was start from scratch, tearing down first, burning away first. Things were just too rotten and compromised to build on.

The only way to solve this problem was turn to a fresh page, a page that had no moronic writing on it.

It would be like sealing up a house (the way the Petersons did last year on Green Street) and pumping in gas to get rid of all the roaches and all the baby roaches and all the roach eggs once and for all. That was the only way to go about it.

You amputated a leg if it had gangrene, to save the rest of the body.

Half measures didn't work with Man the Stupid.

Not that Christopher actually thought all this in one and a half seconds, or that he would have put it exactly in those words, or that he really hoped to build a better world, a new order.

Basically he was a frightened, angry, unhappy child. And then the anger, of course, in the heat of battle, took over, the way anger does, becoming rage and then frenzy and then something like a great hunger that can't be satisfied no matter how fast or how much you eat.

But even so, the Idea was there, and an Idea is necessary. Blood-lust alone—the excitement, the thrill, the siren call of killing—won't wipe away an entire village, city, or nation with the unhesitating, unflinching sweep of an eraser across a blackboard in Mrs. Palmer's class.

And the Idea was definitely in Christopher's head.

He was, after all, in a manner of speaking, of a superior race. He couldn't help but notice that, even when he was very little, just out of diapers. Having upsilon and omicron, unlike animals and people with their paltry psi. Having all these powers, though Mother would slap your face if you flew at a birthday party because you felt energetic and happy, or scoop you out if in the fifth grade you traveled in time with your grandfather and hinted about it at school.

Christopher wrapped himself in armor against the missile and its thermonuclear burst a femtosecond or two before the fuse sent the triggering signal which activated the detonating device and everything within a radius of about a mile was vaporized in a flash of intolerable light. This armoring business wasn't easy, but neither was it a skin-of-the-teeth thing. Close, yes, but not that close. It required fancy footwork, or fingerwork, like tying your shoes at the last minute before a race. True, one wrong move would have cost Christopher his young life, but he didn't make a wrong move, didn't even stop to think he might. The armor worked on the clever energy-moat principle, and when the explosion took place, there wasn't that much subatomic tunneling raising the temperature inside. A few degrees only, a pleasant warmth, toasty.

Kaelin had shown him this trick when they got into an incinerator once, hiding from Jason Bigelow and his sister. It was in the old apartment building that was torn down to make a parking lot for the train station. They closed the heavy metal door after them and sat in the roaring furnace, fire all around. Kaelin was always afraid of Mother, but she loved tricks and sometimes did humorous things like this if no one could find out. Covering her mouth as she shook with silent laughter.

He missed Kaelin more than Buzz, maybe even more than Gramps. (Was Gramps really dead, or was he dead only in this Sea?)

Rolling up his sleeves, setting his jaw, Christopher taught the humans a lesson by giving them an eye for an eye and a tooth for a tooth, and see how *you* like it. He set off the same exact payload—not a molecule more, not a molecule less—in the president's Oval Office, which in another flash of intolerable light effectively erased from Mrs. Palmer's blackboard the capital of our country: the White House, the Washington Monument, the Lincoln Memorial, the Capitol, the beautiful cherry trees, the Smithsonian, the Beltway, and the millions of innocent people who lived there, not to mention the tourists.

In his anger, which was mounting, growing nastier and thirstier, he laughed. About time someone taught those stupid arrogant ugly football bullies a lesson. They had it coming. You can't go around punching people in the arm just because you feel like it, and then grabbing them and shoving guns in their faces.

He peered out of his armor and saw, above the great, steaming, slowly revolving bowl in the earth, a vast pale violet sky and in the sky the biggest, highest tower he had ever seen, an awesome edifice made of oyster gray cloud so thick it looked more like concrete than cloud. There would be a tower just like that now also over the District of Columbia crater, probably visible for a hundred miles in all directions.

A lesson America would never forget.

But, standing at the center and the bottom of the bowl, Christopher felt alone and naked. What would he do without his house, without Wenderoth? Where would he go live now? With Uncle Raymond in Cleveland? Uncle Raymond was so boring, and he had false teeth.

Christopher walked around a large pool of pink glass which was growing duller. Still plenty hot, though.

There were no birds in sight, no mosquitoes humming, there was not one tree.

Why were people so destructive? Was it a stupid ugly ape gene they got from evolution and couldn't get rid of despite all their science?

Christopher heard more whooshing rips in the sky, and with his far vision he saw, behind the missiles, a wedge of bombers climbing from the south, and another wedge coming from the west.

What did it take to teach these humans a lesson? What did it take to get through to these one-track moron monkeys? But that was the point, wasn't it: they couldn't go beyond kill or be killed, they couldn't because they didn't understand anything else, not having the brains, not having the souls.

So Christopher acted on the above-mentioned Idea, because it was logical and seemed right, and he acted with a firm hand and a strong hand. He swept the missiles and bombers from the sky so they wouldn't cause any more destruction and ugliness. Enough was enough. Using ions, he made a Blanket of Death descend on the land from coast to coast, from San Diego to Bangor, from Key West to Seattle, from Duluth to Brownsville, and so on. It wasn't death in general, just death to humans. The plants and animals had nothing to worry about.

Attention please: We are starting civilization over with a clean slate.

Odd, that someone hadn't thought of doing this before.

The Blanket descended noiselessly, like fog, like the biblical Angel of Death going from house to house, except that this time it wasn't only the firstborn.

Children died on the way to school, slumping to the ground with their book bags and lunch boxes beside them. The crossing guards died, too, women in their uniforms and bright orange reflective straps. They dropped where they stood, on the curbs or in the street.

Cars everywhere swerved off highways, expressways, ramps, service roads, side roads, driveways, as the people in them slumped over steering wheels or against car windows.

The radios kept going if it was something recorded, but otherwise they, too, stopped, an announcer ending in the middle of a sentence as he or she pitched forward and banged his or her lifeless forehead. Callers to talk shows died, too, right at their phones. In the middle of agreeing or disagreeing, or confessing, or saying what was wrong with this country and why they hated the president or the right-to-lifers or the bleeding-heart liberals.

Adulterers died in their adultery, in bed, corpse on top of corpse.

Dancers died on the stage, in the middle of a step, graceful as they plunged loose limbed and openmouthed.

Bird-watchers died in marsh reeds, eyes rolling up, letting go of their binoculars.

Homeless people died on city streets, and in the case of some it didn't seem to make much difference.

Construction workers died on scaffolds and rooftops; office workers died at desks and by water coolers.

Surgeons in operating rooms collapsed over their patients, who were equally dead.

People died in elevators (going up), grocery stores (dropping a cabbage or a grapefruit), and airplanes (a head turning as if into sleep). They died at football games, and the players died on the field, the referees not blowing their whistles because they, too, fell like puppets whose strings are cut.

On basketball courts tall, beautiful men died in the middle of jump shots.

Scientists died in their labs, and garbage collectors died with their hands on garbage cans.

Readers of poetry died in the middle of a poem. Books fell, pages fluttering. And people in art galleries folded up on polished wood floors.

Murderers died before they could murder, and their victims, spared, died also. Sometimes murderer and victim fell side by side, as if they were partners.

A mother slapping her child: both died with the slap.

A father and teenage son shouting at each other: both dying with their faces red and fists clenched.

A bride and groom at the altar dropping together before the priest, who also dropped.

A clump of people in black, bent and weeping at a graveside, all falling in unison like stalks, perhaps one or two of them pitching into the grave itself, on top of the coffin.

People partying, half-drunk, packed together, silenced in the middle of a happy roar and tobacco smoke.

Bartenders falling to the shatter of glass. Pool players falling with a clatter of cues, the balls on the felt untouched. Fishermen disappearing without protest into the cold, bubbling stream. Whores dying with their johns on the way up the stairs, both bump-bumping back down. Box-office ticket sellers dying in their windows, and the people waiting on line outside all dying in a line, like dominoes.

A man on a park bench with no one in sight, dying all by himself.

An auditorium full of people in their best clothes all standing and applauding, and all expiring in the middle of a clap, while the celebrity in the bright lights, bowing, bowed lower, lower, then all the way down.

People on toilets reading newspapers dying. People on lounge chairs on cruises dying, a tropical breeze riffling their hair as they dropped their glasses of gin and tonic with a sprig of mint in it.

The world continued turning, but now it turned without people. The world was a much quieter, much simpler place. The rhythm slowed. There were no appointments to keep now, no deadlines to make, nothing to wait for and nothing that could be missed if you didn't hurry.

The digital clocks, unaware of this, powered by lithium batteries good for years, kept flashing their 8s.

Nothing on TV

Christopher has gotten really tired of rats, ants, roaches, maggots, and vultures. Everywhere you turn, it seems, you see something scuttling from, swarming on, writhing in, or flapping over carrion. He realizes that Nature's scavengers are only doing their job, the good work of cleaning up the environment, not letting all that protein go to waste—but it does get depressing when the scenery is constantly skeletons, big and little, being freed gradually from their clothes and meat.

After the Great Purification, he flew to Cleveland. Uncle Horace wasn't there. The bdellium dish on the roof of the house in Shaker Heights was so badly mildewed, it looked like a half-melted ear. The transmitter inside didn't work: no juice. And no voices, not a peep, on the subether. Where was everybody? Hiding? Gone to another Sea without telling him, as punishment?

He flew west, toward the setting sun, which was an unusual orange. He spent the nights in people's houses, choosing houses that didn't have too many bodies to clear away—because even though it was no problem clearing them away, using his powers, it was still uncomfortable. The species had to go and the species went, fine, but it did put a lump in your throat to see a curly blond tot, for example, decomposing on a throw rug before a television set that was on but showed nothing but a flickery gray. She had probably been watching *Sesame Street* or Saturday morning cartoons. Her little jeans and sneakers were so familiar, friendly, next-doorish.

It made you feel sad—and spooky, too, particularly at night.

Sometimes he had bad dreams: dead people crawling out of the loose black earth and coming at him slowly, stiff legged and arms outspread. When a person had a dream like that, it wasn't fun waking up with a pounding heart in a strange bedroom—where the pictures on the bureaus were all dead people, even though in the frames they were healthy and smiling.

Christopher flew over fields of corn, lakes, and burning cities, all revolving and giving off vapor, though in the case of the cities the smoke usually covered the vapor. He stayed at a big hotel in Topeka and watched taped movies and tried beer and his first cigarette. He didn't like beer at all, and the cigarette made him dizzy, then sick in his stomach.

He walked through lobbies that smelled half like cleaning fluid, half like pickled beets. He walked through enclosed malls full of merchandise, stepping around corpses. He took elevators up, escalators down.

He walked down many corridors and in and out of suites.

I need fresh air, he thought, because there was a growing tightness in his chest. Maybe the air-conditioning was going.

His next stop was Salt Lake City. He found the Mormon Temple interesting, impressive, but didn't understand the point of it. That is to say, what the point had *been*—because there was no point now to anything human, was there?

Tired of canned food, bagged food, he was dying for a greasy hamburger, but there was nobody to cook it for him and he didn't know how to do that himself. At one point he tried using the kitchen of a cafeteria in a downtown office building. He turned on the gas of a grill. But when he stepped into the walk-in freezer to get a patty of ground beef, he encountered such a stink that he had to run out gasping and gagging. The refrigeration must have stopped days ago.

On to the Pacific and California. He loved the seals. It was as if they were having an endless birthday party, they were such sleek, pleased, and cheerful animals. Maybe they would be the ones to evolve and take over the reins of civilization. All they needed was opposable thumbs. Christopher liked their faces, their whiskers, and the way they nuzzled each other.

Months have passed. What has Christopher done with his time? Not very much. Everything bores him.

Thinking of Gramps, he went to a library yesterday and actually took out a book on English grammar. He has it open now to dangling modifiers. But it is hard to focus on the page. And it is hard to breathe. Sighing doesn't help.

"Come on, Chris, let's play," says Cathy Carmichael. It isn't the real Cathy Carmichael, of course, just a droid he put together out of omicron. Most of her used to be an owl.

There's quite a proliferation of owls, by the way, probably because of all the rats and mice. Except that these new owls have the wrong color, slightly, and funny eyes. Accusing eyes, almost.

"Come on, Chris."

He puts down the book with a sigh and joins her and Jimmy Barnes and Stupid Loomis, all omicron-made, in a story that has a high-speed car chase and a Nazi spy. Stupid Loomis is the Nazi spy.

Christopher wishes that Stupid could be a little more threatening and nefarious, and he also doesn't like Cathy's constant giggle, but these are only dolls, after all. There are limits to what a doll can do, to what omicron can do. Omicron won't bring the dead back.

They zoom down the highway at ninety miles an hour, Christopher behind the wheel and Jimmy going blau-blau with his .45 and Cathy squealing "Help, help!" in the car ahead as she heaves her chest and struggles against her bonds. Stupid shakes his fist in defiance, but it's not very convincing. There is always something too apologetic about Stupid.

A cloud of buzzards, disturbed by the noise, reluctantly takes to the air.

Both cars are Austin-Healeys, one sky blue, one Lincoln green, removed from a showroom in Los Angeles.

After lots of skidding and bumping and squealing wheels, Jimmy and Stupid shoot each other dead and Christopher gets to have sex naked with Cathy on a grassy hill free of skeletons. Even though they're cousins. It's not really sex—Christopher is still too young for the real thing—but they roll around together and moan, and he gets a hard-on until it starts to rain.

He's glad nobody's watching. This must look awfully dumb.

Sometimes the heroine is Ruby Star instead of Cathy Carmichael, but the giggle is the same.

He's getting older, he realizes. Those inevitable hormones must be kicking in. No pubic hair yet, however.

The best adventure so far was last week in the Everglades. They went there in honor of Gramps, and staged a safari chase with lots of alligators. The alligators were real—but too sluggish during the day, wanting only to sleep, so Christopher set up the final shoot-out scene at night, in the swamp, and then there was all the snapping, splashing, and crunching anyone could want. Stupid had his head chewed off at just the right moment. Jimmy got it all on videotape. The birds shrieked at the intruding children and at the spotlights.

Instead of improving his mind, Christopher spends hours and hours watching movies on the VCR. Horror movies, Harrison Ford thrillers, comedies, foreign films, porno flicks, and even the *Star Trek* movies, which he doesn't mind so much now because he's learned how to drink alcohol. He sits in some rich dead person's living room or den, watches on a big screen, and sips Jim Beam on the rocks. He likes the way Jim Beam makes his lips numb.

It's a pity the bourbon doesn't taste better. It tastes like chalk mixed with milk gone bad.

Christopher would take drugs, too, but doesn't know where to find them. You can't buy cocaine in a supermarket or a pharmacy. A pharmacy might have some drugs, even cocaine, but the names there are all in technical Latin, and Christopher doesn't have the patience to thumb through dictionaries and medical reference books.

The best thing about alcohol is that it makes the room turn in the opposite direction; or it may cancel out the turn altogether, which is really weird.

Sometimes he goes a little nuts and breaks things. Once, using his upsilon, he punched big holes in the walls and roof until the house collapsed around him. Then he had to find another place, flying through cold and snowflakes. Which wasn't that much of a problem—there are plenty of houses available, millions of them. But in a new house there are often unpleasant surprises waiting. One thing Christopher hates, for example, is finding pets starved to death: a dachshund in a bedroom, a canary in a cage. All the goldfish floating on the surface of green scummy water.

There is, naturally, nothing on TV.

"Come on, Chris," says the Cathy Carmichael droid. "Let's play."

He doesn't feel like playing anymore. He doesn't feel like doing anything.

He wants to go home. But going home is impossible, quite impossible. He doesn't know the secret of Gramps's bathroom tiles, you see.

Panda Ray has marooned him here forever.

Christopher breaks Cathy's neck, to make her shut up. Even though she's a cousin. Her body smokes a little as it twitches its last.

He can't breathe.

A month? A year? It's hard to tell how much time has passed, but the skeletons everywhere are all cleaned and white now, so that's some indication. The yellowish white of dry bone.

No ghosts have come to visit. Not Emily, not Gramps.

He did have a dream about Mrs. Palmer, though. She was explaining something. It was important, too, but he couldn't pay attention even though he wanted to. One of the children in the class, in the back, was expanding. Expanding slowly and in every direction, like a balloon. Mrs. Palmer kept on talking and pointing to the blackboard. Christopher wanted to tell her about the kid in the back—already too big for his chair and desk—but he didn't know how to interrupt. It would be such a mess if the kid popped, and the kid was definitely going to pop, and soon, any moment; you could see this by the way his skin was stretched paper thin.

Just before he woke up, Christopher recognized the student. He recognized him despite the distortion in the face caused by the inflating and stretching. It was Pee Wee, sometimes called Half Pint, the Zimmerman kid, who lived in that creepy old house on Wilson or Winston Street. You mean Kaelin's little brother? Yes, that's right, Kaelin's little brother.

We are back in Kansas, sky everywhere, in the middle of an open field. On someone's farm. Someone who is now no one. A strong wind blows out of the northwest, or maybe it's the southeast. Compasses don't work too well in this particular Sea, as you have perhaps noticed.

We are surprised at how different Christopher looks. His hair is darker and coarser than ever. His hands are larger than ever. He stands taller, is gaunt now, and has a slight stoop, as if he is thinking hard about a terribly important problem that unfortunately has no solution.

His eyes are troubled eyes. Hooded, clouded eyes.

He is wandering through a field of composites, the most highly evolved of the plants: daisies, asters, marigolds, dandelions, black-eyed Susans, and ragweed. Could it be the ragweed pollen, we wonder, that has made Christopher's asthma worse?

And, of course, among these botanical specimens is Panda Ray's personal favorite: the sunflower, *Helianthus,* the golden girasole that turns with the sun, turns its head of honeycomb achenes from sky to sky, a round ray-framed mirror of honey following the blazing chariot, also ray-framed, of beautiful, life-giving Phoebus Apollo.

Christopher does not walk any longer with the easy, natural, unself-conscious stride of a child. He has aged. He has slowed down and become both more awkward and more deliberate. Is there a hint of clay or sandstone or shale in his skin, you ask nervously? Not yet, not yet. But his color is not good. He has a cough, too.

Out in the world by himself, poor thing, no parent to minister to him, advise him, or comfort him.

And look how he's dressed. The shirt doesn't match the pants, the socks don't match either shirt or pants, and the shoes don't fit, too tight. Maybe that's the reason he's walking funny. As if afraid of tripping.

He has a splitting headache from too much Jim Beam last night. His face is sour and twisted, his breath bad.

In the middle of the field in the middle of Kansas (Lincoln County), which is pretty close to the middle of the United States of America (not counting Hawaii or Alaska), Christopher Zimmerman bends, sits on the ground, and stares vacantly, stares into space for fifteen minutes or maybe it's fifteen hours.

If you listen carefully, you can hear the child wheezing.

A figure appears on the horizon of the field. Someone else going for a walk, communing with Nature on this late July or possibly already August day. Unless we've lost track completely and it's now September. In any case, late summer.

It's a man, and as he walks, he has to lean forward a little against the wind, which is strong. We say a man, but obviously it can't be a human man, since there are none left, and this makes us look at the slowly approaching figure with extra interest. Who could it be? A relative? Uncle Jack from Cleveland?

When he draws closer, we see the short round form, dark-brown skin, bald head, and potbelly of that enigmatic Cambridge-Oxford personage known only to a select few and to them only as Panda Ray, which name, by the way, comes from Greek philosophy, Heraclitus.

Seeing Christopher, he nods and smiles.

"Hello, Christopher," he said.

Christopher grunted.

"Feeling poorly?" asked Panda Ray, sitting down beside him.

"Why shouldn't I be?" said Christopher, not very politely, as the wind shook the weeds around them. "I'm stuck here. You put me here."

Panda Ray chuckled a liquid, bubbly chuckle. "Yiss, to save you from your evil mother."

"Well now I'm a mass murderer," said Christopher. "You can't get more evil than that."

"Is it not amu-sing, the tricks that fate plays?" The sage from the south of ancient India fluttered his eyes and tilted his head, considering fate with a beatific smile.

Christopher coughed.

Together they listened to the wind whip and roar over the field. Together they watched the black clouds advance over the field.

"It will rain," remarked Panda Ray.

It rained.

Together they listened to the sound of the rain on the field.

"I don't understand the world," said Christopher in the rain.

Panda Ray nodded approvingly. "Yiss, that is very wise of you. Great complex-ity in great sim-plicity. I do not understand it myself."

The rain stopped, the wind abated, and the sky began to clear. In the southwestern part of the sky a rainbow formed against a gray wash.

"God's promise to Noah," said Christopher bitterly. "That he wouldn't destroy the world again."

"The rainbow?" asked Panda Ray, surprised.

"Yes."

"Oh no no no. Your Bible is making up stories again, Christopher. The rainbow was not a promise to Noah, it was a pay-ment to Noah."

"Payment? What are you talking about?"

"Certainly," said Panda Ray, explaining patiently. "This is how it hap-pened. The whole world was des-troyed by the Flood, but Noah and his fam-ily were spared, in the ark."

"I know that," said Christopher.

"Yiss. So the Creator says to Noah to go forth and multi-ply, you see. But Noah says to his Creator that it is not so easy. Everything has been ruined, complete-ly ruined. Such water damage you can-not imagine. He needs to rebuild, to breed the animals, to plant again the crops. To put up the fences and the sheds and the silos. To dig latrines. This takes money, much money."

"Money?"

The Dravidian laughed up and down the Pythagorean scale and wagged his finger. "Christopher, do they not teach you these things in Sunday school? It is money that sets the whole world in motion."

"Money is the root of all evil."

"No no no. Money is the root of all free-dom. A man can do noth-ing, nothing, without money. Surely, Christopher, you are not hearing this for the first time. You are young, yiss, but no longer a baby."

"What does the rainbow have to do with money?"

"But the rainbow has everything to do with money! The pot of gold at the end of the rainbow. Have you for-gotten it?"

"The pot of gold."

"The pot of gold, of course. The Creator says to Noah, 'How much will you need?' And Noah takes out paper and pencil and starts adding up this and that. The chicken coops, so much. The seed, so much. The fodder, so much. The ferti-lizer, so much. And mind, we are not even talking about the labor. It comes to quite a sum, oh yiss. The Creator says okay and makes the rainbow. And *this* rainbow, Christopher," said the Dravidian, pointing a pudgy deep-mahogany finger at the sky, "is *your* pot of gold."

"What will I do with gold here?" asked Christopher. "I can take whatever I want."

Rays of sun streamed from opening clouds, a vibrant yellow spread across the field in ribbons and sheets, and the rainbow before them grew breathtakingly vivid, the red, orange, green, and indigo becoming so pure, so saturated, the colors seemed not real but from another world.

"Not the ele-ment, the ratio," said Panda Ray. "The ratio is more valuable to you now. Go and see, Christopher, go and see."

Christopher got up and began walking in the direction of the rainbow. What else was there to do? Sit and stare some more? There was no school. No appointments on the calendar. No calendar. This direction would do; it was as good as another.

"I don't care about money," he said.

"You will," said Panda Ray behind him. "Money is very interesting. Interest is very interest-ing, compounded. The natural logarithm. The e is like the phi, you know. Both ob-tained by a recursive al-gorithm so simple and so unexpected. Great complexity in great sim-plicity, yiss."

Christopher coughed.

Panda Ray waited for him to stop coughing, then burbled on, speaking more to himself than to the boy. Something about the fluxion of a fluent. Something about money and the beauti-ful num-ber e, and how Euler knew a lot but didn't know about the connection between e and phi, while Panda Ray did, chuckle chuckle, and that Christopher would make a good accountant when he grew up because he had learned the lesson of balance better than most people his age. The voice grew faint, fainter, and then was gone. Christopher turned and saw only the empty field and the warm sun on the weeds and wildflowers. He turned back and continued following the rainbow, smiling to himself about the pot of gold. Panda Ray was funny.

He came to the end of the rainbow, which, oddly enough, was not miles and miles away but right at the edge of the field. The lovely colors of the spectrum, descending, blended and faded into a cluster of ordinary sunflowers.

"No pot of gold," said Christopher, still smiling, "only sunflowers."

But he couldn't believe that the sly Dravidian had sent him here without a reason. What could the reason be? That sunflowers were used as a medicine among the Hopis and Dakotas for respiratory problems? (But how did Christopher know that?) Should he chew on a leaf, on one of the seeds, to see?

He tried both, stepping among the sunflowers as if entering a maze. But it was a friendly maze, not like that awful Hall of Digital Mirrors in the fun city of the future. There is something rather homey, unfancy, backyardish about the sunflower.

Christopher chewed. Fairly tasteless stuff, slightly bitter. Did it help his wheezing? Hard to tell. Maybe it did. Unless it was simply the heat of the slowly revolving summer sun relaxing his chest. He walked and chewed, and began to notice something interesting about the sunflower heads.

About the florets of the capitulum.

They were arranged in spirals. Spirals that went both ways, intersecting to make a kind of whirling grid. So that your eye went in this direction, then was drawn halfway in the opposite direction. They were logarithmic spirals, too. Equiangular. Does logarithmic spiral ring a bell? It seems to, yes.

And the seeds along the spirals, they were packed together like cells of a honeycomb, like tiles.

Tiles.

There was gold here, all right, not the metallic kind or the pigmented kind but the numerical kind, honey-rich, essential gold in the form of the square root of five plus one all divided by two. A mystery how and why it got into the sunflower. Maybe it was because each corolla of the disk flowers had five lobes, five united petals. Or maybe it had to do not with pentagons and pentagrams but simply with the way things grew around a cylinder or out from an apex, making room for other things as time passed, positioning themselves with optimum economy.

In any case Christopher understood, if only intuitively, that this was his ticket out: the rope thrown to him so he could pull himself finally out of the dread quicksand Sea of Isn't.

As the breeze rustled lazily in the grove of steaming sunflowers, he sank his eyes and all his attention into the largest head and let his mind shift from one family of spirals to the other, from pattern to counterpattern, all in gold and divinely angled, until his eyes swam and he hung between two symmetries, undecided, unfocused, but not really undecided and unfocused, because at the same time he was as tense as a spring in a mousetrap or bear trap, ready to snap and pounce and grab and hang on for dear life to the first cosmic string that came his way.

Part Three

Pythagoras being asked, how a man ought to conduct himself towards his country, when it had acted iniquitously with respect to him, replied, as to a mother.

—STOBAEUS

Be It Ever So Humble

His point of entry was the field off Green Street. The light hurt his eyes, made him squint. So much light. Apparently there was a lot more light in Is than in Isn't. He hadn't noticed this difference before. He must have been in constant dusk all that time and grown accustomed to it. Also, he experienced difficulty walking: at each step the ground wasn't quite where he expected it to be. He actually fell twice, idiotically, like a clown, before he reached the sidewalk and the street. He realized the problem: the ground wasn't shifting in any direction; it was stationary. Likewise the trees, the telephone poles, the street signs, and everything else. They were in exactly the same position they occupied a moment ago. And if you stood and waited, they were still in the same position. It made his stomach queasy. A sparrow flew by. Watching the sparrow, he felt better. Movement. Keep your eyes on moving things, Christopher, and take deep breaths. This will pass. You will acclimate—you will get your landlubber's legs.

He walked carefully along Green, turned right at Carter, into the shade of old maples and oaks. The shade was easier on the eyes. What season was it? How long had he been away?

The narrow street was a tunnel: thick trunks on either side of a ceiling of gnarled boughs. He turned left at Wilson. The pavement, broken in many places, each section at a different angle and on a different level—forget roller-skating here—was green with leaf stains and patches of moss. Ants crawled; acorns crunched underfoot.

Mother was on the screened-in porch, her crossword puzzle in her lap.

He took a deep breath and blew out. He closed his eyes for a moment. Opened them.

He crossed the street to 54, proceeded past the high hedge, went up the slate walk, up the steps, and to the front door.

"Christopher's here," announced the doorknob in psi.

"Yes, I know," thought Mother, swinging on her seat, pencil poised over puzzle.

Then he was in, and after a few steps was facing her, was not more than three feet from her.

She looked into his eyes, and he looked back, his eyes straight into her eyes, not hiding, and he saw all her power and all her wisdom.

"I could kill you," she said quietly.

"I know," he said. "I'm your son. My life belongs to you. You took it once, and you can take it again."

"I'm a monster," she said.

"I know," he said. "I'm a monster, too. I'm your son."

Debra Zimmerman nodded. She was satisfied with his reply.

The trees rustled overhead like surf. The wind in the leaves was one of the most beautiful, most peaceful sounds in the world.

"There won't be any need now to neutralize you," she said. "You've done it yourself." She adjusted the rust red scarf around her shoulders.

He was relieved, but, to tell the truth, not that relieved. He hadn't been that afraid to begin with, really. Because it really didn't matter—this was the point—what she did or did not do regarding him. It was her decision. If Mother gave him dinner, he would eat. If Mother didn't give him dinner, he wouldn't eat. If Mother grounded him, he would be grounded. If Mother scooped him out, he would be scooped out. It was her decision.

Mother was his creator.

She didn't need to ask him if he was going to fly anymore at birthday parties or half-joke, half-brag at school, in front of humans, about having traveled to other centuries and other galaxies. She knew he wouldn't. Not ever again. She knew that the rules of the house were safe, completely safe, with Christopher now.

"And Gramps?" he asked, remembering the fly trapped in the glass and running out of air.

"Your grandfather didn't make it to Golden Years," Mother said.

Gramps didn't need air anymore.

"He had a stroke," Mother said.

Poor Gramps.

"You can visit him in the cemetery. We buried him not far from Mrs. Palmer, as a matter of fact." Mother filled in a word, 84 down, letter by letter. The lines on her forehead were all straight, horizontal, and parallel, a musical staff without notes.

"I'll go to school tomorrow," Christopher told her.

"That's a good idea," said Mother, the features of her face not moving.

"I was thinking. . . ."

"What were you thinking?"

"I was thinking I might become an accountant."

"Oh?"

"Numbers are interesting, and accountants make good money."

Mother filled in another word, 13 across, filled it letter by letter, a long word beginning with D. Her pencil never lost its sharpness. A surreptitious bit of upsilon there, no doubt. She said as she wrote: "That's nice, dear. But you don't have to make your mind up right away. You're only in the sixth grade."

"Sixth grade?"

"You were ill a long time, Christopher. I'm glad you're better now." She looked up and smiled a mild, noncommittal smile.

The audience was over. He nodded and backed out.

In the hall he met Father, who was on his way somewhere.

"Oh, hello, Christopher," said Monty Zimmerman, wincing, embarrassed.

"Hello, Father," said Christopher.

"Uh—everything all right with your mother? I mean . . . between your mother and you?"

From the dining room you could hear the clock ticking, the antique captain's clock atop the sideboard. A peaceful rhythm.

"Everything's fine," said Christopher.

"Ah, good," said Father, touching his mustache. "Good." At a loss what to do next, he nodded, muttered to himself, then put out his hand for a handshake.

They shook hands, father and son.

It was the first time Christopher had ever shaken hands with his father. As if they were two grown men there in the hall. Allies. It was a strange feeling but not unpleasant. To Christopher's surprise, Father had a warm hand.

Monty Zimmerman said, "Well, I have to be going. Good." And awkwardly, very awkwardly, he was away and gone.

Christopher passed the living room. He saw that there was no fireplace and no portrait over it. No bogus Uncle Martin or Marvin winking at him knowingly. The credenza was locked, as it should be. Everything stood in its correct place. No washing machine and drier to walk around in the foyer.

He climbed the steps to his room, three flights, thirty-six steps in all, and shut the door behind him. He took a breath. He went to the closet, opened it. Buzz looked up and thumped his robot tail. Good.

Christopher made a resolution then and there: He would be better to the dog in the future. More attentive. He would buy the dog a faster, newer computer, maybe a Mac. He would get a job delivering newspapers, save up for it. He would give Buzz more capability. Play with him more. Poor Buzz. The liquid-crystal eyes were dull but full of devotion. And not one atom of reproach.

Christopher put his books in order for the next day. He combed his hair. He rested in his bed. The bed didn't move.

The bed was all right angles, just as the ceiling and room were all right angles.

At dinner (meat loaf, mashed potatoes, peas) four sat, one at each side of the table, at each point of the compass. A balanced and symmetrical arrangement. There was talk, first, about the high school homecoming parade next month. Kaelin was on the committee. Not that she asked to be or ever wanted to be. Brian had been on the committee last year, so they approached her, chose her. They said they needed a Zimmerman.

"A little social activity will be good for you," said Mother.

Christopher noted that the food tasted like food, not like chalk. This was nice but disconcerting. He also observed that Kaelin avoided looking at him—much in the way people avoided looking at cripples or the severly retarded on a bus. People went to ridiculous lengths—hiding behind a book, absorbed in a thought—to pretend not to see crutches, humps, and misshapen, drooling mouths jerking past them.

Not one mention, at the table, of Christopher's long absence. Not even the most indirect allusion to it.

Brian was doing well at Indiana, it was reported.

Forks clicked on teeth.

Father said something about office memos and a waste of paper. He waved loosely, not finishing his sentence.

The sound of decorous chewing and swallowing.

Mother said something about Mrs. Wells's lemon cake and Mrs. Wells's lumbago.

Pass the salt, please.

Kaelin said a few things but nothing to Christopher. What was wrong?

The milk tasted like milk.

After dinner he returned to his room and reviewed his adverbs for an hour. Trying not to think about Gramps. Gramps would be with Emily now permanently. Emily would look after the old man.

Trees rustled outside Christopher's window to a cricket chorus. High on the roof the bdellium dish hummed subliminally, Mother at the transmitter again talking to Mrs. Fxn.

Christopher got into his pajamas, brushed his teeth, turned off his light, and lay in bed, waiting for Kaelin. She didn't come up. An owl hooted. He listened to the crickets.

It was a long night, a night unbroken by sun.

He realized, too, that the days here would not be interrupted, from dawn until dusk, by any interpolation of the moon and stars.

This would take getting used to.

He sighed.

In the distance he heard a train horn. It made him sleepy.

He thought of Panda Ray.

When he finally fell asleep, Christopher dreamed he was walking on slippery stones, between gray boulders, through mist, near a lifeless sea.

Too Much Science Fiction

At Lincoln Elementary the tiles on the walls are a pastel terra-cota color again, and the air smells not of sauerkraut, motor oil, and feces but of apples, beaverboard, and poster paint. An improvement, we think.

Honking, tootling, and hair-raising squeaks come from the band room, where Mr. Moskowitz is doing his duty manfully again at morning rehearsal. They don't pay that man enough, I tell you.

Betty is busy in the main office: paperwork for little Christopher Zimmerman, who is not so little anymore. This is his first day in the sixth grade, after being out for months. The note from Dr. Hill, stamped, goes into his file. And he has to see Mr. DiVincenzo today, too.

Mr. Sykes has assigned the boy to Mr. Humphrey's class. Mr. Humphrey is a new teacher, young and full of idealism and great ideas. The idealism and great ideas won't last long, Mr. Sykes knows, but he sees that the young man also has a sense of detached humor, of irony. Humor and irony will temper the inevitable bitterness when it comes. Teaching is a tougher job than most people think, not because of the children or grading papers but because of the discouragement to your soul.

"Here you are, Christopher," says Betty, giving him three sheets of paper—a white sheet, a pink sheet, and a green sheet. "It's room sixteen." Room 16, a coincidence.

In the hall, Carole Harrison says hi. Christopher holds up a hand, acknowledging.

From a group Ken French calls, "Hey, Chris! I didn't recognize you!"

Mr. Humphrey turns out to be loud and nervous. Christopher likes him but can see right away that there will be a discipline problem. A teacher should never show fear to a class.

Mr. Humphrey takes the three sheets of paper and points to an empty chair.

Christopher sits.

"Why are you squinting so much?" asks Beverly Hopkins in the seat behind him.

Christopher shrugs.

Meanwhile, down in the boiler room, Mr. Sykes is saying to George: "Christopher Zimmerman came to school today."

"So?" says George, who is at his workbench and in the middle of repairing a lamp. The custodian hasn't changed a bit: beer belly, shirt coming out of his pants, the same old smell of cigars, stale sweat, and hops.

"You should see him," says the principal. "So sober and businesslike. No more devilry in his eyes."

"So?" says George, annoyed. "He was sick. Sick for months. He was at death's door."

"Death's door my foot," says Mr. Sykes. "They scooped the child out."

"I don't want to hear this."

"You can tell, you can tell. It's not the same person in there."

George gets up and wipes his hands on an old rag. His callused, tobacco-stained fingers are more like claws than fingers, and the top joint of one of them is missing. An accident in a machine shop when George was young.

He is angry, indignant.

"Damn it," he whisper-growls to the principal. "Are you getting pleasure out of this? What's the matter with you? Are you on their side or ours?"

"Of course not," Mr. Sykes huffs, then looks around. "Of course not."

"Christopher was a good kid," says George. "No harm in him."

"Maybe he talked too much," says Mr. Sykes in a low voice. "Maybe he was disobedient. You know they don't tolerate that."

"If you ask me," mutters the custodian, "we should get a high-powered rifle, a couple of high-powered rifles . . . and from behind . . ."

"I don't want to hear this," says the principal. "I didn't hear what you said. Not a word." And he leaves hurriedly, pale, straightening his tie.

When the science teacher comes—it's Mr. Dunst, who used to be at the high school, so maybe he was demoted—and when he tells the class about molecules, acids, and bases, Christopher listens like all the other students: half-interested, half-bored; sometimes with a glimmer of comprehension, most often presenting an impenetrable wall of fatalistic inadequacy and stubborn ignorance. He doesn't sit back and smirk. He doesn't raise his hand and say that on Blithró they have this neat corkscrew polymer that's an acid at one end and a base at the other.

At lunch, while on line in the cafeteria, Christopher is approached by none other than Billy the Bully and Stupid Loomis.

"Who's this?" asks Billy, pointing with a thick, big-knuckled finger.

"It's Chris Zimmerman," says Stupid. "Remember him? Half Pint."

"Oh yeah. Half Pint. He's not a half-pint anymore, is he?" A laugh.

"Up with your sleeve," Stupid orders Christopher. Sometimes they do this even in the cafeteria. No one pays attention. It's boys being boys.

Christopher makes a fist and lifts it in front of Stupid's face. The fist doesn't have much in the way of knuckles, maybe, but it's definitely a fist. And Christopher's eyes are steady, and his jaw is set.

"Tough guy," says Billy.

They're both bigger than Christopher, but he says to them, and his voice doesn't quiver in the least: "Go pick on somebody else, you assholes."

"Tough guy," says Billy.

Stupid flashes a black look and is ready to say something threatening to the kid, like, "You just made a big mistake, Half Pint. Wait till after school. You're dead." But now he sees the fist in a different light and reconsiders, changes his mind. Sure, they could beat up Half Pint behind the school, no problem. But he would hit back. This wasn't the type—you could tell—who ran home crying. There would be a fight. There would be bloody lips and noses on both sides.

"Asshole yourself," says Stupid, but with a certain respect, and he and Billy the Bully move on to easier prey.

After lunch Christopher has to see Mr. DiVincenzo.

The psychologist pats him on the back and takes him to the conference room next to the cafeteria, from which you can hear plates still clattering and nutritionists chattering. He closes the door, blocking out the noise, and invites Christopher to have a seat at the table.

Christopher looks around. The brown lie detector was over *there*. Jimmy was smacked in the face and cowered over *there*. And Carole peed on the floor, weeping, over *there*. Except that none of it really happened. Or if it did, at least not in this Sea, which is all that counts.

No smoke rises from the conference table, not the barest wisp.

"Christopher," says Mr. DiVincenzo, opening a folder, "you've been telling stories in class?" This is an evaluation.

Which stories does he mean? Christopher wonders. It was so long ago.

"Shakespeare in a dress," says the psychologist, looking over some notes. "Dinosaurs with ESP. Mathematics on other planets. Very imaginative."

"Well," says Christopher with a slight, self-pitying smile, "I guess I was reading too many comic books at the time, too much science fiction."

"Ah," says the psychologist, understanding, sympathetic. He is familiar with the too-much-science-fiction syndrome. "And now?"

"Oh," says Christopher, "I got out of that. But I guess I overdosed on it a little."

Mr. DiVincenzo is amused and gratified by the expression *overdosed*. Kids say the darnedest things. Overdosed on science fiction: how well put and how cute.

"I don't know," Christopher goes on, "I'm in the sixth grade now. With all the competition in the world today, I guess, I don't know, it's time I got more realistic."

"Well," says Mr. DiVincenzo, "you're still young."

"I don't know," Christopher says, "kids are looking into colleges sooner every year. Early admission and all that. And look at the Japanese."

"True," says Mr. DiVincenzo with a sigh. "Sometimes I wish our children didn't grow up so fast. It's because of computers."

Christopher nods, commiserating. As if the psychologist has said something sad and deep about childhood and the modern age. As if computers are something he doesn't approve of, either. Christopher doesn't tell the psychologist that his dog runs off a computer. He is not even tempted to. He has grown up a lot, our Christopher has.

Mr. DiVincenzo leans over and tousles his hair. Christopher has passed the evaluation.

On the way out, the psychologist asks, "Something wrong with your eyes?"

"Oh no," says Christopher. "I was in a dark room for a while, when I was sick. I haven't adjusted yet."

Mr. DiVincenzo is amused by the big word *adjusted.* Kids do indeed grow up awfully fast. Old before their time. And yet, for all that, they remain kids, don't they? "My advice to you, Christopher," he says, "is to get some exercise. Fresh air in your lungs. Put some color in those cheeks. Take up soccer. Soccer is an excellent game."

Christopher nods, as if soccer is exactly the sport he has been thinking of taking up.

And maybe he will. Why not? A sport is good camouflage.

Also, when you do what people suggest, they immediately stop worrying, fretting, thinking about you. You are on their side, you are one of the good guys. The Zimmerman kid? He's all right.

Toward the end of the day, Mr. Sykes appears and takes him in tow. The bright yellow school buses are lined up, waiting. The bell will ring any minute.

"Your first day in the sixth grade."

"Yes, sir."

"All better, from the double pneumonia?"

"I feel fine, Mr. Sykes."

"You like Mr. Humphrey? He's new."

"He's great."

"Wonderful. We're glad to have you back, Christopher."

"Thank you."

"I hear you're interested in accounting, and you're also thinking of taking up soccer."

"Yes, sir."

"Wonderful . . . Quite a change."

"A change?"

"In you. Overnight."

"Oh."

"It happens, with children your age. They wake up one day, and bam, they're a completely different person. Keeps us parents and educators on our toes, I can tell you."

"Yes, sir."

"It was the same with your brother, Brian."

"Brian?"

"Bam, overnight, changed."

"He's going to be a patent lawyer. He's at Indiana."

"Yes, I know. He was a handful before."

"We're proud of him."

"I'm sure you are. I'm sure you are. Well, there's the bell. Run along, Christopher, run along. My regards to your mother."

And the principal of Lincoln Elementary purses his lips and shakes his head as the child runs to the bus.

Brother and Sister

Moonlight. Midnight. The door creaked slowly open in Christopher's room, and a shadow slinked in. The shadow held its breath—and held, in its hand, a flashlight. Kaelin finally. Christopher pretended he was asleep.

It was his flashlight she had, the old dented metal Eveready, and he was willing to bet it contained no batteries and no bulb, just a low moany whistle resonating inside. She had come to give her brother the flashlight test while he slept, as they once did to Brian, together, the night Christopher began his insane escape.

He snored a little as she crept up to his bed on tiptoe. It wasn't often he got to play a trick on Kaelin, the master of tricks.

Gingerly she took his hand from the blanket and placed it over the upturned flashlight. There was a click. He opened one eye and looked at the ceiling.

There was no full moon of sad orange light, the light that had not a ripple or kink in it, as if spilling from a can of paint. No moon of orange. Not so much even as a sliver or thread of orange.

"You're awake, aren't you?" she said.

"You thought I was scooped out," he said.

"Well, you acted like it."

"You're not doing a bad job of that yourself."

They looked at each other in the darkness.

She got into bed with him and put her arms around him. No sobbing or sniffling, but her cheeks were all wet, as if she had just put her face under a tap.

"You have all your upsilon and omicron," she murmured.

A breath.

"I thought I was the only one left," she murmured.

Then she couldn't say anything for a while, not even in a murmur.

Moonlight. Mother talking to Mrs. Fxn over the subether. The trees rustling.

"There's some of Mother in you now," said Kaelin.

"She's in both of us," said Christopher, staring at the blank ceiling.

"At least we're not dead," said Kaelin. "This is better than being dead, isn't it?"

"I don't know," said Christopher, thinking of Gramps, wondering.

They listened to the crickets and the tree frogs for a while. They smelled the leafy smell of the night. You can't do that if you're dead—or can you?

"We can't go anywhere," she whispered, or maybe thought it rather than said it, for safety. "We can't run away."

"We shouldn't," he thought back. "Mother is right, Kaelin. I learned that the hard way. We're bombs—atom bombs. And atom bombs shouldn't be loose. They have to be wrapped up very tight. They have to be kept under lock and key at all times, Kaelin."

A breath.

Another breath.

"You're soaking my pillow," he said.

"I'm sorry," she said.

They held hands, brother and sister, and looked out the window together at the moonlight on the treetops.

Good-bye, Gramps

We are in the East Carlyle Cemetery. There is birdsong, fresh air, and a lot of lawn in every direction, which is just what you would expect in a cemetery. Two well-dressed FBI agents stand behind a tree, which is probably not what you would expect in a cemetery. The agents are peering through field glasses and listening hard on their earphones—the tombstone of Cesar Porter has been bugged with a highly sophisticated, nearly microscopic bug. It's very state-of-the-art, but they listen in vain: the kneeling child says not a word.

"You know what I think, Calv?" says Agent Hornwood finally, clearing his throat.

"What, Calv?" asks Agent Pliscou.

"I think we're wasting our time here."

All the kid has done is kneel and put a hand on the ground, on the grass, moving blades of grass between his fingers, brushing an ant off his hand, all very natural things for a kid to do at a grave. He kept his hand there for a few minutes, and now it's on his forehead, which has lowered. A hand supporting a bowed head—what could be more natural than that? It's a time-honored attitude of grief. Well, but it was the kid's grandfather, after all. The two may have been close. They may have had good times together. They may have gone fishing together. They may have bonded despite the big difference in age.

Pliscou relaxes a little inside and thinks that maybe he will get through this investigation in one piece and not be turned into a screaming human pretzel that pleads, pleads, pleads for oblivion.

He crosses his fingers.

Maybe they are barking up the wrong tree and there are no superhuman monsters after all in this sleepy central Pennsylvania town. Children sometimes do drop dead on playgrounds. And babies in cribs sometimes stop breathing, just like that, for no reason. There's a name for it.

Pliscou thinks that if he gets through this investigation in one piece and they don't have to go straight to another town in another state where there *are* superhuman monsters, this time for real, who can stop your heart at a distance and do unspeakable things to your body before you die, he will get himself reassigned. When he volunteered for this duty, he was feeling pretty grim and reckless, because of Mary Beth's leaving him, but he doesn't feel that way now.

Thinking of Mary Beth and the sharp pain of unrequited, disappointed love, he sympathizes with that boyfriend they questioned, Henry Parks. No, not Henry—Harvey. Harvey Parks. Kaelin Zimmerman had told the boy she was grounded and that her mother said she was too young to go steady. Even though at her age, nowadays, plenty of girls went all the way.

They sure do lay down the law in that Zimmerman family, don't they? But that isn't such a bad thing, Pliscou thinks. Young people would be better off with more discipline.

Calvin Pliscou thinks that he will not only get himself reassigned but maybe even leave the FBI. Why should he keep putting his life on the line? At one point he thought it was exciting, heroic, to carry a gun and arrest people. Not now.

His mother had wanted him to be a doctor.

The FBI agent who looks like a Jehovah's Witness in a typical suburb thinks he wouldn't mind going into education. He pictures himself as a teacher at a school in Middle America, a school like Lincoln Elementary, where the biggest danger is getting hit with a spitball. The children would all look up to him when he told them he was once an FBI agent and carried a gun.

"Did you ever shoot anybody?" they would ask, eyes bright.

"Let's make a deal," he would answer with a wink. "You do all your adverb homework for tomorrow and I'll tell you about the time I almost got killed busting up a drug ring."

"Mr. Pliscou," the parents would say on parent-teacher night,

"We don't know how you straightened out our Johnny. It's a miracle. We can never repay you."

Families would invite him to supper and eligible daughters would flirt with him. He would take Harvey under his wing—a decent, no-nonsense kid—and tell him, hey, cheer up, there's more than one fish in the sea.

"Wait," says Hornwood, "Christopher's saying something."

Pliscou turns up the volume on his earphones and listens hard.

"Good-bye, Gramps," Christopher says. He gets up and brushes off his knees. He turns and walks away, past the agents, who crouch behind the tree to keep out of sight.

"That's it?" asks Pliscou, his cheek against bark.

"That's it," says Hornwood with a grunt. "C'mon, Calv, let's go have a beer."

Pliscou could do with a beer.

Michael Kandel has published three previous novels, including *Strange Invasion,* which was a finalist for the Philip K. Dick Award. He is also an accomplished editor and has been nominated twice for the National Book Award for his translations of Stanislaw Lem. He lives in Long Island and currently works for the Modern Language Association.